HARLEM MOON
BROADWAY

Also by Brian Keith Jackson

The
Queen of Harlem

BRIAN KEITH JACKSON

HARLEM MOON

BROADWAY BOOKS

NEW YORK

A hardcover edition of this book was originally published in 2002 by Doubleday, a division of Random House, Inc. It is here reprinted by arrangement with Doubleday.

THE QUEEN OF HARLEM. Copyright © 2002 by Brian Keith Jackson. All rights reserved. No part of this book may be reproduced or transmitted in any form or by any means, electronic or mechanical, including photocopying, recording, or by any storage and retrieval system, without written permission from the publisher. For information, address: Broadway Books, a division of Random House, Inc.

PRINTED IN THE UNITED STATES OF AMERICA

The figure in the Harlem Moon logo is inspired by a graphic design by Aaron Douglas (1899–1979). HARLEM MOON and its logo, depicting a moon and woman, are trademarks of Broadway Books, a division of Random House, Inc.

This book is a work of fiction. Names, characters, businesses, organizations, places, events, and incidents either are the product of the author's imagination or are used fictitiously. Any resemblance to actual persons, living or dead, events, or locales is entirely coincidental.

Visit our website at www.harlemmoon.com

First Harlem Moon trade paperback edition published 2003

Book design by Claire Vaccaro

The Library of Congress has cataloged the Doubleday hardcover edition as follows:
Jackson, Brian Keith.
    The Queen of Harlem / Brian Keith Jackson.
        p. cm.
    1. Harlem (New York, N.Y.)—Fiction. 2. African Americans—Fiction. I. Title.
PS3560.A2117 Q84 2002
813'.54—dc21
2001047233

ISBN 0-7679-0839-2

10 9 8 7 6 5 4 3 2 1

For Juan H. Gaddis and David Paul

Acknowledgments

With gratitude to Eraka Bath; Christopher Beane; Elma Blint; my agent, Faith Hampton Childs; Renee Cox; Jay Evans; Shelly Eversly; my editor, Janet Hill, and the rest of the Doubleday/Harlem Moon family; Joe Mejia; and Carl Swanson.

Our worst fear is not that we are inadequate. Our deepest fear is that we are powerful beyond measure. It is our light, not our darkness, that most frightens us. We ask ourselves, "Who am I to be brilliant, gorgeous, talented, and fabulous?" Actually, who are you not to be?

MARIANNE WILLIAMSON

Y o. Yo wassup?" asks a young man, planting himself in front of
me. Though the temperature hardly warrants it, he's already
wearing his new black parka, with fur trimming the hood. The coat
is his business suit, different from the one I wear but a business suit
nonetheless. "You cool?" That is all he says, and I fully understand the
nature of the weather report.

I smile, somewhat tempted by the offer, but I pass with a simple lift
of the hands. The moment does find me cool, so the young man, with
a swagger and a sway, pushes off on his way. He doesn't take it personally; in his business, and in mine, a no is a yes, an offer away.

"Great day, huh?" says a guy walking by with a briefcase.

"Yeah," I say. "Can't complain."

"I hear ya. Have a good one."

"You too."

Autumn has always been my favorite season. It's when time turns
back on itself, if only for an hour.

Spring forward. Fall back.

I sit on the stoop of the town house, checking out the refurbished Marcus Garvey Park, which has been renamed Mount Morris. The leaves, going through their changes, sway with the breeze in the air as though Billie Holiday is singing "Autumn in New York."

I cherish the moment because I haven't been back to this street, haven't been back to New York, in four years. But here I sit where it all began.

A group of kids on the sidewalk across the street are double-Dutching, maybe hoping to one day take the crown back from the Japanese team. They are screaming with delight and the sting of the frayed extension cord they use goes unnoticed. They are used to its touch.

I bob my head to the sound of the cord slapping the concrete; my dreads swing to its cadence, almost as though my turn is coming up. Watching the kids, I'm loving their natural high.

An old woman tosses bread crumbs for the pigeons, and their velvet coos attract a swarm and they settle on the sidewalk at her feet. All the pigeons look alike to me, but I'm certain the old woman can spot a few of her favorites, her "babies"; perhaps the ones that most resemble doves. The pigeons begin to scurry as a car passes, but the little girls across the street double-Dutching never miss a beat.

M r. Randolph?"

"Yes," I say, standing, closing my journal.

"Diane Turner," she says, sticking out her hand. "So nice to meet you. Sorry I'm tardy, but this area is booming and I've had to show four other town houses today. Of course, this one is the prize."

"That's fine. I was having a great time just sitting here checking things out."

"Yes. The neighborhood has changed drastically in the last several years. This town house is a jewel." I suspect she knows what time it is, but she takes a look at her watch. "I actually have another client coming to see it in an hour. Shall we?" Diane Turner walks up the steps. I follow.

"Didn't that park used to be called Marcus Garvey?" I ask.

"Yes. Well, actually it was Mount Morris Park first, then it was renamed Marcus Garvey Park in 1973, but due to the current changes in the area they thought it would be best to again call it Mount Morris. Full circle, wouldn't you say?"

"Yes. It seems so. Malcolm X Boulevard hasn't been renamed, has it?" She smiles but gives no answer.

"After you," says Diane Turner, opening the door. "As you can see, fabulous." She places her hand behind her ear. "Just listen. You hear that? That's the sound of history."

Though the place has been renovated it's still as familiar to me as a childhood scar.

"I see you've brought a notebook," says Diane Turner, glancing at my old journal. She looks like a fancy black doll in her tangerine designer suit and matching suede shoes. A black and gold silk scarf covers her neck, and her lips are painted into a permanent smile. "That's wise. It's amazing how much people forget."

"Yes. It's just something to refer to."

"You said you're new in town?"

"Somewhat. But I like the area."

"I'm sure you'll enjoy New York. Harlem is definitely the place to be. It's as the kids say, 'All that.' You'll find this town house to be a worthy investment. The best space for the buck. It's all in the details."

"You've got that right."

"I don't normally advertise, but I used to be the only broker handling properties up here. White brokers wouldn't touch it with a gloved hand when it was just shit. Anyone can appreciate the harvest, but few have seen the seeds I've sown. We do what we can. I'm sure as a young brother, and a lawyer no less, you understand."

"Yes," I say, catching her eye. "I think I do."

A cell phone rings and I reach inside my jacket pocket. "Oh, that's me," she says, taking her black alligator purse off her shoulder, digging inside. "This will only take a sec." Then into the phone, "Diane Turner . . . Hello, dahling. How are you? . . . Yes . . . Well, we do what we can . . . Um huh . . . Well, I'm showing another house at the moment . . . Yes, of course. Hold on." Diane Turner covers the phone, then whispers to me like telling a friend a secret, "Listen, hon, a couple interested in a property around the corner—mind you, not nearly as fabulous as this—is waiting for me. They want to take another look. Do you mind if I just—"

"No, please. Feel free to go. I'll just make myself at home."

"Clever. Clever," she says, slapping me on the arm playfully. "I feel good about this. I think it's going to work out with you here." Diane Turner winks at me. "I have another appointment to show the house in an hour, but I'll try to be back before then. I think this deal around the corner is about to come together. A lovely couple, they. Did you say you were married?"

"No," I say. "I'm not."

"Well, FYI, a great many gay people have moved into the neighborhood. Follow the gays, I say. They really are the best people. Just fabulous. Give gays a ghetto and they'll fix it right up . . . Not that I'm implying you're gay, but if you were, just know, it certainly wouldn't be held against you."

I open my mouth to speak, but Diane Turner with a hold-that-thought gesture returns to her phone call. "Hello. Yes, I'll be right there . . . Nonononono, don't be silly. Anything for you . . . I'm just around the corner. I had a feeling you would want to take another look."

Yes, another look. But for me it was more than that.

I'd been staying at Jim's East Village apartment for two weeks, but as we sat in his favorite bar on East Fourth Street downing dollar drafts, the air was let out of the keg.

"Listen, Mason, it's been cool having you crash, but if you wanna keep kicking it in New York you're gonna need to find your own place."

Jim was your average hipster whose claim to fame was that he was the first white guy, that he knew, to have dreadlocks. All summer I had been twisting my hair, trying to attach myself to something associated with black heritage.

"I know. I've been looking," I said. "I've checked the ads every day."

"Fuck the ads," said Jim, holding up his empty mug to the tattooed bartender. "Just tell everybody you meet that you're looking. It's the only way. That's how I found my place."

The "place" was a railroad flat. At least that's what they're called in

New York. In the South it's called a shotgun house. But at that moment it was more than I had.

I'd crossed out all the possible ads but one remained:

HOUSEMATE WANTED
TO SHARE TOWN HOUSE
450/month. Rarely home
No. 20 W. 120th St.
Appt. 4–4:15, 15 October

I'd circled it as a lark. Sure, I was going to go to Harlem, at some point, to check it out, but I'd never really considered living there.

"Please be sure to take all of your belongings when leaving the train. And be mindful of your wallets, for the hand in your pocket may not be your own." Voice over the intercom of the 6 train, tunneling through Manhattan's East Side.

I got out of the subway at 125th Street, and the rush of color, fabric as well as skin, filled me like a Jamaican patty. The air was different, alive. Incense filled my nose, and the different languages and accents felt good in my ears.

Harlem.

"Dreads?" said the West African woman, stepping up to me. "You want dreads? Twist?"

"No, thank you," I said with a smile as I walked on, avoiding the rolling tumbleweeds of hair that hadn't made it onto someone's head.

"Yo. Yo, playa. Wassup?" said a voice. I turned around as he stood on a stoop. His three friends stayed on the steps, sipping Forties and sporting their latest bubble coats. "You I-ight? You need something?"

"Nah, man. I'm cool. Thanks," I said, stopping, hoping to strike up a conversation. Bond with the brothers.

" 'I'm cool. Thanks,' " he said, not at all trying to cover his mocking tone. His friends started laughing like Richard Pryor was doing a show. "Yeah, I see. You one of them uppity niggas. Probably get your shit delivered. Look at this motherfucker," he said, turning back to the peanut gallery. "He look like one of them niggas they always have in an ad, peeping out from behind the white boys. Like he don't care they got his ass stuck in the back. 'Just so happy to be here, massa.' Black boy blending."

I smiled, trying to brush off the situation. *That* I was used to, but not this.

"Your name's probably Theo. You a Huxtable?"

"Nah, man. It's not like that," I said, trying to change my voice, deepen it. "My name's Mason."

" 'No. My name's Mason.' "

"Malik," said one of the guys on the stoop. I glanced over at the guy, happy for the interruption. "Give the brother a break."

"Brother? This nigga ain't no brother. You ain't from up here, are you?" asked Malik. I wanted to just walk away but I didn't want to turn my back on him.

"No," I said. "But I'm checking out a place, though."

" 'I'm checking . . .' Nigga, you better head on back downtown. Harlem ain't for you. You too soft." He pushed me hard in the chest and I stumbled back. I couldn't smile anymore. At the end of the street I could see a cop car turning the corner and rolling our way.

"Malik," said one of his friends. "Chill, man. Damn."

"I'm just fucking with this li'l nigga." Malik looked me up and down, then started laughing. He reached out his hand and I shook it, feeling the calluses on his palm as he slid his hand from mine and headed back to the stoop.

The cop car stopped but the policemen didn't get out, fully aware that their presence was more than enough. "How's it going, fellas?"

"It's all good," said Malik. "Just keeping it real, ain't that right, Theo?"

He changed my name so easily; he saw me as Theo, and as far as he was concerned, that's who I was: a black TV character from the eighties, living in a brownstone, successful parents, beautiful sisters, no troubles in the world. Theo Huxtable, easy as that. "Fine, Officer," I said, using this as an excuse to start walking away. I felt Malik's eyes on me, but I just walked on, hands jammed in my pockets, a slight ache in my chest.

I thought of going back to the ads, back downtown, back to something familiar, but I wasn't going to let one incident stop me. Still a man, in Harlem, I marched on.

M y steps weren't as strong as they were before running into Malik and they became even more strained when I turned the corner off of Fifth Avenue onto 120th Street. Standing outside of the town house was a mostly white crowd, all looking attentive, ready to claim the space. I stopped for a moment, nervously twisting my hair; dreading rejection.

Black hair is hard work.

As I stood there it was like Malik had left his friends on the stoop and was standing in front of me, Forty in hand, then spitting in my face, "Black boy blending." I crossed the street and went into Marcus Garvey Park. I took off the sweater I'd gotten in Ireland and stuffed it in my backpack. I pulled out my shirt and T-shirt and let the tails hang. There was no way to hide my loafers so I took off my belt and pushed my khakis down as far as they could go without falling off.

The park was hardly a telephone booth and Superman I wasn't, but with a slow swagger I walked toward the group standing outside of the town house like I belonged in the neighborhood and they were mere loiterers. "Wassup?" A few people nodded their heads but didn't say anything. I made my way to the back of the crowd hoping that being set off from the rest would draw attention to me, praying that on this trip a whale in the distance is more alluring than those circling the boat.

We didn't have to wait long. At four o'clock the front doors of the town house opened. A woman stepped out and my body straightened and I shifted my weight from foot to foot to try to get a better look.

She closed the door and walked down the steps, leisurely as though an aria was ending, the cadenza on its way. She had on a fitted black sweater, a gray ankle-length skirt with a slit up the side, and tied around her shoulders was a light blue cardigan. Her hair was high on her head, as though pulling up her neck, where a strand of pearls pulled it all together.

"Women," she said, looking over our heads. She said it like it was the only word worth saying. "You may leave."

My penis had helped me survive the first cut of the apartment hunt bris and I was thankful for it.

"I gather you boys are here to see me," said the woman, a gleam in her eyes. Her voice was intimate and soothing. Chocolate mocha ice cream. A few men started to leave. I guess it wasn't their cup of black oolong, but I felt like honey ready to melt into the mix. Stir it up.

"You and you," then pointing with eyes only, way in the back toward me, "and you. The rest of you, thank you." She did this with ease, no exuberance, no explanation. It was like I'd called on God and he'd put me on hold, but at least Mahalia Jackson was singing while I waited. I pulled up my sagging pants as I made my way up to the front, stoked to be one of the You's. I could feel the eyes on me and I loved it. *Who da man? Who da man? How ya like me now?*

Hello," she said as we stood in the entryway. "I'm Carmen England." "Richard Downing," said one of the guys, wearing a designer pin-striped suit and spit-shined shoes. He'd gone all out and I started to worry.

"Nice to meet you," said Carmen, then looking at the other guy.

"Scott Franklin," he said. His dark hair was cut short in the back and the sides, but he'd left it full on top. He had huge dimples and couldn't seem to stop smiling.

"A pleasure," said Carmen, then she looked at me. "And you?"

"Ma-Malik," I said, tugging on my pants, slightly slouching, giving aloof. "Malik Randolph."

I instantly felt alive. I didn't care that it wasn't my name, but just saying it made me feel powerful. Assertive. Assured. Just the name alone made me feel as though I could walk down the streets of Harlem without scorn or ridicule; bubble coat on my back, forty-ounce in my hand. If I wasn't going to get the place, it wasn't going to be because I was blending.

"Wassup?" I said, extending my hand to her.

Carmen arched her eyebrow, then said, "Never extend your hand to a lady unless she offers hers first."

I dropped my hand back to my side and started rubbing it against my pant leg, hoping that would salve the sting before it began to swell.

"Sorry."

"Don't be. It's nice to meet you, Mamalik."

"What? Uh, oh," I said. "It's just Malik."

"That's very seventies. Power to the people."

"You know," I said, trying to compete with Scott's smile. "Gotta keep it real."

M y twists and the way I was wearing my clothes would have made my mother have a fit and it would have even made those at Johnny's Barbershop, an institution in Layton, Louisiana, pause. Though appointments weren't taken at Johnny's, people would line up for hours before the shop opened to be one of the first to take a number.

Clovis was the most skilled barber and always cut my hair. If you wanted any style, Clovis was your man. But he never got to try them fully on my nonthreatening fade.

There was always lively conversation going on, but once the soap operas started, all attention went to the television on top of the "pop" machine. These men were as avid about their "stories" as any woman and were loyal to the CBS lineup. They would talk about when Nikki was a stripper before marrying Victor or when Mrs. Chancler had her first face-lift, long before she met Rex, or they'd talk about Billy and his drinking problem. They'd shake their heads at the woes of the television rich.

But whenever I'd walk into the shop they'd want to know what was up with the "Randolph boy." I don't think many of them knew my first name, but they knew, or knew of, my father and I was his son.

One day I was getting a haircut because I was going to Baton Rouge to represent Layton in the Louisiana State Spelling Bee. I'd told Clovis and he made a point to share the news. As usual, the old men sitting in the chairs that lined the wall, beneath the coat hooks and old posters of old hairdos sure to come back, were encouraging.

Clovis finished my cut, put the stinging green rubbing alcohol around the hairline and brushed me down with talc powder. He removed the barber's cloth and I stepped down from the chair, but before I could start to leave, Joe motioned me over.

Blue-eyed Joe was a fixture in the shop. He'd take the lunch orders and phone them in to Marianne's, the soul food joint a few doors down. He also swept up the different textures of hair that had fallen around the base of the chairs, all becoming one.

Black hair is hard work.

The bluish haze coating his left eye was how he got his name. No one knew if he could see out of it and no one ever asked. Mr. Joe never said more than he had to.

He patted the fold-out chair next to him. I sat, but he didn't look at me. He kept looking at the action in the pool hall in the back of the shop.

"Don't ever smile too big when thangs going good for you," said Joe. "We's proud of you here, hear?"

"Yes, sir, Mr. Joe."

"Just know, ever'body in that world out there ain't gonna be like that. Some people, Colored or other, ain't never gonna want to see no black man looking too happy. God speed."

Joe turned away from the pool hall and looked up to the television set. As I opened my mouth he put his hand up to stop me.

As the World Turns was starting.

C armen showed us the room available for rent. It was small, right across from the kitchen and under the stairs, but a window looked onto the garden. I knew I could work with it.

We followed her back down the hall and into "the parlor." I looked around, taking it all in. The gilt mirror over the mahogany fireplace, the wainscoting, the decanters on the drinks cabinet, the ceiling cornices, the Oriental rugs and the pocket doors that closed off another room. The smell of the old didn't bother me.

She eased down onto the edge of a chair and motioned for us to take a seat. Richard headed for the chair to her right.

"Not in that chair, dear heart," she said. "It may not appear so, but the arm is loose and I can't be bothered to have it mended. I broke it when I was a child. When fine things begin to fall apart, only then do they reveal their true essence. Trust." Richard made his way over and joined us on the sofa.

"So. What is it that you boys do," she said, and after a brief pause, "for a living?"

I listened, getting nervous, as they spoke. Scott was a model, Richard a lawyer. Carmen focused on them with debutante attention and it took everything I had not to start twisting my hair. When they finished she looked at me.

"I don't have a job." I found myself thinking, *Oh, now you wanna tell the truth*. I could feel the sweat huddling in my armpits, ready to fall like rain from a dark cloud on a New Orleans afternoon. "Yet."

Carmen laughed and the other two guys relaxed in their seats, all of us certain that I'd blown my chance.

"I just got to the city a couple of weeks ago," I said, forgetting that I was trying to be cool, trying to be down, trying to turn this dead end into a cul-de-sac. "But you know, I have some leads and I do have enough for the deposit and the first month's rent. As soon as I find a crib I'll focus on the job, but you need shelter." Then against my better judgment I mumbled, "It's hard on a brother out there."

Carmen looked at me for a moment like she was a doctor examining an X ray, trying to see if there was something she missed, seeing if I'd break. "Well then, it's evident to me that you're in need of the place more than these two gentlemen."

"Yes," I said. Victory mine.

"And an excellent winner to boot," said Carmen. I sunk into the sofa. I knew this outburst would make her change her mind. But she smiled and said, "I like that. Modesty is a learned affectation, wouldn't you say?"

Relief.

Carmen got up from her chair and the two guys stood, knowing they had to keep looking.

"It was nice of you to come," she said, like a host at the end of a party. She touched each of them on the back and walked them to the entryway. "You're both fine young men and I'm certain neither of you will have any difficulty finding a place."

I heard the front door close. The sound of the lock made me wonder what I'd gotten myself into. I sat waiting for her to come back into the room, but she didn't. She walked down the hall like she'd forgotten I was there. I wasn't sure what I should do, but I got up and quietly walked to the door and looked down the hall. I didn't see her.

"Ms. England," I said, like being alone in a dark empty house and asking if anyone is there. "Ms. England."

I heard a noise behind me and I jumped. "Please. Call me Carmen," she said, sliding open the pocket doors that separated the parlor from the dining room. She had a bottle of champagne and two flutes. "I suppose we're housemates, which is cause for champers."

"Sounds good," I said, walking back to the sofa. I sat then stood, trying to figure out which was best. I decided to stand. She opened the bottle and when the cork flew off she screamed like it was New Year's Eve, then poured for two. She walked toward me until she was just a few inches away and handed me a flute. "Cheers."

"Cheers," I said, focusing on the flute like it held a magic potion.

She took her finger and placed it under my chin, then lifted my head. "You should always look in the eyes of the person you're toasting. If you can't have a connection with the person with whom you're toasting, then you really shouldn't toast."

"Oh, I'm sorry." I was nervous, certain I was doing everything wrong and would soon be back on the hunt.

"Don't be." She moved in a little closer. "Let's try it again. To us," she said.

"To us."

She took her first sip and this time I held her gaze for as long as I could. The champagne had warmed in my mouth before I was able to swallow. I moved away and walked back over to the sofa and sat down. She walked around the room as though looking at everything for the first time. Her champagne flute swung in her hand like a pendulum and I was ready to be hypnotized. I watched every move: the gleam of leg peeping out of the slit of her skirt; the red of her painted toes peeking out of her shoes; the way her tennis bracelet slid down her forearm when she raised the flute to her mouth; the lipstick kiss on the rim. I watched and she didn't seem to mind.

She picked up the champagne bottle from the mantel, refilled her glass, then walked over to me and topped off mine. I watched as the bubbles reached the top of the glass but refused to fall over. She put the bottle on the coffee table. I could see my mother coming over and picking it up. *That's why we have coasters.* I took a swallow of the champagne, trying to shake the image of my mother out of my mind. Carmen walked back to her chair and finally sat. She leaned back and crossed her legs, letting her arms rest on the chair's. I sat back on the sofa, more for support than comfort. I was trying to think of something to say, but I didn't have to.

"I don't have staff here, but you should know that I do have a cleaning lady, Rosita, who comes in once a week. The way she acts, one would think she owns the place. I make every effort to see that I'm not home when she arrives." Carmen took a deep breath, and when she released it, she said, "This maison de ville has been in my family since Harlem was chic, lost its chic, then became chic again, and that's a damn long time. Uptown real estate is becoming popular and people are starting to pay cute money for properties. 'Gentrification.' Such a nice-sounding word. Much better than 'Take your shit and get.' "

I started to relax; the champagne didn't hurt. "You know," I said, "I didn't think I had a shot at the place."

"Really. You were my favorite from the beginning."

I perked up a bit. "Why's that?" I asked, reeling out the line for an ego pat.

"Just a hunch. I can't quite put a finger on it, but I saw something familiar in you."

"Gotta keep it real."

"Yes. I believe you mentioned that."

"And one hand does wash the other," I said, pulling out the race card.

"Indeed. But two hands wash the face." This almost knocked me through the sofa, but I took it and slowly eased back. "But if you must know—" She stopped then said, "What's your name again?"

There it was. I'd forgotten that little detail. My grip tightened around the champagne flute. I thought of coming clean, telling her the truth. But I was in and I wanted to savor it. Wanted to live in Harlem. Wanted to experience her. I ran my hand over my twists and those words came back to me: *Black boy blending.*

"Malik. Malik Randolph."

"Yes, Malik. Right. You see, the model was definitely eye candy and would have been a nice bauble on my arm, yet white boys that age can be gorgeous one day and ass-ugly the next. So a proper five-to-ten-year scan is always necessary. Trust."

I felt drunk, but not just from the "champers." She downed the rest of her flute, then held it out toward me. I picked up the bottle, walked over and refilled her glass.

"You're too kind," she said, touching my forearm. I felt the hairs rise under my shirt. I walked back to the sofa and put the bottle on the coaster, then I moved it, trying to stay in the moment, remain cool, appear at ease. If she didn't mind a water stain, why should I?

"As for the lawyer," she said. "He's probably just out of school. Columbia, perhaps, which means he's nothing more than a well-dressed gofer. He's definitely from a good northeastern family because the firm he mentioned rarely lets outsiders roast marshmallows at their fire.

"In a few years he will have moved up in the firm, and as this is a rather small town, I will more than likely run across him again, socially. He'll pretend to forget his experience here today, but will be a good little soldier and play nice, realizing that I may prove helpful in the future. And even if he's engaged to some poor girl who will have done more than just put in her time for his grandmother's ring, he'll still want to fuck me."

I laughed. I had to. I'd always found something sexy about a woman who could say "fuck" without hesitation, claiming it, owning it.

"You are a sweetie," she said, getting up and walking over to the sofa. She sat down. I was about to move over, but I caught myself and eased back into the cushions, opening my legs wide and placing my arm along its top like I imagined Malik would do. *Just chilling.*

"You're a southerner, aren't you?"

"Yeah," I said. "I'm from—"

"Wait. Let me guess." She placed her index finger behind her ear as if trying to pick up the radio waves of my accent. "Mississippi!" Her answer wasn't presented as a question so I was more than happy to let her be right. Why not? If I could be Malik, I could be from Mississippi. It was a sister state.

"Good ear."

"Never question a woman's skills," she said with a self-assured glow. "Southerners are so respectful and well behaved. Everyone knows their place. Lovely."

My mood suddenly turned and I began to feel uncomfortable. I felt defensive, but I forced a smile. My life had been built on staying in my place, not rocking the boat. But I wasn't in the South. I was in New York, in Harlem, in a house with Carmen, trying to change the subject, trying to change.

"Thanks for the hookup," I said. "I really needed a place and you don't have to worry about the rent."

"I'm not worried about that. I bet you're a hard little worker bee. We like that," she said. She put her hand lightly on my leg and I flinched. She smiled. "I think it'll work out wonderfully."

Carmen again held up her empty glass and I picked up the champagne bottle and refilled it. The last drop went to her.

"Move in when you like. The key is on the hook near the door," she said, standing. "Be a dear and let yourself out. It's time for my nap."

She walked out of the room and started up the stairs. I sat there for a while longer, almost like I was waiting for permission to get up, be dismissed, waiting for direction from Carmen England.

·3·

The sign in the window on Malcolm X Boulevard read, *Free Ear Piercing*. *That seemed rather clear. Argue free. No Thailand haggling.* "So it's free." "Yes, the piercing is free, but the studs are ten dollars." "Then it isn't free." "The piercing is free." "No it's not." "The studs cost ten dollars. The piercing is free." "Okay. Fine. I only want one, so that's five dollars." "No. You have to buy the pair." "But I only want one." "I can't separate the pair." "But . . ." "Look, you either want the shit or you don't." *I think that's what they call Harlem clarity.* "All right. I'll take one in each ear. But you should change the sign. I can see the studs being free and the piercing being ten dollars. The piercing is a service, but—ouch . . ."

This wasn't the life my mother had planned for me. Much to her dismay, I'd deferred a year from law school. I loved the law, its rhetoric and usage of ironic gentility, something I'd nurtured while growing up in the South. I just wasn't sure I was ready to start a life based on tort and fine print.

"Then tell me, Mason, why did we pay for that trip around the world? As far as I know, Stanford is in Palo Alto, not New York," she'd said over the phone, forgetting the mileage she'd gotten out of telling everyone I was "traveling abroad." But none of that mattered now. I was heading to Harlem.

When I got to the town house on move-in day, there was a limousine parked outside. I nodded at the driver as I climbed the steps and pulled out the Tiffany key chain I'd gotten for graduation. I got a rush as I stuck in the key, wondering if it would work, and when the lock turned, I looked back at the driver, letting him know I was home.

When I walked in, two suitcases were in the hallway, which made me think she'd taken on another housemate. I started feeling like a child not wanting to share. My duffel bag suddenly felt heavier and made my shoulders sink.

". . . a spectacular meal. Spectacular. I got the caterer's name. The table setting, the flowers. Everything." It was a woman's voice, but I was certain it wasn't Carmen's. Her voice had stayed with me for the last five days. This wasn't chocolate mocha. It was lime sorbet.

"The salad, oh, Carmen, the salad was so fresh you could still smell the Mexicans."

Then there was a laugh. I remembered that laugh.

"Wassup?" I said, standing in the doorjamb of the parlor. A woman was sitting in the room with Carmen. Her hair and face were perfectly done as though she'd just come from the salon.

"Oh, hello," said Carmen. "You've made it. Malik, this is Judith Steinman."

"Hello," said Judith Steinman.

"Wassup?"

"Malik is a southerner. From Mississippi," said Carmen.

"Oh, how wonderful," said Judith Steinman. "I've always liked southerners. Not the women, though. Bitches. All of them. You've definitely got to hide your pearls around those girls. Pure evil. Walking around like a bowl of sugar, but if you dig deep enough you're sure to find a saltine."

"Now, Judith, don't frighten the boy," said Carmen.

"It would take more than that," I said.

"That's good to know," said Carmen. "We were just about to leave. Judith has invited me on a girls' getaway."

"Yes, I can always depend on Carmen to be up for a getaway."

"I hear ya. She's been there in a pinch for me too," I said, trying to hide my disappointment. I had been waiting for my reunion with Carmen and already she was about to leave. I had to remind myself that her ad had read, Rarely home.

"Where are the rest of your things?" asked Carmen.

"This is it. I travel light."

"How I envy you," chimed in Judith Steinman. "Try as I may, I still have so much luggage."

"Malik, why don't you join us for a drink before we go?" said Carmen, extending her hand, signaling for me to come into the parlor.

"I-ight," I said, putting down my duffel bag.

"Sit," said Judith Steinman, patting the sofa next to her. She downed the rest of her drink.

"More wine, Judith?" asked Carmen.

"Well, maybe just half a glass."

"I'll get it," I said. I quickly stood up, taking Judith Steinman's wineglass, but I was moving too fast and as I walked by I hit my shin on the coffee table.

"Ah," I said, trying to hold it in.

"Are you okay?" asked Carmen.

"That's got to hurt," said Judith Steinman.

"Uh-huh. Fine."

"Good. Would you get me a bit more too?" said Carmen, handing me her cocktail glass.

"What's your poison?" I asked.

"Ice cubes," she said, then added, "floating in Jack Daniel's."

"So I see you've already made the switch to brown," said Judith Steinman suggestively. I looked over and she was looking at me.

"Yes, the brown liquors are dangerous," Carmen said. "But I love them, so what can I do? It's the season. So finish telling me what happened."

"Oh, yes. Yes. Divine . . ." To take my mind off my shin I focused on the drinks and their conversation. "We'd just walked in from the dinner party and the phone rang. I answer it and it's Daniel Cumming, you know, the novelist, and he says he's in the neighborhood and has a 'friend' with him. I should have known something was suspicious."

I walked over with the drinks. I gave Carmen hers first. She looked up at me and touched my hand as she took the glass. I walked over to Judith Steinman and gave her the wine. "Thank you," she said, again patting the sofa next to her. "Nothing for you?"

"Nah, I'm cool."

"This is more than half a glass," she said, taking a sip. "That's probably best. Save us all some steps." She turned her attention from her glass and back to Carmen. "I should have just come right out and told him it was late and he couldn't come by, but when a prize-winning novelist calls, you can't just turn him away. Let's face it, you can lunch on that for at least a week, particularly if he's drunk and depressed, which with him is usually the case."

"And how else are you going to end up in one of his books?" said Carmen, shaking the ice in her Jack Daniel's.

"Exactly," said Judith Steinman, raising her glass. "So he comes up and has this handsome young man with him. Just delicious." Judith Steinman looked over at me like I was hanging on a hook in a meat locker. "Completely yummy. I knew he had to be a hustler, or I think they call them escorts now. Who cares? A whore is a whore no matter what you call them." I looked over at Carmen and she met my gaze, took another sip of her drink and then looked back at Judith Steinman. "But I knew he had to be one because Daniel, bless his heart, can write his foreskin off, but I've seen boils better looking than he is, so no boy like this one could possibly be interested in him unless there was some monetary exchange. But I'm not one to judge. Oh, that's a lie. I do judge. That's my job." Judith Steinman let out a shrill laugh, then continued, "Daniel started telling me all the gossip, hardly gossip at all, really. Just a rehash of the same tired stories he's told me a thousand times, but they get better each time, so at least it's entertaining. The hustler, *Johnnie,* for one seventy-five an hour, you'd think he could come up with something more original than that. Well, *Johnnie* is just sitting there smiling, adding nothing to the conversation but looking around the room, being appropriately doe-eyed and attentive, so David—David's my husband," she said to me, touching my biceps and giving it a slight squeeze—"David says to the hustler, 'Let me show you around the apartment.' So Daniel and I stay in the living room and we're chatting having a good laugh and two drinks later I realized that David and the hustler weren't back, and our apartment ain't that goddamn big."

Judith Steinman chugged the last of her wine.

"Can I get you some more?" I asked, looking for any reason to get up.

"No, that's plenty," she said. "We've got to be going," then after a thought, "Maybe just half a glass." I looked over at Carmen and she put her hand over the top of her glass, letting me know she was fine. I got up, my shin reminding me to watch the coffee table, and walked back over to the drinks cabinet. I couldn't believe how easy it was for Judith Steinman to tell her story in front of me, a stranger, but it almost seemed like she enjoyed the added ear. I didn't mind because I knew once she stopped, Carmen was going to leave.

"So I go storming through the apartment and I hear this groaning in our bedroom. Thank you," she said without missing a beat as I handed her the glass. "I opened the door and there they were going at it. It was as though the Discovery Channel had come to East Seventy-ninth Street. I was completely taken aback."

"Yeah, I'd think catching your husband in bed with another man would be surprising," I said, trying to add to the conversation. Relax.

"Oh, who cares about that?" she said with a flip of the hand. "Everybody knows David swings both ways. What surprised me was the look of excitement on his face. I hadn't seen that look since his last prostate exam." She took another drink of her wine.

"So you kicked the hustler out?" asked Carmen.

"Oh, no. He was already paid for so I had no choice but to have a turn myself."

The driver came in and took Carmen's suitcase to the car, then escorted Judith Steinman, who had managed to "half" her way through an entire bottle of white wine, down the steps.

"I shouldn't be gone more than a week," whispered Carmen. *A week?* "You were perfect in there. Make yourself at home." She kissed me on the cheek, then rubbed the lipstick away, but her scent stayed with me as she made her way down the steps to the car. When she slid into the backseat she waved, then I heard laughter.

Limousines and laughter.

Transition is exhausting. I'd planned on just taking a nap, but the sun shining through the curtains and the blue fluorescent numbers on my night table made it clear that a new day was donned.

The coolness of the season made me hug the duvet and I smiled as I looked at my little room. I stretched my body, balancing on my stomach like a baby too young to know stiffness.

I wanted to chill in the warmth of the duvet, but my bladder forced me up. I walked into the bathroom off my bedroom and stared at the mirror over the basin, angling my head in different directions, looking for the most alluring pose. I imagined Carmen standing next to me at some exclusive event, giving over for yet another photo. I could see the caption: Socialite Carmen England and unidentified young friend at . . ."

I rubbed some conditioner and hair food in my palms and ran them over my growing twists. I rotated the studs in my ears. I looked at myself and smiled. It was a big smile and I didn't think Mr. Joe would mind. It was a private smile, a smile that offended no one.

·4·

In Harlem, Prep was played so the clothes I was used to wearing weren't going to cut it if I wanted to fit in. I'd hit 125th Street, the epicenter of Harlem. Merchandise from stores, and a few cars, spilled out onto the sidewalk, urging and prompting the power of the black green, and I had worked my way up to three shopping bags of baggy jeans, shirts, hooded sweatshirts and a bubble coat.

"What about kicks?" asked the salesman as I started walking out with my bags, the Notorious B.I.G. blaring from the speakers, adding a bop to my stride.

"Yeah, I been kicking it," I said, feeling particularly down.

His "nigga please" look showed he wasn't buying it. "Nah, man. Kicks."

I followed him downstairs and he swept out his hand and before my eyes appeared a whorehouse of shoes, each fighting for my aesthetic attention.

"What size?"

"Twelve."

There was only one shoe of each pair on display, but most of those were chained down, which I guess was to prevent fashionable amputee shoplifters.

The salesman came back with several boxes and pulled out a pair of construction boots.

"New to the city, huh?"

"Yeah," I said, lacing the boots. "Came up from down South."

"Yeah, then you gonna need some good shoes. Niggas be walking. These are the bomb," he said, tapping the steel toe. I stood up, looked in the mirror. I put my hands deep into the pockets of my new baggy jeans, slouched a bit and angled to my side.

I looked good.

"Yo, G!" said a teenager, touching the shoe on the wall next to the mirror. "Check out these new Pumas. Damn."

"Yeah, Jimmy's been kicking those," said his friend. "Natasha bought 'em for his ass."

"That nigga be having all those ho's buying him shit. I need to find me a honey like Natasha."

"How you sound?" his friend asked, then looked around at the rest of us. "Ever since they got them new uniforms at Micky D's, this nigger think he all that."

"I-ight. I-ight," said the other guy. "At least I got a job, nigga. And I'ma remember that shit the next time you come in looking for a hookup on the food."

"You know I'm just playing with you. I been looking for a job. I even went down to the unemployment office to fill out an application, but them niggas wasn't hiring either."

The two guys started laughing, then butted fists. All forgiven, they rolled back upstairs.

"I'll take the boots," I said, still wearing them and walking over to the tennis shoes the guys were looking at. "These are pretty cool. I mean, they're the bomb."

"Yeah, they the bomb," said the salesman, reassuring me. "You'd be stepping style in those."

"I'll take them."

"You wanna put these on your credit card too?"

"And you know it."

Loving Harlem. Had lunch at this great restaurant; a diner really. M&G. Soul food. Today's special was oxtails. Wasn't feeling that adventurous. Had eggs over easy. Sat at the counter and when the waitress came over she asked, "How you feel?" I love that. How you feel? . . .

A woman came in, sat next to me. "How you feel?" "Girl, my head hurts." "You want a BC?" "It ain't a headache, my head just hurts. Needs time to heal. I can't afford the real deal so I had to settle on the ghetto face-lift. Cornrows. That girl did them so tight I can barely move my head. When I got in the chair she was arguing with one of the other girls and talking that French. They do good hair, but all I have to say is don't let no angry Haitian get up in your head." And that's how she felt . . .

Carmen was out of the house more than a father who owed child support and I had no choice but to start getting to know the hood.

The vibe in Harlem ran through me and I started to feel at ease, stepping out, cruising in my new urban wear. Seeing all the black faces was like a needed shot, but it left a reaction. I was no longer the only black person around, but even in that I felt like a curious traveler, flipping through a guidebook for direction.

During the day the streets were swarming with activity: the young guys rolling dice and pitching coins or the older men playing the bones, framing the double-five in hand until the right time to slam it down on the makeshift table with the joyful and needed cry of "twenty-five." But like a small town, once darkness set in, the workday done, pedestrians retired to their homes, and few of them were town houses.

On Sunday, fresh from service, the lovely women in their pinned hats, crowns, really, with Bibles under arm demanded my attention. In Harlem, churches and beautiful people were much the same: it was impossible to take ten steps without seeing one.

Mount Olivet, 1907. St. Martin's, 1888. Bethelite Community, formerly the Harlem Club, 1889. St. Andrew's, 1891. St. Ambrose, originally the Church of the Puritans, 1875. Greater Bethel, originally the Harlem Free Library, 1892. Metropolitan Baptist, originally New York Presbyterian, 1884. St. Philip's, 1911, an effort of two black architects, one of which, Vertner W. Tandy, was the first black to receive an architectural registration in New York State. Abyssinian, where Adam Clayton Powell Jr.'s spirit still thrives, 1923.

Many of the other buildings lining the streets were like corpses waiting to be identified by more than just posters for albums, concerts and malt liquor. But the churches remained a presence, almost screaming, *I shall not be moved.*

The Studio Museum in Harlem became my Metropolitan Museum, and when I walked along 125th Street, the music pumping from stores and cars made me think of the Savoy dance hall, "the Home of Happy Feet," where race didn't matter, but your moves did. It was a sole thing, a swing thing, a dream thing.

As I walked by the Apollo Theater, in a blink I was back in the Renaissance, back when black was the beginning of all true things and definitions were redefined.

In everything I could see the determination in Jacob Lawrence's colorful migration and over "The Walls of Jericho" I could feel "The Weary Blues" of Langston Hughes as Bessie Smith's voice spilled out onto the dapper streets.

I thought of Zora Neale Hurston, a southerner true. I imagined a hearty laugh coming up from her toes, where a real laugh roots. From the first time I read her work, I'd longed to be her man; longed to be back there to assure her her words were appreciated, long before they stopped blooming from her fingers and mouth.

I walked for hours, drawn by the power found in lore, and when I got back to the town house the past was replaced with the present. Carmen wasn't home and I was back, in my solitude.

·5·

U m, what's that smell?" asked Carmen, coming into the kitchen, giving me a lift like finding a twenty in the pocket of a pair of pants you haven't worn in a while. She was dressed casually, wearing jeans and a crisp white oxford shirt, and a silk bandanna tied around her head.

"I didn't know you were home," I said, hardly able to curb my enthusiasm. It had been almost a week since I'd last seen her and even then our conversation was brief. She had been on her way to a Halloween party, where she went as Cat Woman, looking as soothing as silk against a naked body. "It's chili."

"I didn't mean to startle you. I've been upstairs most of the day. I guess I didn't hear you come in. I wish I'd known, I could have used the company."

Carmen walked over, took the wooden spoon from me and tasted the chili. "Um, very good."

"Cooking is a part of growing up in the South," I said, adding cayenne. "In New York the first thing people ask you is, 'What do you do?' But in Louisiana we wanna know what you had to eat." I failed to tell her that that question was just as revealing.

"I thought you said you were from Mississippi," she said, opening the door to the deck and looking out onto the garden as though it was a marvel.

"Yeah," I said. I kept stirring as steam brimmed from the pot. I felt sweat make an appearance but the breeze coming in from the door dried my brow as quickly as the moisture appeared, tightening like a mask over my face. "But my grandmother lives in Louisiana and I was living down her way before I came up here."

I watched as the tomato sauce rose to the surface, bubbled and popped. *Hot air.*

"Oh. And how is the job going?"

"It's all good," I said. My knees immediately began to ache, a product of Catholic guilt, whenever I spoke of my job; particularly since I didn't have one. "It's been slammed. For a café, the tips aren't bad. There's nothing like cash in hand."

"Great," said Carmen, closing the deck door. "I'm glad that things are working out for you."

"What about you?" I asked. I didn't want to just come out and ask her about her job. She'd never mentioned one. It was a tricky question, one that would definitely get me a cross look from my mother, who believed it inappropriate to talk about money, but I was intrigued by this creature who seemed to just float through life, free.

"What about me?"

"I was just, you know, wondering . . ."

"You mean do I have a job?"

"Yeah," I said, unable to look at her.

"I live in New York."

She then walked over to the refrigerator and opened it. "What is this?" she asked, pulling out a bottle and holding it up as though she'd found a body.

"A Forty," I said proudly. I'd started stocking forty-ounce bottles of Ballantine ale, high-end malt liquor.

"A Forty? And it's in here, why?"

"To get my buzz on."

"Get your buzz on?"

"Yeah, gotta have my Forty."

Carmen put the bottle back in the refrigerator as if it carried a virus, closed the door and shook her head. "At first all we wanted was forty acres and a mule, now we're drinking Forties and acting like asses. Life and its twists." She rubbed my head and started to walk out of the kitchen.

"Oh, I've been collecting your mail. It's on the counter." Carmen walked over and picked up the mail. I watched her because I'd seen a guy's name on many of the envelopes. Christopher Langley. I was sure he was the guy I'd replaced. She leafed through the mail and said nothing but "Thank you" as she walked out of the kitchen.

I'd been an obedient child and always did as I was told. This made me somewhat passive, yet I knew the difference between being passive and being unaware, being seen and being invisible.

I didn't see a rated-R movie until I was seventeen because my mother told me not to. Seventeen was the age restriction; it was right there in the commercial. So it wasn't a case that I could argue and win.

Mothers love to point out to other mothers the inappropriate behavior of a child; other than their own. It may be with a nod, a raised brow or an offhand remark behind a smile. But as I was the only black boy in most of my environments, my mother never had to concern herself with that.

I was an obedient child and always did as I was told.

Before I was born, Jonathan Scott Randolph, my father, once had aspirations of being a painter. I'd never seen him pick up a brush, not even to paint our house, but nonetheless he'd told me about his dream.

I was ten years old and on a Saturday afternoon we'd gone up to the attic. He showed me some of his work. Cubist—a period long gone. Mangled tubes of paint were in a wooden shoe box along with more than twenty different brushes. He unrolled the canvases, one by one, and a light—faint, but a light nonetheless—appeared on his face. I could see him recalling another time, a freer time, a time of youthful possibilities. But when the sixties were nearing an end and the promise of change had been killed in Dallas and then Memphis, life presented itself to my father and he put away his canvases and clogs and opted for an M.B.A. instead.

"It's hard to root on rock," he said, rubbing my head.

He'd done what he had to do. He grew into his name, it didn't grow into him.

D inah Washington's voice was coming out of the speakers, the candles were lit, a bottle of wine, long confined, was breathing. Though I usually ate at the kitchen table, alone, except for my journal or a copy of the *Amsterdam News,* Carmen insisted we use the dining room.

"I hope you don't mind my musical selection," she said, walking into the dining room from the parlor where the turntable and records were in a cabinet under the bookshelves.

"Yeah," I said, "Dinah Washington. Old school. You can't get much better than Ruth Jones."

"Impressive," said Carmen. She pulled out the chair directly across from me at a table for eight but with its leaves added could be extended to a friendly twelve. Even with that much room, Carmen's presence made the mood intimate. I thought of making a grand gesture by sweeping everything off of the table and pulling her onto it. The thought relaxed me. "You even know her real name? I wouldn't expect someone your age to appreciate Ms. Washington."

"You know. I get around."

"I bet you do," she said.

"Nah. My old man was down with jazz," I said, passing her a bowl of chili. "He played it like it was going out of style."

"Thank you. It smells delicious." Carmen poured some wine into my glass. I didn't reach for it.

"That bottle doesn't look like MD 20/20," I said. I could see that it was a 1989 Château Talbot. I'd had it in France. "I wouldn't waste it on chili."

"Don't be silly," she said. "Yes, it's a far cry from a Forty, but this bottle has been around waiting for a special occasion. Look at it as congratulations for your job."

I couldn't appreciate the gesture and it evidently showed on my face, and under the table I was rubbing my knees. She picked up the linen napkin and placed it across her lap, then I did the same, as though following her lead.

"Would you like to lead us in prayer?" she asked. This took me by surprise. I hadn't expected Carmen to be religious and again my face failed me. "Don't look so surprised. I pray."

"Nah, I just . . ."

"As Billie used to say, 'Hush now, don't explain.' "

Slap.

Her posture changed, slumping then rising just a bit, but not to full capacity. She took a sip of her wine, then said, "Don't judge me just yet, Malik. This candle still has plenty of wick. Trust." She looked at me for a moment, then bowed her head. "Dear heavenly Father, thank you for this meal we are about to receive and the company in which it is shared, for neither is granted. In your name we pray."

"Amen." This, I said alone.

Heeey," said Carmen, putting her wineglass on the coffee table and oozing up from the sofa as though the groove had nestled in her lower back, making sitting impossible. "This is my song. Dance with me."

She didn't have to ask twice. She took my hand and we walked to the front of the fireplace, not yet cold enough to be lit. I stood for a moment looking at her, not certain how close to move in. "I don't bite."

"Too bad," I said. I put my hand around her until my palms, sweaty and anxious, rested firmly against the small of her back. She draped her arms over my shoulders and we inched closer until our stomachs kissed.

"That was a lovely meal," she said in a tone as if she'd just taken the first bite. "Thank you."

"It was just chili."

"Take the compliment. Take it. Knowing how to accept a compliment keeps them coming." It wasn't a reprimand; her tone was as soothing as Dinah Washington's voice. Our bodies fit, moving magically as we slowly swayed, lento sostenuto, circling in one spot, my hand sliding to the groove at the small of the back. Sometimes the shortest songs say the most, and we remained silent until the last line, when Carmen's voice blended with Dinah's, "And this bitter earth may not be so bitter after all."

The record stopped and the sound of the turntable clicking didn't detract from the mood. We swayed in silence a while more.

Another album played; another bottle of wine opened. Carmen and I went out on the deck off the kitchen. Though new to New York, I was aware of the value of outdoor space, of nature in a place where the fires that had blazed in Harlem did little to enrich the soil. Yet, in this glaring city, stars were still visible.

The wine, deceiving, made the fall breeze exhilarating; kind caresses to the skin.

"Is this Nancy Wilson?" I asked, leaning against the railing. Carmen had positioned herself in one of the deck chairs, cruising into the night.

"No. Little Jimmy Scott."

"That's a man?"

"Some have debated, but yes."

"Stop tripping. It's Nancy Wilson."

"No it's not. Nancy sounds like him, but he's the true diva. I saw him a few years ago. Divine. It was a lovely evening."

"Bet," I said.

"It was a surprise, actually. Christopher had gotten tickets. He knew I loved Jimmy."

The name made my ears arch like a dog hearing food hitting his bowl. It was the first time she'd mentioned him.

Christopher.

"I'd gotten dressed up, looking particularly fetching, as is my wont," she said, putting her feet up in the chair and placing her chin on her knee. "He kept saying that we were going to see someone special but when the car pulled in front of Tavern on the Green I thought it was a joke. No one goes there anymore."

A Mona Lisa smile graced her face as she put her leg back on the deck's floor. She put down her wineglass, sat straight up and stared into the beyond as though Jimmy was about to appear before us.

"He looked adorable but fragile and you wanted to hug him. Even though he was long in age, all the glitz in the place paled to his presence. Tears filled my eyes and I'm not one to cry."

"Damn," I said. "There's always something slamming to do in this city."

"If you've the money," she said, again joining me from her reverie. "If he does another show, I'll take you. We'll make an evening of it."

"Bet," I said, sitting on the top railing of the deck. "I'm surprised you don't have anything going on tonight."

"Oh, there's always something going on, but one must pick and choose. Opting not to go is often better than being there." Carmen leaned over and touched my knee. "This is our night. I barely know a thing about you."

"Not much to tell."

"Then make something up," she said, getting up and grabbing my arms, feigning to push me off the railing.

Then make something up. Those words sat with the wine and forced me to utter, "That's usually easier."

"Rough life?"

"No more than anybody else," I said, certain this was true, certain I could convince myself.

"But it was yours."

"Yeah." I looked down at the deck, focusing on the crevices between each plank, believing I could seep through as my bones and spine seemingly deteriorated.

"Why did you have to live with your grandmother?"

"What?"

"In Louisiana."

"Oh," I said, taking a sip of my wine to give myself a moment to think. "My moms had a breakdown. We don't know why. She just went into this depression. Bipolar, I think they called it. She wouldn't leave the house and thought everyone was out to get her. The pills helped, when she took them, but she was always tripping, and sometimes she got scared of me. So my old man shipped me off to live with my grandmother."

I stopped for a moment, looking up at the stars, waiting for God to reach down and pluck my ear. Carmen said nothing, but looked at me attentively as though she were in a UNICEF commercial and was urging others to write a check in support of this poor disadvantaged boy. I could feel the chili churning in my stomach.

I stepped down from the railing and turned away from her. I found myself fighting the urge to say, "See, what had happened was . . ." or "See, I had told her that . . . ," becoming nothing more than a child trying to thwart punishment, but other words found their way into my mouth.

"We didn't have any insurance and with the doctors and the medicine, money was tight, so my old man pulled some strings and got me a job at the refinery, but I wasn't feeling that. One day I just woke up and thought I'd come up here. Check it out. Maybe try to write."

"That was brave of you."

Bravery implies a choice. We sat silently. I couldn't add any more. Luckily, I didn't have to.

"Today I was in Central Park," she said. "It's always pleasant in the fall. The colors are breathtaking. I walked around the reservoir and over to the Great Lawn. I had no destination in mind. I was just walking, consumed by the beauty of it all. But I ended up near the playground that Diana Ross funded. I stood at the gate watching all the little kids playing. One can't help but smile when one sees kids. They give one hope."

"Yeah. Do you want kids?"

"I wouldn't be a good mother."

"How do you know?"

"Some things one just knows. But I just stood for about ten minutes and watched the kids play. The West Indian nannies were all sitting on benches, talking but keeping an eye on the kid that belonged to them. There *was* one mother sitting in the playground. She was sitting away from everyone else. But she got up and went over to get her daughter and told her it was time for them to go. She took the little girl's hand and led her out of the playground.

"One could see that the little girl wanted to stay, she had such a long face. Her mother tried to placate her and asked, 'What's wrong?' and the little girl, this innocent little girl, just as they were walking by me, looked up and said, 'I want a black mommy like everyone else.'

"I wanted to laugh, but I couldn't. I couldn't laugh. The look on that mother's face! I'll never forget it. I can't describe it, but I'll never forget that look."

Carmen stood up from her chair. She rubbed my head, then worked her way down to my chin before letting go. She gave my arms a reassuring embrace, then walked to the door.

"Thanks again for the meal," she said, turning back toward me, and almost as an afterthought, "Always remember, Malik, what you do or where you're from is irrelevant. What's important is knowing what you're doing and where you're going."

"And how do you do that?"

"By knowing who one isn't." I was certain she had read through my story and was just placating me. Carmen looked at me for a moment, then turned to go inside.

I sat on the deck a while longer but as I walked to my bedroom I suddenly felt consumed by my evening, our evening. I lit some of the Blue Nile incense I'd bought from a street vendor on 125th, and watched as the ember released its smoke, snaking through my small room, yet not at all constricting. I opened my journal, hoping to write, hoping to decipher what I had felt, experienced, but no words would come. I closed the journal, defeated and torn, and for the first time in a long while, I got down on my knees to say a prayer. My fingers automatically wrapped together, tightly, as though concealing a rare black pearl, certain that if the world knew I had it, it would be taken away, its value beyond me. My knees immediately began to protest against their contact with the hardwood floor. As I prayed, I wondered if Carmen was on her knees too. I also wondered how many people, other than my grandmother, still got on their knees every day. I prayed and the words flowed. A journal can only do so much.

·6·

Though I knew I could get by on my credit card and allowance, the last few weeks I'd done more than just hang around the town house modeling my new urban gear, drinking Forties and pining for Carmen. I had made an honest attempt at finding a job, deciding that working as a waiter would allow me to meet people and still give me ample time to enjoy the city and Carmen.

I'd been told that getting a restaurant job downtown had little to do with past experience and everything to do with having the right look, and since ethnic was in, "at the moment," I didn't think I'd have a problem.

I'd gotten dressed in all black and stood in the mirror, yanking and pulling my clothes, expending a great deal of energy to evoke casual. I'd gotten résumés printed up, as restaurant jobs are like auditions and some places even feel the need to take a Polaroid of you. It's about the look.

One place had a Help Wanted sign in the window near the door. It was a modern restaurant, trying to evoke Belgian bistro, and it was dimly lit to compliment even the most uncomplimentary patron. Bottled water centered each table, signaling that tap was for cheap people and cheap people were not allowed. The waiters were setting up for the dinner shift and their uniforms looked custom-made.

I took some deep breaths, refusing to be defeated, walked in, picked up the sign, hoping to indicate their search had come to an end. After numerous restaurant visits and no job, I was a bit delirious, and when the woman at the host stand finally acknowledged me, you would have thought I was Pontius Pilate and she was Jesus.

I held up the sign. All of the wait staff stopped what they were doing and looked at me nervously. I could hear my father saying, "Nothing bolsters employee productivity like a Help Wanted sign."

"I'd meant to take that down," said the woman at the host stand. She took the sign from me and put it behind the stand. "But you can leave a résumé and we'll keep it on file."

I, remaining positive, left my résumé and went to a few other places in the area. But later, still jobless, as I walked back by the bistro the sign had been put back in the window, for all, and me, to see.

I looked at the woman inside. She stared at me for a second, then walked out of view.

Everyone told me that if I wanted a restaurant job I had to have the right look.

I walked to the subway station and stood on the 1/9 train platform. Everyone looked exhausted, agitated. Announcements were made through the intercom but the words came out muffled, useless static. People strained their ears toward the speakers and became annoyed by the lack of communication, but I began to laugh, and as I thought of every restaurant I'd gone in that day, Travers came to mind.

Travers Kendall and I had become friends when his family moved to Layton from Boston into the house next door to ours on Elmwood

Drive, becoming the second black family in the neighborhood, prompting other For Sale signs to shoot up like poplar trees. This didn't surprise Travers. Boston had prepared him.

One day we'd gone to the mall and were walking around Dillard's department store. There was Muzak playing but it was suddenly interrupted by a sweet voice that crooned, "Number twenty-three. Number twenty-three. Pick up in Men's."

Pretending he was an employee, Travers walked over to the store phone on the wall in the men's department, picked it up and punched in some numbers. I tried to stop him but he pushed me away.

The Muzak continued, then it stopped and I heard Travers over the public announcement system.

"Number twenty-three. Number twenty-three," he said, taking on the same tone of the woman we'd heard moments earlier. Then in his own voice he said, "Two young niggers in the men's department. Watch 'em."

As the words echoed through the store, as well as in mind and conscience, Travers dropped the phone and we ran out of the store, laughing all the way until we made it to the parking lot, where we climbed into my car and sped away.

The 1 train pulled into the station, breaking me of my thoughts of Travers, thoughts of Muzak, thoughts of home, of Louisiana, thoughts of rejection. Laughter. The muddled words of the subway intercom seemed less important as people boarded the train, just enough energy left to push and shove, jockeying for position; nearer to being home, to familiarity if not comfort.

D amn," said Jim as I opened the front door of the town house. "Check out this fucking place."

"What did I tell ya? Sweet, huh?"

"Hell, yeah."

I showed him the parlor, the kitchen, then my room. I could tell he was already impressed but I'd been saving the prize.

"Come on. You've got to check out the roof," I said, walking down the hallway and heading toward the stairs. When we reached the second floor Jim stopped at Carmen's door. "What's this?" Carmen had posted a sign: ROSITA: DO NOT ENTER.

"Rosita is the cleaning lady," I said, still heading upstairs. "I don't think they get on, but it's probably one of those love-hate things from too many years of knowing somebody."

"And are these bedrooms?" he asked as we climbed to the third floor.

"I guess. I don't know. The doors are locked."

"Spooky," said Jim, pushing down the handle of one of the doors.

"Don't. I told you they're locked." I knew very well the doors were locked. I'd used a paper clip, a screwdriver, and had even bent a butter knife, trying to pry my way into one of those doors. For the first time in my life I was disappointed that I hadn't taken shop class in high school. "It's a big house and she was living here alone when I moved in, but mail keeps coming for some guy named Christopher."

"But he hasn't come by to pick it up?"

"No. I don't think so. I haven't seen him."

"She probably murdered him and he's chopped up in one of those rooms in a trunk filled with coffee beans so you won't be able to smell him when he starts to rot."

"You really need to lay off the pot."

"Okay. But if you disappear, I'll know where to tell Five-O to start looking."

We climbed the last few steps that led to the roof. I opened the door with a pride-filled flourish.

"Look at this fucking view," said Jim, scanning the 360-degree view.

"Yeah. You should see it at night. All of the buildings downtown are lit up. It's the bomb."

"Damn. At first I was, like, why is he moving way uptown? But this place is slamming," he said, then, adding the highest of compliments, "I'm jealous."

"Thanks."

D on't sit there," I said when Jim started to sit down. "The arm's broken." He moved over from the ailing chair to the sofa and pulled out a cigarette from his pack of Parliaments. "You can't smoke in here."

"But there's an ashtray right here. She must not care."

"Maybe so, but I've not seen her smoke and I don't want to risk it."

"But there's an ashtray right here."

"I know but it's probably for guests." Jim gave me a look. "Look, I told you, I'm trying to make a good impression. If I get kicked out of here I'll have to move back in with you."

"I'll wait," said Jim, taking the cigarette out of his mouth. "This place is pretty cool. What does she do?"

"She lives in New York. That's job enough."

Jim could easily relate to this. His mother, Reeva, had the same occupation. I'd met her at one of Jim's gigs. He was surprised she'd come out and I didn't understand until she said, "Goodness, I haven't been below Forty-second Street since 1968."

Jim was the heir of a pharmaceutical company and it was almost impossible to pop a pill without his name being on or associated with it. The intake of his family alone made certain the company would always prosper.

"This used to be her grandparents' place. That's all I know," I said. "But listen, I need a favor. If you call and she answers or is around when you're here, I need you to call me Malik."

"Malik?"

"Yeah. I told her my name was Malik."

"Why?"

"It kind of slipped out."

"Saying 'I love you' while fucking somebody for the first time is a slip. That I can see. Been there. But another name?"

"The two other dudes up for the place were really uptight and I wanted to stand out, and this isn't downtown and one thing led to another and the next thing I knew I was Malik from Mississippi with a bipolar mother and a father who wanted me to work at the refinery."

"But your father is the president of the refinery."

"I know that. But Carmen doesn't."

"So let me get this straight," said Jim, flipping his cigarette between his fingers like he was practicing a magic trick. "What you're saying is, it's okay for you to stink up the place with your bullshit, but smoking might upset her?"

"It sounds worse than it is. When we met at that pension on the Rambla you said you liked traveling because you could reinvent yourself, totally escape from the scene."

"Yeah, Mason, but—"

"Malik."

"What?"

"Call me Malik."

"Okay, *Malik,* but I could be someone else in Spain. I'm back in New York. People know me here."

"Yeah, but I'm still traveling," I said. "I don't plan to do this for life. I'm gonna tell her, I just can't tell her now. Look at this place. She'd probably kick me out."

"This is some crazy shit," said Jim, quickly lighting his cigarette. I couldn't refuse him. I needed his cooperation.

"It's not a crime. I'm paying rent. So I changed my name, big deal; so have half the people in this city. I made stuff up and she filled in the blanks. It's no big deal."

"Save it for law school, because they might buy that at Stanford but I'm not buying it here."

The front door opened. I jumped from the chair, waving my hands through the air to dilute the smoke, wishing I'd lit incense to cover the smell, only adding to the list of deceptions.

She walked into the doorway of the parlor.

"Oh," she said, looking at me, then noticing Jim. "You've got company."

"Uh, yeah. Jim Ross. This is Carmen. Carmen England. I didn't know you'd be back so soon. Sorry."

"Don't be," said Carmen. "You don't need my permission to have a guest." She walked into the room and headed toward Jim on the sofa. "Oh, the day I've had. Can I trouble you for a ciggie?"

"No prob." Jim smiled at me as he pulled out a cigarette for Carmen. He flicked his lighter and she cupped his hand as she leaned toward the flame. Carmen took a long drag, then expertly blew out the smoke through her nostrils.

"I didn't know you smoked," I said.

"I used to smoke religiously," she said, flipping an ash into the ashtray, "then I saw a photo of what it does to the skin. I couldn't have that. Not that I'm against plastic surgery. I refuse to judge anyone who feels the need to change a few things in order to make one feel better. It drives the economy."

I looked over at Jim and it was my turn to smile, which made him blow smoke in my direction.

Carmen took another drag on the cigarette and dabbed it out in the ashtray. She got up from the sofa. "Nice to meet you." She gave him a curious look. "Jim Ross. You look familiar. You wouldn't happen to be related to Reeva Ross, would you?"

"Yeah," said Jim, putting out his half-smoked cigarette and immediately reaching for another. He looked over at me, and I knew he understood that needing a change wasn't so peculiar. I could now be Malik, but he was Jim Ross. Inheritance comes in many forms and always with a price. "She's my mother."

"I thought so. How is Reeva?"

"Peachy keen," said Jim.

"Wonderful," said Carmen, extending her hand to Jim. "A pleasure to meet you."

After seeing Jim off I walked back into the town house. Carmen looked down from the landing of the second floor almost as if she'd been waiting for me to return. "Aren't we just stepping in high cotton now?" said Carmen, walking down the stairs. "How do you know Reeva's son?"

"His name is Jim."

"Yes, but he's Reeva's, regardless. How do you know him?"

"I know people," I said a bit abruptly, upset that she wouldn't think the likes of me could know anyone she'd consider worthy. But I didn't want to raise suspicion. "Just from downtown. He comes into the café where I work," then quickly adding, "How did you know who he was? Do you know his mother well?" I could just envision Reeva walking into the town house one day, blowing my cover.

"Just socially. I see her at this or that. I remember seeing him at some benefit his mother was chairing. The Rosses are a bold-print name."

"And you remembered him?"

"Yes. Certain names you never forget," she said, and I had to divert my eyes from hers. "Besides, white boys in tuxedos are commonplace, but a white boy with dreads in a tuxedo is blue-chip stock. Trust. Don't let his 'I'm down' routine fool you. He's a walking ATM. Boys like that I can read like a book."

"I'll have to take your word on that," I said. "He just seemed like a cool guy to me."

"Oh, Malik. You'll learn in time."

"Yeah. I guess I will."

Got mugged. It was exciting. As I write this I can't help but laugh about it.

It was late. Streets empty except for the smell of White Castle ham-

burgers. I'd been over at a bar, Nikki's, and was walking home via 125th Street. I've always liked empty streets, when it feels like everything around me is mine. I had on my headphones. Listening to Sista Souljah.

I saw him. He passed me. I wasn't paying too much attention, which was my bad, but my mind was on the music, the power of the words. I remember looking up at the Hotel Theresa. It's an office building now, but in 1960 it housed Castro during his U.N. visit because he was too afraid to stay at a downtown hotel. He knew Harlem was safer. Even Khrushchev came to call.

The guy came up behind me. Pushed me against the hotel. My back slammed against the wall. He had his hand in his jacket pocket, which bulged out toward me. That caught my attention before I even looked at his face. I was certain I was about to get shot. I began to think of the hot metal piercing my skin. He ripped the headphones off my head and the CD player from my belt. I kept looking at his pocket and then I looked at him and for some reason I wasn't scared. He wasn't big, he didn't even seem threatening. I mean, I could have taken him, particularly now that I'm sitting safely at home. He moved in close, reaching for my back pocket, and as he brushed against me I lightly touched the bulge in his jacket pocket, but felt no gun. It was just his hand. As his other hand reached for my wallet, I pushed him away, and then again, but more aggressively, I reached right out and squeezed his pocket. "You don't have a gun." "What the fuck you doing?" "That's not a gun. It's your hand." I have to laugh. What in the hell was I thinking? I sounded like I was three years old. You don't have a gun.

I watched as he walked away. I'd stopped him from taking my wallet and I didn't care about losing the Walkman, but for some reason, I don't know why, I screamed at him, "Listen to the CD. Okay? Listen to it. We've got to stop doing this shit to each other." For some reason I hoped my words wouldn't be as barren as the Harlem streets. I started walking toward him, still telling him to listen to the CD. I'm sure he was thinking, "Damn, of all people, I had to pick this annoying moth-

*erfucker." He turned back, looking at me as if I'd just broken out of
Bellevue. "What, you gonna follow me now?" "No. I just want you to
listen to—" "Right now?" "No. Just listen to it." "Okay. Damn. I'll
check it out." He kept walking away and I didn't move from my spot
until he turned the corner. It wasn't until then that I realized that I'd
just been mugged. It was then that I realized that I'd gone so far as to
touch his pocket where a gun could have been. I can still hear those
words coming from my mouth. You don't have a gun. It was a thrill.
I can't help but laugh. But it was a thrill. I wonder if he checked out
the CD.*

*I was exhilarated by my mugging and the adrenaline was rolling
through me. I popped into the Lenox Lounge. Nightcap. The music
made me think of all the jazz that my father used to play, but seeing
it live and feeling it brought it all to the forefront.*

*Jazz is about the moment. It's never played the same way. The
breaths are different. The mood is different. The audience is different.
Jazz is about the moment. As I listened I knew no matter how much
I tried to alter myself I wasn't jazz. I was an album or a CD mass-
produced, distanced from the reality of the struggle.*

*The mugging came back to mind and it wasn't so humorous any-
more and the saxophone player let me know it as he wailed.
Bittersweet. I thought of all those jazz greats, many of whom died
young. Too brilliant to be understood. Too stubborn to care. Hustlers,
really. Nothing to fall back on but their music and mother wit. They
could travel the world, honored by kings and queens, only to return to
the U.S. with their music and the shackles that came with being black,
being brilliant.*

*Now those jazz musicians are glorified. Albums and CDs pose no
threat. I'm trying not to be a mere moment pressed or burned in time,
but sitting there, I knew I wasn't jazz.*

*The same gaze that chilled the hearts of many jazz greats has now
turned toward rappers. They too are dying young. It's hard not to be
understood. But understood by whom?*

Years from now, the rappers will be looked at differently and many of them won't be here to see it. I wonder how I will be seen. How will I see myself?

The music weighed heavily on me as I walked the dark streets of Harlem, heading for home. I was suddenly afraid. I was no longer laughing. I hated that Castro felt safer in Harlem in 1960 than I did in that moment. A sigh of relief came as I climbed the steps to the stoop. Opened the door. I walked down the hall and Carmen was sitting in the kitchen, the window providing the only light.

"Hey." She jumped a bit. She looked at me and a pinch of a smile appeared, but she wiped her cheek as she looked away. She was dressed for an evening out; black crepe de chine, but her feet were bare. She didn't say anything. I opened the refrigerator and hoped to get a good look at her face from the light. "Long night?" Still no answer. "I sure did." She continued to gaze out the window. "I was at the Lenox. The bartender had to school a guy." She still said nothing, but I wanted to talk. I needed to talk about my evening. "See, he was leaning on the bar and the bartender kept saying, 'Mind your back.' She kept saying it, but the guy didn't get it. So I told him that he shouldn't turn his back on the bartender, that if he was gonna stand there taking up real estate, he oughta face the one overseeing it or let someone else in." Still, she said nothing. I failed to tell her the guy was me. Mind your back. *Still, she said nothing. "All right. I guess I'll go to bed." I started to walk toward the door, then finally, "This is a beautiful house, isn't it?" "Yeah. It's great. You're lucky." "I am, aren't I?" "Are you okay? Did something happen tonight?" She picked up her glass of Jack Daniel's. Walked to the window. "No. Sometimes I just like to dress up. It's cold out there. But this is a great house, isn't it? It's warm in here. I am lucky." "Yeah." "Yeah." She turned around. Looked at me. She was making me nervous. I looked at her and wondered if it was possible to sleepwalk with open eyes. She turned back to the window. "Tell me. What do you think is more difficult: being on the inside looking out or on the outside looking in?" "I don't know, Carmen. I guess it de-*

*pends on what you're looking at." "Good answer." Then without any
hint of how she felt about it, like just another comment on the weather,
"It's starting to snow." I walked over to the window. Stood next to her
as the first flakes of the season started to fall. White silence. "Do you
think it will stick?" "That remains to be seen." She downed the rest of
her drink. "Good night." "Good night."*

   Good night.

· 7 ·

*This city is a peculiarity, a place where chameleons do as they do;
a veritable island of strangers hoping to become less so as they
scurry to get where they have imagined they should be; a place where
even a spiderweb can appear beautiful with the right light reflecting
upon it, but what light is reflecting on me? . . .*

"Damn it!" screamed Carmen, coming down the stairs.

"Wassup?" I asked. She started walking down the hall toward me in
a robe and slippers at a pace that buffed the already shiny hardwood
floors. Though the green facial mask strained her voice, crack lines appeared at the corners of her mouth, a result of her screaming.

"Kip. He's canceled for tonight. At this hour! Fags. They tend to be
loyal and a hell of a good time, but the moment they meet someone it's
'Sorry, girl. I can't go out tonight.' Carmen walked into the kitchen but
before I could follow, she returned. "Malik. I know you have your own
life, but could you do me a gigantic favor and go out with me tonight?"

I wanted to scream out that I was available, but I didn't want to sound too eager. "I was supposed to hang out with . . . forget it," I said. "I can bail on that. Yeah. I can roll with you. If you need me to."

I'd seen Carmen leave the town house numerous times, always stylishly dressed with the of-the-moment fashionable cocktail purse with just enough strap to fit on her shoulder. She'd wake from her constitutional nap, make a few phone calls to decide which evening's event she'd grace. Sometimes I'd followed her around the house, hoping that my presence would instigate an invitation. Those nights I'd merely remained the doggy in the window. But suddenly it appeared my breed had become fashionable. It was time for my walk.

"Wonderful," she said, kissing me quickly on the lips. Her mask smelled like avocados and though I hated avocados I wanted to eat it up. "Come upstairs. We've got to get dressed."

She grabbed my hand and I followed closely as she turned the corner at the top of the stairs and went into the first door. Her bedroom. I stood at the door as though there were an invisible field keeping me from entering. This was the first time I'd seen the room.

It was surprisingly messy. She was always so put together that I'd assumed that that would carry over into every aspect of her life, but open suitcases were on the floor with clothes flooding over.

"Going on another trip?"

"Oh, no. That's from the last one."

Carmen quickly disappeared into another room. As I walked in I stepped on an alligator mule, which made me start walking as though the floor would devour me. I thought of all the other men who had stepped into this room and wondered if they felt the same way I felt simply standing here.

My focus immediately shot to the bed and as I had imagined, it was the centerpiece of the room: a mahogany four-poster, sheathed with a mosquito net like the one I'd slept in at a hotel in Chiang Mai. White sheets, a white duvet and two king-size pillows rested on top while a plethora of small multicolored throw pillows were haphazardly scattered about. I wanted to run over and jump in the bed, roll through it, smell her scent, but the sight of her skin pulled my attention to another part of the room; a camel to water.

Leaning in the corner was an image of Carmen. She was on her stomach stretched out and arched on a chaise lounge, and her arms were positioned beneath her, embracing herself; naked yet not. A fur throw was draped up to her shoulder blades and though the pose appeared submissive, the controlled look on her face suggested otherwise.

As I walked toward the photograph, I slipped on one of what seemed like dozens of magazines on the floor. Even in a photo she wasn't going to make it easy to reach her. I stared at the picture, looking deeply into her eyes, attempting to see the reflection of the others lucky enough to be there during the shoot. I began to wonder what the photographer had said to her as he captured this creature for perpetuity. I felt a quiver in my stomach like the rush from an amusement park ride.

"You like?" she said. Her face had been washed of its mask. "Those are from my modeling days."

"Yeah," I said as I rifled through the other frames, each a shot of Carmen. "They're slamming. You should hang them. Represent."

"I did have them up but I like them better like that. Piling art in the corner adds balance to the room." Her attention quickly turned away from the photos. "Put these on. What are you, thirty-two, thirty-four?"

"Yeah," I said, a bit surprised how easily she was able to size me up, but more surprised she had men's clothing. She tossed me a pair of gabardine pants and a blue cashmere sweater.

"Then get dressed." Carmen again left the bedroom but I was uncertain as to whether I was to change there or go back downstairs. But having gained access to her room, I didn't want to leave, so I slid out of my construction boots and dropped the baggy jeans that had become the staple of my wardrobe. I stood in my boxers for a moment, hoping she would return, but something told me Carmen preferred briefs.

"Have you ever been to an art opening?" she asked, her voice drifting from the other room. At that moment, I wanted to rid myself of Malik, and step into my rightful gabardine, cashmere, art-opening place. "Nah," I said. "Never had much use for it."

"Then you're in for a treat," she said. "Could you come zip me up?"

"Yeah," I said, walking through a dressing room, a bathroom and then on to another room, which was a den. Carmen was perched on a settee.

I walked over to her, she stood, turned her back toward me, and lifted her hair. The tiny quarter-moon-shaped birthmark at the base of her neck stared back at me. Holding my breath, I reached for the zipper. I put my other hand on her waist. My pulse was evident in my fingers and I could feel the bottom of her rib cage. Expanding. Deflating. My mouth dried as I pulled up the zipper. I let my thumb brush her skin all the way up to that birthmark, providing the slightest eclipse.

She released her hair, which smelled like almonds, then turned toward me. She looked me over, then came close and pulled up the zipper of the pants that I had unintentionally left undone. "One turn deserves another," she said, her eyes smiling. After ridding me of any chance of exposure, she put her fingers between my stomach and pants, pulling the waistband to gauge the fit. I moved toward her and she didn't back away.

"Perfect," she said, the smile now appearing on her mouth.

"Couldn't be better." I closed my eyes and started to lean my face toward her. With no contact, I opened my eyes to see her back. She walked out of the den and I caught my breath. When she returned, she handed me a suede jacket.

Butter.

"You clean up very well," she said. "It even makes those things on your head look good."

"Thanks."

The phone rang.

"Could you get that? I think the phone's in the bedroom on the night table."

I ran through and picked up the phone. "Hello," I said. "Hold on."

"Who is it?" she whispered, coming into the bedroom, while putting on her earrings.

"Who this?" I asked, taking a protective tone, but the name hit me like high altitude on a smoker's lungs. "Kip."

Carmen lit up as she walked over to get the phone. The ease with which she could walk through the clothes and magazines on the floor amazed me. She didn't say hello, just, "Yes, darling, I still love you."

I sat on the bed watching her. I grabbed one of the pillows, holding on to whatever hope I had in keeping my invitation.

"So, he canceled on you, did he?" she said, enjoying the moment. "Imagine that. That's what you get for sitting by the phone waiting for a piece of ass. The most damaging wounds are self-inflicted."

Though she was speaking to Kip, the words seemed to penetrate the pillow I was holding and hit me in the chest, the weight more than a feather. Kip said something and Carmen's laugh filled the room. I tried to smile, hoping to add to the jovial atmosphere, but I sat with Sabbath stillness.

"No, dear. You're as late as last season's fashion. I've already found another companion for the evening." She winked at me, enjoying her power play. "That wouldn't be right, now would it?"

Carmen came over and sat next to me on the bed, leaning in until our arms touched. She placed her head next to mine so I could hear the conversation.

"Who is he?" asked Kip, his voice oozing with curiosity. "Have I met him? Is he cute?"

"He's called Malik," said Carmen, moving from the bed. I wanted to get up but she was succeeding in teasing both of us. "Yes, very attractive. He's a southerner and a bit green, but I'm sure I can whip him into shape." Kip said something else, and again Carmen laughed before adding, "Trust."

Carmen hung up the phone and tossed it on the bed.

"He can go with you if you want. It's cool," I said unconvincingly. For effect, I began taking off the suede jacket.

"Oh no you don't," she said, walking over and pulling the jacket back over my shoulders, then running her hand down my arm until she held my hand. "I have to teach him a lesson. Calling me up at the last minute. Who does he think I am? Ever since he booked that job on the soap, he's been a bit big for his Capri pants and on a man that's never cute. Well, that's not quite true. John Wayne pulled it off wonderfully, but Kip is no John Wayne."

"He's an actor?"

"Don't tell me you've never heard of John Wayne. I must really be getting old."

"No. I mean Kip."

"Oh. Yes. He's on a soap, though he likes to call it a daytime drama. He started out as the misguided, criminal element, son of one of the maids, but received so much fan mail that three months later he miraculously had the background to be a resident at the hospital and getting to fuck the white women on the show; an act itself. So shed no tears for him. It's you and me tonight."

Which subway are we taking?" I asked as we walked downstairs. The look Carmen gave me almost made me certain she was about to change her mind about my going.

"No, dear. These shoes aren't made for walking," she said with a giggle. "They're sending a car. These babies are from-the-house, to-the-car, to-the-event, to-the-car, back-to-the-house shoes."

That's what she may have called them, but in my neck of the woods they were still known as come-fuck-me pumps. And like standing in one of the many Harlem fish markets, I was ready to take a number.

Carmen rested her hand on my thigh as we sat in the backseat of the Lincoln Town Car, floating through the belly of Manhattan.

"All over this despicable city there are what we call Six to Eights," said Carmen. "These events start at six and end at eight, usually followed by a more selective affair. For those of us who are as tight as a Massachusen's jaw, we call it dinner."

The car crossed south of Houston and pulled up in front of a gallery on Greene Street. A large crowd was gathered, while three identically dressed pixie stick-looking girls were flipping through their clipboards determined to keep the crowd corralled.

I started to hop out of the car, but Carmen held my arm until the driver opened the door. As she stepped out, she put on her sunglasses. I slid across the seat, quickly following, and as she reached back for my hand she turned to me with a slight laugh as though I had said something funny and whispered, "Walk with me, not behind me."

The walls of the gallery were empty; nothing hanging and I seemed to be the only one looking for the art. I scoped the corners to see if anything was positioned there. Nothing.

"Where's the art?" I asked Carmen as she grabbed the last California roll from the passing tray.

"You're standing on it."

I looked down and through the hordes of black shoes I saw what had to be thousands of cards and invitations. The show was entitled "You're Invited." The artist had taken ten years of invitations he'd received and dumped them on the floor.

I walked around the space examining the invitations.

A wedding.

A magazine launch.

A first view.

A premier.

But one invitation made me stop. The lettering was beginning to blur from drops of careless wine. I bent down and could see that it had been the invitation for the inauguration of David Dinkins, New York City's first black mayor. Now, just like all the other invites, it was nothing more than another piece of history to walk on.

· · · · ·

The gallery was buzzing and cameras were flashing. There were several familiar famous faces: a few of-the-moment novelists, models and even a popular movie star who insisted on holding up the wall while looking forlorn.

Even in her impossible heels, Carmen glided through the crowd like an Alvin Ailey discovery. I watched her and watched others watch her. I felt pangs of jealousy, but was simultaneously pleased that others could appreciate her.

"I think that guy likes you," I said to her.

"Who?" she said, excited by the prospect.

"That guy over by the column." He was holding his empty wineglass down in front of him like it was a beer bottle, and his black leather pants, laced at the crotch, left little for the imagination.

Carmen nonchalantly looked over at the man. He puckered his lips and kissed her from across the room. She smiled, then looked away.

"Satan," she mumbled.

"You know him?"

"No. But Satan isn't going to be ugly. He's gonna look just like that man. Trust."

"Maybe it takes one to know one," I said.

"Cheers," she said, clinking her wineglass to mine. "You're a quick study."

"I've got a good teacher."

"The very best." We both laughed and when I looked back at the man he seemed to deflate, certain the laugh was targeted at him. I recognized the defeat in his face.

Though the opening was to end at eight, at 7:45 the mass exodus began. I spotted Carmen's burgundy raw-silk shawl heading toward the door and I quickly began to walk through the crowd, bumping into people, apologizing as I did.

"Excuse me," said a voice. I hadn't noticed her, but when I stopped she demanded my attention. Copper-toned. Her hair short and natural. She had on a pantsuit, but no shirt, providing a glimpse of breast. The outfit made her look more sophisticated than her age would warrant—she looked my age, but she wore it well. I was certain she was a model.

"Yes," I said, almost forgetting about Carmen.

"No," she said with a coy smile. "I didn't want anything. It was just that you said, 'Sorry,' when what I think you meant was 'Excuse me.' That would be the appropriate expression when you're trying to get around someone."

"My bad," I said, stunned by this beautiful semanticist.

"I didn't mind."

"Then, excuse me."

"Sure."

I backed away from her before turning to try to catch up to Carmen, but I did the "look back" and she was still watching me, then I did the "look back, look back" and she covered her smile with her hand. She had me on the line and didn't have to pull too hard because I was ready to jump into the boat. I stopped and started walking back toward her. I relaxed into a homeboy stroll, minus grabbing my dick, but on closer inspection I knew I would have to step correct with this girl and I'd better slow my roll.

At my approach she stood as firm as Lady Liberty.

"Oh, there you are," said Carmen, grabbing me by the arm and looking at the girl. "Hello."

"Hello," she said.

"We have to go now," said Carmen. "I can't be caught here at the very end and we've got to get to the dinner."

"Okay," I said.

"Are you invited to the dinner?" asked Carmen, looking at the girl.

"No."

"Um." Carmen took my hand and started leading me out.

"What's your name?" I asked as we walked away.

"Kyra."

"Later, then." I didn't know where I'd see her again, nor did I expect to, but I'd always wanted to be able to throw my head up and say, "Later."

Kyra continued to watch me. I wanted to talk to her but I let Carmen lead me out. I may have been in New York, but I was still a southerner and if we knew nothing else it was "dance with the one who brought you."

C armen and I hopped into the Town Car and rode down to a White Street building owned by the Invite artist, "a gift of his parents." Though the opening had been jam-packed, the party was smaller and more selective. This was New York, but I was familiar with these full-name affairs. My mother had hosted many and I was accustomed to the routine: compliments on attire, followed by people asking what you've been up to, hoping the answer isn't more than they've been up to, then when all that is said and done, it ultimately turns to what in university catalogs should be called Cocktail Conversation 101: Proust.

The only difference was this was New York, not Louisiana, and I didn't know anyone, and no one made an effort to engage me.

Carmen had positioned herself on one of the sofas and was holding court, so I walked around the impressive loft, imagining what I'd do to it if I lived there. I caught snippets of conversation, hoping to segue into one, but I felt like the title character of Ellison's novel.

At the party this girl said, "I just don't get ghetto." She was sitting in a group resembling a liquor advertisement hoping to appeal to the next generation. My generation. "I mean, rap I like. But ghetto? I just don't know." The guy next to her sneered, "It's the same difference." "Same difference. What exactly is that?" asked another girl, giggling and spilling her drink, which made her laughter escalate. No one gave her an answer. They moved on to the next conversation. But I knew the answer.

Same Difference: The difference is the result one obtains by sub-tracting two numbers—e.g., seven minus three equals four—which conveys the notion that although two quantities, positions, events, items—e.g., seven minus three and five minus one—don't look alike, they are, indeed, the same. Four does equal four. Thus, we have the term "same difference." That's the rap.

I positioned myself by the bar and watched Carmen work the room. Two women came over and ordered drinks. They both had on pumps, tight jeans with a belt, and a white shirt with a scarf tied around the neck; throw in a baguette and a beret and they could have been French.

"Who is that?" asked one of the women. "She looks familiar."

"I forget her name, but I think she lives up in Harlem."

My ears perked. I looked back and saw they were looking at Carmen. I wanted to tell them her name, prove myself knowledgeable, in the know. But I remained silent.

"Yes, I think I met her once. I believe someone told me her parents had opened all of these Laundromats uptown, then sold them off, making a killing."

"No. I think it was real estate."

"That's it. I met her once with that photographer. Christopher."

"Oh, yes. I think you're right. Where is he? I haven't seen him in a while."

"I don't know, but he's evidently come to his senses. Just look at her. She's a bit much if you ask me."

Who asked you? I looked over at Carmen and she waved and blew me a kiss. I stuck out my tongue in a particularly vulgar way and she laughed. The women looked at me and put their drinks on the bar.

Yeah. Yeah. Get to stepping.

They walked away from the bar and again I looked over at Carmen, who had continued watching us. She looked concerned and was trying to read my face. I forced myself to smile and motioned to the bartender. She seemed to relax a bit and lifted her glass, shaking it.

"Ice cubes," I said, turning to the bartender. "Floating in Jack Daniel's."

W ho's that?"
"Niku Henu," said Carmen, putting her compact back in her bag.

"What's his story?"

"Morning glory."

"No. Really."

"Actually, Niku has been deemed *the* black artist of the moment," she said. "This is a big night for him."

"Did he have an opening too?"

"No. More of a coming out. You see, this is Mr. Henu's first public appearance after a two-month visit at Hazelden."

"Is that an artist colony?" I asked, attempting a joke. But again, Carmen assumed I knew no better.

"You could say that," she said. She took a sip of her drink. "Hazelden is a rehabilitation center and though Niku's time there was supposed to be hush-hush, it's rumored that his gallery leaked the information to the press."

"So he was on drugs?"

"No. He's too high-end for that. Niku doesn't do drugs. He does narcotics. Would you like to meet him?" A look of excitement filled her eyes as though the devil had climbed his way through her ear and happily sat, legs crossed, on the right side of her brain.

"All right," I said, trying to appear noncommittal. Carmen placed her drink on a table as we walked across the loft toward Niku, who was surrounded by a tony crowd.

"Those vultures swarming around him are collectors checking to see if there's any meat left. They've been shelling out cute money for his work hoping that Niku would follow in Basquiat's footsteps."

"He's that good?" I asked.

"Something like that," uttered Carmen.

I suddenly became starstruck, thrilled that I was about to meet someone being compared to an art icon. A black someone making it in the arts.

Niku Henu looked like a black Andy Warhol. He had on cake makeup, two shades lighter than his skin, and I couldn't tell if his hair was his own.

"Carmen!" said Niku. I could feel the entire room turn to look at us. The collectors opened a space for us so we could move in, and Carmen and Niku embraced and air-kissed, neither wanting to muss their makeup. "It's been a while, but as I'm sure you know, I've been on a bit of a sabbatical."

"Yes, I did hear mention of something like that. You know how people gossip. But you look wonderful."

"The Midwest is a very healing place," he said, taking a drag on a cigarette, then quickly exhaling. "I've never felt better."

"I bet. Every time you go on one of your little sabbaticals your prices skyrocket." Niku and Carmen laughed and embraced again, and the bulls and bears, a half-beat later, joined in before eventually exiting stage right.

"Still the same old Carmen," said Niku.

"Who else could I be?" she said, leaning on the wall next to Niku. "You know you can't bear kissing those collectors' asses."

"Hey, some of us have to work for our supper."

"Touché," and as though remembering I was there, she said, "Speaking of, this is Malik. I've taken him under my wing."

"Just make sure you don't fall out of the nest," said Niku, looking at me.

Carmen's smile disappeared but resurfaced as she said, "He's never heard of you."

"How refreshing," said Niku in earnest, extending his hand for a limp shake. "Nice to meet you."

"You too," I said. "Carmen says you're being compared to Basquiat."

"No," said Carmen. "What I said is that the collectors were hoping he'd follow in Basquiat's footsteps."

I stood with them for a while as they continued to talk and bask in each other's repartee, and eventually another crowd circled them. I slowly moved out of the loop, lacking in contribution. Some people collect, some steal, and information, not money, makes the difference. Of that I had little to offer.

That party was phat?" I said as we walked out of the building. "Thanks for letting me roll with you."

"Just another night," said Carmen with slurring ennui. "They need flavor in their lives and that's what I provide. There's little excitement in blending."

Black boy blending.

"I hear ya. But I'm sure it's more than that."

"That's sweet," she said, grabbing my hand. "That's very sweet." The November air seemed drastically cooler than it had moments earlier, a cold breeze lurking around the corner. Carmen's focus drifted away from me and gloom clouded her words as though assessing the truth behind them.

Winter was coming.

I pulled up the collar on the suede jacket but Carmen walked on, holding my hand.

Hunched in the doorway of a nearby building a woman attempted to get her lighter to conquer the breeze. When it obliged, adding a glimmer of light to her aquiline face, I could see the flame heating the whitish rock and the gray smoke filling the burned black tube.

White. Gray. Black. A solemn palate.

This was no show on television or using the term "crack" in jest. This was right in front of me and my facade was just that.

Carmen didn't appear fazed by the sight, but it was ambushing me, and though I instinctively moved forward with Carmen, my eyes were stenciled on the woman. She looked up at me with a terse stare and her mouth fell open as though reproach was mine. But her high set in and a euphoric smile presented itself, freeing me of her aspersions.

"Crackheads have the best cheekbones," said Carmen after we had passed the woman. "It's a hard way to get them, but one has to admit, those cheekbones are flawless."

I thought of all the sucked-in cheeks I'd seen since my time in New York and not all of them were from crack, but addiction is addiction is addiction and the appearance isn't always the same.

Before I could respond to Carmen I saw a cab coming up the street, and hoping to impress her with my resourcefulness I ran to the corner and threw up my hand. The cabdriver rolled down his window.

"Where ya going?" he asked as I walked toward the rolling car.

"One Hundred Twentieth Street," I said proudly. He didn't so much as grant a reply. He simply shook his head, rolled up his window and drove off. The driver was black. I stood in disbelief, a haze of my own. Carmen said something but I was focused on the taillights of the cab, and her words were intangible.

White. Gray. Black.

Darkness is never as quiet as it is made out to be.

·8·

Resistant to waking, on an early mid-November morning, an eerie sensation swept over me like the buzz of a bee too nearby. I gradually opened my eyes. The woman had her hand scrupulously positioned in the crevice between her hips and torso as though the indention was made for that very purpose. I sprung to a sitting position, trying to cover my share of inheritance.

"Oomph," she muttered with a look of disgust as she walked out of the bedroom.

Sleeping naked wasn't my usual modus operandi, but in the town house, with the nearest blood ties a thousand miles away, I felt comfortable in my nakedness and the laying on of hands associated with my youthful needs and desires. But "Oomph" isn't exactly what you want to hear when someone has just seen you naked.

I got out of bed, picked up a pair of jeans and a thermal top from the floor, slid them on and walked across to the kitchen. The woman was standing with a mop in hand. I realized she had to be Rosita, the cleaning lady. I'd not seen her before, yet every Wednesday I'd return home to find my bed made, my room cleaned.

Rosita stared at me, then shook her head. "XYZ," she said. I looked down and pulled up the zipper of my jeans. Embarrassed, I took a step around her, and her head quickly turned back, providing a Siberian breeze.

"I just wanted to get some juice."

"Oomph," she uttered, but that was enough to keep me from taking another step. I stood leaning on the doorjamb between the kitchen and dining room, left foot propped atop of right, like a child being reprimanded, shrinking to absorb the blows.

"I'll wait until you're finished. No rush. Take your time."

She said nothing and as I crossed the kitchen to go back to my room, on her back swing the handle of the mop hit me in the stomach. I bowled over; more out of surprise than actual discomfort. No apology presented itself. Again, just "Oomph."

"Is Carmen here?"

"No," she said, refusing to look at me. "She's not here when I come." Rosita put the mop in the bucket and leaned the handle against the counter. She took a firm stance and gave me a good once-over. "I don't like her and she don't like me. This is business. I miss Mr. Christopher. He's a good man, but it's not my business. I just clean. It's business."

"You must be Rosita," I said, feeling that incorporating her name would add a sense of cordial familiarity.

"My name is Rose. Not Rosita. She tell you my name is Rosita?"

"Maybe I got it wrong. She just mentioned—"

"Well, ha, ha, ha. She's so funny."

Rose was a short Latina who barely came up to my chest. She was wearing the two sisters, Polly and Ester, and they stuck to her rotund body like the skin on an onion.

"How old are you?"

"Twenty-one," I said proudly, sucking in my stomach and sticking out my chest.

At hearing my answer, it seemed that some of the air left her portly body. She shook her head as though I'd said there had been a death in the family.

"Oomph. Barely on solid food."

Rose walked past me, crossed the hall to my room, and upon entering she stopped. "Every week it gets worse. Your momma would be ashamed."

She was right. My mother was adamant about having things in their place, particularly me, but I'd been enjoying my mess. It was mine.

"You don't have to clean in here," I said. I hurriedly started to fix the bed, anything to distract her eyes from the room's disarray. She watched and I could feel her soften, dough in an oven.

"You're young," she said, walking to the other side of the bed. "I can see there is goodness in you." Rather than helping me fix the bed, she pulled the sheet off, ripping it from my hands, singeing my fingertips. "Her. There is no help. You're not the only one. She has many men friends." I bit my lip trying to stifle a laugh.

"Oh. You think it's funny. Ha, ha. Sin is no laughing matter."

"No, ma'am. You've got it wrong."

"Oomph."

Before I could regain her favor, the phone rang. I stood there for a minute, wondering whether or not Rose would get it, but by the third ring she gave me a less-than-Christian look, making me more than aware that answering the phone wasn't one of her duties.

I ran into the kitchen and picked up the phone off the wall. "House of the Holy One."

"Uh, hello. Yes. May I please speak with Mason Randolph."

"Uh. No speak English," I whispered, hoping Rose wouldn't hear me. But my mother was unrelenting. "Mason? Mason, is that you?"

"Yes," I said, regressing.

"Why did I have to call who-knows-where to get in contact with you? I called that Jim at least twenty times, and he was useless. Thank goodness for that sweet girlfriend of his."

"I was going to call as soon as I got settled in . . ."

"Settled in? I was told you've been out of that Jim's apartment for over a month."

I turned around and Rose was standing right behind me giving me the evil eye.

"Do you mind?"

"Don't you speak to me like that, young man."

"I wasn't talking to you, Mom."

"I should hope not," she said, but this only piqued her interest. "Who are you talking to? Who's there with you? Mason, answer me."

Rose wouldn't budge and though I tried to turn my back, that didn't help. She walked in front of me, made a face, then from behind her back pulled out a dustpan, revealing the evidence that proved I didn't believe or care whether Catholics went to hell for masturbating. I'd usually discard the wipe-up wads in the morning when I got up, but Rose had come in prematurely.

"Oomph."

"Mason!" my mother said as I placed the phone back to my ear.

Whaaat? "Ma'am."

"God loves you," said Rose. "Accept Him into your life and receive His glory."

"Who is that?"

I covered the phone again and shushed Rose as politely as one can when shushing. "Uh, it's a Jehovah's Witness," I whispered as I turned my back to Rose. "I was trying to get rid of them when you called."

"Jehovah's Witness?" said Rose with contempt and crossing herself. "Jehovah's Witness?" She came right at me, shaking her stubby finger in my face until it, like a moving pencil, appeared rubbery. She kept screaming and though I could get the gist of her Spanish, it didn't block out my mother on the other end of the line.

"Listen, Mom, I'm going to have to . . ."

"Mason, what's going on? Where are—"

". . . call you back."

· · · · ·

After leaving a rosary hanging on my bedroom doorknob, Rose eventually left the town house. Though certain to receive the wrath of my mother, I had no choice but to call home. Luckily my father answered—a rarity in our house, as my mother has always been phone warden.

"M.R. How's it going?" I could tell he was trying to be light, but his voice was somewhat taxed.

"Hanging in there."

"Hang up," I heard my mother say. I knew she was perched like a canary at my father's shoulder, refusing to pick up one of the numerous extensions at our house. "Hang. Up."

"Hold on a minute, Joyce," said my father. "I'm sure there's a perfectly good explanation."

"Explanation? What explanation can he possibly offer?"

"Mom," I said more to myself than actually wanting to vocalize it.

"You want to speak with Mom?"

"No. I—"

"I don't want to speak to him," said my mother. "He has no appreciation for anything we've done for him. Why should I talk to him?"

"Joyce."

"Don't Joyce *me*. You've always been Mr. Willy-Nilly with him, now he's up there all mixed up in who-knows-what. It sounded like some kind of cult."

"Dad, I'm not in a cult. Tell Mom I'm not in a cult."

"We *would* have to be the only black family we know with a child in a cult," said my mother. "There's always one." *It never seemed to matter that I was the only one before.* "There's nothing more pathetic. Tell him I'd better not see him on *60 Minutes*. I refuse to have Ed Bradley making snide comments about us next year at Jazz Fest. I won't have it."

"I'm not in a cult," I screamed, hoping my mother could hear, trying to reach her.

"Just calm down," said my father. "Everyone just calm down."

"I'm sorry." Heat rising, I slid down the wall and sat on the floor in search of cooler air. "I'm not in a cult. I've found a great place. That was the cleaning lady. She's very religious. That's all."

"What's he saying?" I heard my mother ask in a failed attempt at whispering.

"Joyce, if you want to talk to him then pick up the phone. If not, let me get to the bottom of this."

"Listen, Dad. Everything is cool. I was going to call you at the office, but I've been working and—"

"So you've gotten a job," he said. "See, Joyce, M.R.'s gotten a job."

"It's just part-time, but it's great and gives me time to focus on some writing I've been doing." I knew bringing up the artist angle was a soft spot with him and would make him conjure his painting past.

"That's great," said my father.

"Why hasn't he called?" asked my mother. "Where is he living?"

"Harlem," I said before he could relay her query.

"That sounds great, M.R." I could hear the excitement in my father's voice. "He's living in Harlem."

"Harlem?" asked my mother. I then heard a noise, which I imagined was my mother fainting, but in fact was the front door of the town house. I assumed it was Rose returning for the second half of her revival.

"Dad, I gotta get to work, but, uh, listen, this job really doesn't pay that well, and New York is more expensive than the other places I've been traveling. I really want to keep writing, but I'm running a little short . . ."

"What's he saying?" asked my mother. "We've invested far too much for him to be living in Harlem. It's dangerous. He's not doing drugs, is he?"

". . . so if you just have Caron deposit a little more allowance into my . . ."

"I won't stand for it. Jonathan!"

"Hello?" It was Carmen.

I tried to remain calm as I cupped my hand around the phone.
". . . account. Just a couple hundred more a month would be a great
help."

"Malik?" said Carmen. "Are you here?"

"In the kitchen," I said, covering the phone.

"I hope he isn't asking for money, because that is out of the question." My mother had managed to scare off any young secretary that
my father ever had and had handpicked Caron. She was in her mid-
sixties and homely, and she had a mustache, which, unlike my mother,
she made no attempt to conceal. But she kept my father's office intact
and my monthly allowance was always deposited on time.

"Sure. That sounds great."

"What sounds great?" asked my mother.

"He was just saying he was going to call your mother."

"Thanks, Dad. Good looking out."

"What?" asked my father.

"Good looking . . . nothing. Just thanks."

"Malik. Did I have any calls?" asked Carmen as she walked toward
the kitchen. I stuck my head out of the door to signal I'd be with her
in a minute.

"I gotta go, Dad. I'll call soon. I promise."

"Jonathan, let me talk to . . ."

Just as I hung up, Carmen entered the kitchen. "How you feel?" I
said, a bit winded, yet trying to remain steady.

"Hello," she said with a curious eye. Her shoes were dangling from
her hands, slightly brushing her thighs. "What are you up to? Were you
talking to another woman, trying to make me jealous?"

"No," I said with an uncomfortable laugh.

"It wasn't Christopher, was it?" she asked, looking concerned.

"Uh, no. It was my old man. I was ready to get off anyway."

"I understand," she said sincerely. "How's your mother? Better, I
hope."

"Uh, yeah. She's doing the best she can. Thanks," I said, then somberly, "I'm sure she'll be all right."

"Just hang in there. We all have our crosses to bear." She walked out of the kitchen. It was time for her nap.

I walked toward my bedroom and Rose's rosary still hung on the door waiting on me. As I took it off, I couldn't help but mumble, "We sure do."

·9·

W*ent down to Jim's last night. He had some people over. It was an okay time. Lots of drinks and enough pot to send a drug-sniffing dog into a coma, so of course the high led to cartoon talk. Everyone was into the Road Runner. I didn't care for that one. I would have if the coyote had won once, but he never did. Somebody mentioned the Peanuts. Everyone had a favorite. Lucy, the cranky one, or Peppermint Patty, the butch one, or Linus, the smart, insecure one, and of course Charlie Brown. They even mentioned Marcy, forever "sir"-ing her way through the scene. But no one brought up Franklin. I always thought of Franklin, always looked for him out there in center field.*

Though Carmen's life lacked any foreseeable schedule, having told her that I had a job made it necessary to be out of the house as much as possible.

I had anointed the Hungarian Pastry Shop on Amsterdam Avenue, catty-corner to St. John the Divine Cathedral, as my favorite uptown café. It resembled a Juan Gris painting as the patrons, Columbia students and bearded intellectual sorts, slumping over papers and periodicals, leisurely sipped their lattes and teas.

"Mind if I share this table?" I asked.

"No prob," he said, moving his books to the side. "But we might have to get a permit."

"Why's that?" I asked, sitting down.

"Two black guys sitting at the same table may constitute illegal assembly."

"True that," I said. "Malik." It now came out as easily as though I'd been born with the name.

"What up, Malik," he said. "Malcolm. I think I've seen you around campus."

"Uh, no. I'm not at Columbia," I said.

"Oh. My bad. I just thought . . . Maybe I've just seen you here or around the way."

"Yeah, maybe," I said. "I live in Harlem."

"Me too. On 136th."

"I'm 120th. So you're at Columbia, huh?"

"Yeah," he said, now looking as though he was embarrassed to admit it.

"Good one. What are you studying?"

"I'm doing my M.S. at the J school and getting my J.D." My eyes lit up, but I think he mistook my expression. "Oh, my bad. I'm getting my master's in journalism and doing the law school thang."

Before I could assure him I knew what the initials meant, a girl walked up to the table.

"Hey, X. What's up?"

"Trying to make it."

I looked down at my copy of *The Best of Simple,* attempting to exclude myself from their conversation.

"Vee, this is Malik."

"Hey, Malik."

"How you feel?" I said, feeling particularly cool.

"Oh, you know. Same old shit."

"I'm gonna get a refill," said Malcolm, getting up from the table. Vee sat in one of the chairs and immediately began to interrogate me.

"What program are you in?"

"I'm not in school right now."

"Oh," she said, looking at me to access if she should be talking to me. "How do you know X?"

"From around the way."

"I like your accent. Are you from Brooklyn?"

"No. Louisiana."

"New Orleans?"

"No. Layton."

"I've never heard of that. But I love New Orleans. It's the Paris of the States. My sister went to Tulane. It's a nice place to visit, but the South is scary. My father went down there in the sixties to help with the cause."

"What cause is that?"

"You know," she said, looking at me with disbelief. "The cause. We have a photo of him marching side by side with MLK, Jr. He even got arrested for drinking out of the Colored water fountain. He was one of the first to ever do that. I asked him what that was like and he said, 'Tasted the same.' Tasted the same. Isn't that funny?"

A *hoot*. "Yeah," I said, trying to look back at my book.

"Only in the South could someone like David Duke exist. Doesn't it embarrass you that your home state could tolerate such racism?"

"Not really," I said, locking on her eyes. "At least I know where he stands. There's comfort in that."

"I guess," she said. I could tell this wasn't the answer she had anticipated. She turned away from me uncomfortably, looking for a familiar face. Malcolm came back with his coffee refill and sat down.

"So, X, my folks are out of town next weekend and I'm having a few people over. Why don't you come by?"

"Sounds good. I'll give you a call."

"Cool," she said. She got up from the table and kissed Malcolm on the cheek, then leaned over and kissed me. Everyone in New York kissed one another and I'd not yet grown accustomed to that practice. "Nice meeting you, Malik. Welcome to New York."

"Thanks."

"Sorry to leave you hanging like that," said Malcolm. "She means well, but can get in your face. She's poli sci, political science major."

"Ain't no thang," I said.

"So you just moved up here?"

"Yeah. From Louisiana," then quickly adding, "Not New Orleans. I'm from Layton."

"Really. I got people down in Layton. Do you know any Baileys?"

I did know some Baileys. Elizabeth and Darrell Bailey were friends of my parents'. They partnered one of the most prestigious law firms in the state and I'd clerked at their office during high school.

"Yeah, I know the Baileys," I said, impressed.

"I've never been down there but we all have a trail that leads back to the South."

Hearing this made me know Malcolm was good people. Most northerners I'd come across had automatically assumed the South was backward and though at times I'd felt the same, it was home and I'd always defend it without regret.

You oughta know the score by now.

"You're a native New Yorker?"

"Uptown, baby," said Malcolm, pushing his hands up in the air. "Born and bred."

"I can't imagine growing up here. I mean, New York is great, but it seems like a sink-or-swim kind of place."

"True that," he said. "Some just have larger life jackets than others."

. . . . .

How you feel?" I said, opening the door. Malcolm had become a good friend, furthering my belief in happenstance. He'd come over to pick me up so we could head over to the Apollo for amateur night.

"Trying to make it," said Malcolm. "I kept looking at the address to make sure I had it right."

"Yeah, this is it. Come on in. You wanna beer?"

"Nah, I don't drink," said Malcolm.

"Oh," I said. "We've got Coke or O.J."

"Coke is cool."

"How was Vee's party?" I asked as we walked toward the kitchen.

"It was all right. I didn't stay too long. But this girl Kyra came in just as I was leaving. I thought of going back in but I'd already made a pretty big exit so it would have been too obvious."

"I hate when that happens," I said, but I was interested in hearing more about Kyra. The girl I'd met at the art opening was a Kyra too, but "a Kyra" isn't necessarily "the Kyra." "Who's Kyra?"

"This babe from school. She's got it going on. I get hung up every time I see her but she's a look-but-don't-even-think-about-touching kind of honey and she's completely out of my field of play."

"That's crazy," I said, hopping on the counter. "You just have to step up. Take a chance. What she look like?"

"Ah, man. Butter. Smart, beautiful. She's definitely got it going on." I wanted him to be more descriptive, give me statistics, but he seemed distracted. "Nice place."

"Oh, thanks," I said, now oblivious to my surroundings. "I just rent a room here. You'll have to meet my housemate. She's something else."

At hearing myself say that, I realized that that was exactly what she was and nothing summed it up better.

Carmen was something else.

"So it's just the two of you living here?"

"Yeah."

"Damn."

"Come on," I said, jumping down from the counter. "You've got to see the view from the roof."

"This whole place is hers?" asked Malcolm as we climbed the stairs.

"Yeah. It used to be her grandparents'. I think they were in real estate or Laundromats. I'm not sure. Have you ever heard of any Englands?"

"Nah. Are they black?"

"Yeah," I said, surprised by his question. I opened the door to the roof. "Great, huh?"

"Yeah," he said, closing his jacket. This was far from the reaction Jim had shown.

"The hawk's out tonight, but it's worth it," I said, stepping out onto the roof. "When I came to New York I didn't even think about living in Harlem. I didn't even know I was going to be staying in the city. I was just passing through, but I knew I wasn't ready to go back to Louisiana. But Harlem. Man, it must have been great growing up here."

"It had its moments." Malcolm's steps were tentative as though he was afraid of heights.

"Did your folks go to Columbia?"

"No. My mother works in Food Services on campus."

"Oh," I said, attempting to regain some sense of balance; adjust my assumptions.

"I used to walk to campus to pick her up. But I'd wait outside, and seeing all those white kids walking around made it seem like Mars. It's weird having this great school butting the ghetto. Whenever I'd see a black student he always looked like he was just trying to get where he was going without anyone noticing. But my moms would always say that I was gonna go there one day."

"She must be proud."

"Yeah. She's worked hard for it. For most of the kids on campus, college is just what you do. There's no other option. But most of the people I grew up with are either sixed or behind bars and I don't mean the gates at Columbia."

"At least you don't take it for granted."

"Trying to make it," he said in a tone that fell somewhere between hope and cynicism.

"I hear ya."

"But some days are tougher than others. Like today. I was sitting on the steps out in front of Low—the old library on campus—and I was flipping through the paper and I saw this ad for tours of Harlem." Malcolm looked toward the lights of downtown as though a world away; taunting and teasing. "Sunday tours to a Baptist church, then soul food afterward. All for $39.99.

"It made me think of when I was growing up on 145th and Lenox. My grandmother would send me down to the corner store and I'd see these buses pass through with eyes looking out at me. There I was on display, a freak show, while they all sat safe and secure behind the comfort of glass and steel."

The view of downtown was no longer appealing to Malcolm. He turned his back on it like a lover after a breakup and nothing could be salvaged. He leaned against the ledge and dug his hands deep into his coat pockets as he looked in the direction of where his grandmother used to live, where even life as a child was far from simple.

I still focused on the jewels of the city twinkling in the night. The Chrysler Building. The World Trade Center. The Empire State. This was the world I'd always imagined when thinking of New York, but this was no Times Square broadcast and even the ageless Dick Clark couldn't smile the mood away.

"I could only imagine what the tour guide was saying about a people he only read about but would never know. What he said about the black experience. What he said about me, that little black boy standing there watching bus after bus go by.

"Sometimes I think maybe I read too much into things, seeing something that's not there. Maybe I do, but what if I do that fifty per-cent of the time. What do I do about the other fifty percent?"

Malcolm finally looked over at me, remembering that he was speak-ing to more than just the night, more than just the darkness.

I had nothing to add and his silence turned me away from down-town. Then, as if on cue, we both headed for the door that led back downstairs. Back down to the town house on the hill.

M orning," said a voice. I turned around to find a white guy walk-ing into the kitchen.

Christopher?

He was naked and had a grin that said he was pleased with himself. He opened the refrigerator and took out the carton of orange juice—juice I'd bought. "I didn't know anyone else was here," he said. "Are you Carmen's brother?"

"No. Housemate," I said, a tinge of jealousy creeping in.

"Gotcha," the guy said, walking over to the sink, then opening a cabinet, as though he was at home. I tried to distract myself from his naked presence by placing the coffee grounds into the stove-top es-presso maker. I twisted the top on and turned on the burner, wishing I could take his hand and stick it on the flame.

He had what I'd describe as the prep school voice: always delivered from the throat and at least an octave deeper than necessary, simulating authority.

"The glasses are . . ." He didn't wait for the words to leave my mouth before he placed the carton to his own. Again, I thought of my mother. Yes, chagrin would have definitely consumed her if she'd caught a naked guest in the kitchen, but she would have chalked it up a simple mistake, something she could later turn into a cocktail party anecdote, but drinking out of the carton was always out of the ques-tion.

In his Adam and Eve wear he took four Adam's apples' worth of juice, then said, "Tad."

"What?"

"I'm Tad."

"Nice to meet you, Ted."

"No. Tad."

"Yeah. Ted."

"No. Tad," he said. I began to simmer. I knew his type well and could tell he was enjoying this and had probably depended on this miscommunication as a way of appearing charming and unique, but I couldn't believe that Carmen would be so gullible as to fall for it. "T. A. D."

"Oh." *Tiny Ass Dick.* "My bad," I said halfheartedly. It wasn't my fault that he was unable to enunciate. I wanted to take a knife from the wooden block and slice him to pieces. "Malik."

"Great place you've got here."

"No complaints."

"Gotcha."

"Is Carmen here?"

"She's upstairs," said Tad, taking another swallow of orange juice before adding with a signet-ring grin, "Still in bed. Probably needs the rest."

Asshole.

He offered me the juice. I didn't want any but I walked over to the cabinet, pulled out a glass, and held it out toward him, hoping he'd get the message.

"Thank you, dear," said Carmen, walking into the kitchen and taking the glass from me. She was wearing a red silk paisley robe and the contrast to her skin was complementary. Her hair was pulled back into a ponytail and I didn't want to think about what caused her glow.

"Hey, sexy," said Tad, handing her the carton of juice. Carmen gave him a polite smile, the equivalent of a pat on the head, and took the

juice but didn't say a word. She waved the carton at him, then at me—
the nearest thing to an introduction she was willing to provide.

"Yeah, *Tad* and I have met," I said.

Tad pulled Carmen toward him, holding her around her waist.
Carmen didn't resist, but didn't seem to find any pleasure in his action.
She walked away from his grasp and sensing that their time together
was over, his smile, like a good shake of an Etch-a-Sketch, vanished.

"Last night was fantastic," he said. *Fantastic? Who says "Fantastic"?*

"Yes it was. But it's morning now."

What? No, gotcha?

"I was just—"

"Yeah, yeah," she said, taking his arm and giving him a smack on the
ass, creating a backside blush. She pushed him out of the kitchen and
followed him down the hall.

I leaned out of the kitchen door and said, "See ya later, Ted."
Carmen looked back at me and winked. I walked back to the stove. The
coffee was ready.

· 10 ·

I can't believe you've lived here all your life and have never peeped this," I said to Malcolm. We'd gone down to the Upper West Side to see the balloons for the Macy's Thanksgiving Day parade.

"Never thought about it."

We walked through the hordes circling the Museum of Natural History and when we reached the corner of Eighty-first and Central Park West I heard someone scream, "M.R." I kept walking, certain the voice didn't pertain to me. But then again, "Hey, M.R."

I turned around to find Justin Lee behind the barricades that provided privacy for the tenants of the twin-towered Beresford and the other apartment buildings along the street. Behind the barricades kids set up cookie and hot chocolate stands while their parents mingled, providing a suburban feel in an urban full-service setting.

"What are you doing here?" asked Justin, leaning on the barricade. "I thought you were in Palo Alto, getting your law school on."

"I deferred. I took a trip around the world, ended up here."

I was happy to see Justin but anxious as well, fearing my two worlds were about to collide, and I tried to brace myself for the oncoming meteor shower.

I glanced over my shoulder at Malcolm, who was standing about twenty feet away, buying a pretzel from a vendor.

Justin and I had been suitemates in Orin Hall during college and we had often sat around wallowing in the tunes of Prince, R.E.M., Depeche Mode, Sade and, on particularly jovial days, Kate Bush.

He had been the first black editor in chief of the *Mohawk,* the campus daily, and the first black captain of our national-champion water-ski team.

"Look at your hair," he said, jostling my twists, which now held a few cowrie shells. "I like it."

"Thanks. You still look the same."

"Hey, once a seersucker, always a seersucker."

"True that," I said. "How's NYU?"

"Kicking my ass. I don't know who thought it was a good idea to put a school in the middle of the Village."

"I see your parents hooked you in style," I said, scanning the building.

"I don't live here. I came up with a friend."

"A friend or a *friend*?"

"Just a friend."

"Still holding on to that dowry, huh?" We both laughed and then on the periphery I saw Malcolm standing next to me, which made me wish I was like one of the balloons floating on a tether—away from it all. "Oh, sorry. Justin, this is Malcolm. He's up at Columbia doing his M.S. and J.D."

"Good one. I thought *I* was an overachiever," said Justin. "How's it going up there?"

"Trying to make it."

"I hear ya, man," said Justin, shaking Malcolm's hand. "Do you know Kyra Jamison?"

"Yeah," said Malcolm, looking over at me. "Just in passing."

"She's upstairs. M.R., you should meet her. She'd be good for you. She's smart, great-looking, good family. Her father's a heart surgeon."

"Probably to mend all the hearts his daughter has been breaking," said Malcolm.

"Oh, I see you *do* know her," said Justin with a laugh.

"Yeah. But I doubt she'd give one of us any play."

"What do you mean?" asked Justin.

I could feel my heart pumping behind my eyes. "He just means she's—"

"There you are," said a guy walking up behind Justin.

"I just ran into an old friend. This is—"

"M.R.," I said, jumping in. Justin had never called me Mason, but I couldn't risk it.

"We went to school together," said Justin. Malcolm looked at me.

"Dale," said Dale, automatically stretching his hand over the barricade, giving me an assessing look, and evidently my attire didn't wear well with him.

"This is Malcolm," I said.

"What up?" said Malcolm.

"The balloons," said Dale.

"I was just telling M.R.," said Justin, jumping in to break the tension, "that I thought he and Kyra would make a good match."

"Really?" said Dale, hardly concealing his reservation. "You should come back upstairs."

"You live here?" asked Malcolm, taking a bite of his pretzel.

"My parents live here. I live downtown, but every year they throw a party for the blowup." Dale said this as though talking to himself and he didn't want to be seen socializing with us.

"Hey, if you're not behind the barricade you have to move along," said a cop.

"Okay, Officer," I said.

Justin looked at Dale, waiting for him to invite us in, but no invitation was extended. "We should get back upstairs anyway," said Dale. "There are some people you should meet."

"Yeah, all right," said Justin, glancing at the cop that stood there waiting to escort us away if we didn't move. He pulled me in for a hug. When we let go he rubbed my twists again. "So look, I'll see you around, okay?"

"Bet," I said.

Justin turned and headed toward the door of the building where Dale was waiting. Dale put his hand on the small of Justin's back and they went in.

"You know them?" asked Malcolm.

"Just Justin. He's good people."

"I can't figure you out," he said as we walked through the crowd toward the C train, the blue line.

"Hello, Mom," I said, initiating a call I knew was overdue, but an absolute must on a holiday. "Happy Thanksgiving."

"Same to you," she said. She sounded relieved to hear my voice. "I was hoping you'd call."

"Sorry I couldn't make it down, but they needed me at the café and I needed the money," I said, holding on to the charade of having a job.

"I understand," she said, which shocked me. I knew I'd dialed the right number and the voice was definitely my mother's but I still looked at the phone with surprise. "Let us know if you plan to come for Christmas."

"I'll try."

"If it's a matter of the ticket, we can send you a round-trip."

"I will," I said, then added, "Let you know." I was still not certain how to gauge her. I had set myself up to be on the defensive but her playbook had miraculously been rewritten.

"How is New York?" she asked.

"It's great. I'm having a good time." I wanted to elaborate, wanted to share the details with her. I wanted to tell her about the restaurant in Chinatown that Jim had taken me to after hours where the kids and older people played mahjong, while in the back room at twenty dollars a hand I'd lost hundreds of dollars at the blackjack table. I wanted to tell her about St. Nick's pub where jazz played until early morning. I wanted to tell her about getting mugged and how I'd fought back. I wanted to share it all with her, with someone other than my journal, and though she seemed open, I didn't think she'd understand. I didn't want to follow the script of most of our conversations—short and to the point. I wanted more than that, needed it, but couldn't bridge the gap.

"That's nice," she said. "Did you volunteer today?"

"No," I said, feeling somewhat guilty about neglecting what had become a family tradition. "I didn't really know where to go. You were always the one who set that up."

"I see."

My mother had seen to it that every Thanksgiving and Christmas we'd volunteered to drop off food baskets to families who wouldn't have much of a holiday without one. I used to see the way the children looked at me when we arrived at their door. The adults always seemed thankful for their boxes, but the kids would stare at me as I handed them a toy that wasn't on their list. I wasn't Santa. I never forgot their faces as they watched us drive away. I couldn't tell if they wished they could come with us to the land where gifts and food came from, or if they were just happy we were leaving.

One year we'd gone to the door of a house and one of my classmates answered. The surprise on both of our faces was evident. He was the only freshman on the varsity football team and his popularity was beyond refute.

"Great game last Friday," I'd said, trying to slice through the awkwardness as my father handed him the box of food. He mumbled his thanks and my mother wished him Happy Thanksgiving.

The next week when I saw him at school he walked over to my

locker as though he wanted to say something. But he didn't. A crowd of people passed and said, "Good luck Friday night." His demeanor changed from somber to popular, as he raised his head to acknowledge his fans. When they made their way down the hall he looked back at me for a second longer, then walked away.

"So what are your plans?" asked my mother.

"Mom, please," I said, bracing myself for the onslaught.

"What? I meant, what are you doing today? For Thanksgiving."

"Oh. I'm going over to a friend's. Malcolm. He's studying law at Columbia. Good guy."

"At least someone is making use of their opportunities."

"My being in New York is an opportunity. People are more than just a piece of parchment."

"Not when it comes to getting a job."

"There's time. I've not forgotten about school."

"I should hope not."

"Mom, I don't want to argue."

"I'm not arguing, Mason. Why is it that every time I say something pertaining to your future, you think I'm starting an argument? I am your mother, and contrary to what you may believe, I want what's best for you."

"I want that too. I just need time to figure out what that is. I'm trying, okay?"

"That's all I ask."

"Listen, is Dad there?"

"No. He's on the golf course," she said, irritation coating her voice.

"Then just tell him I called."

"I will," she said, then after a chilling pause, "You do realize that you have more than one parent who loves you?"

"I know, Mom," I said. "I've got to go. Malcolm's mother is expecting me and I don't want to be late."

"Your grandmother is here. Can't you take a minute to say hello?"

"Bet."

"What?"

"Yes, put her on."

"Hello?" said my mother's mother.

"Hello, Granny. Happy Thanksgiving."

"Mason, is that you, baby? How are you doing up there?"

"Great, Granny."

"That's wonderful. I hope you've got your thermals on. I don't ever go nowhere but I watch the Weather Channel. It gets cold up there."

"Yes, ma'am. I'm bundling up."

"Wonderful. Just remember to layer. That's the best way. Then you can pull something off if you get warm. And don't forget a hat. Cover up your head."

"I will. Don't worry, Granny, I'm fine and I'm going to try to make it down for Christmas."

"Wonderful," she said. "I'm gonna leave a little something here for you with your mother."

"That's okay, Granny," I said, imagining the holiday envelope she'd gotten from Hibernia Bank, the face of the president staring out through the opening. I could even see her asking for the piece of candy that small-town banks still give out, "for my grandbaby."

"Thank you, Granny."

"You're welcome, baby. And you be careful up there and watch out for those fast girls. Use a condom every time."

"Momma," I heard my mother say.

"What? Ain't nothing to be ashamed of. The boy is grown and there are gals out there who'll claim they on the Pill . . ."

"Momma."

". . . and the next thing you know she'll be bringing him on a talk show on national TV talking about 'You my baby's daddy.' Is that what you want to happen, Joyce?"

"No, Momma," said my mother, defeated.

"That's right. Use a condom. And be careful because I saw on the TV these New York women who were not women at all. They were men who looked like women. Really beautiful, though. And they brought their boyfriends on national TV to let—"

"Momma. That's enough," said my mother.

"Okay. Okay. Hold your water. I'm just trying to tell the boy to use a condom every time, and it might not be a bad idea to get a night-light."

"I will, Granny," I said, trying to contain my laughter, hardly able to believe she and my mother were related.

"Wonderful. Just wonderful," said Granny. "Well, I better get off. I don't want to run up your bill. I love you, baby."

"I love you too, Granny."

"You wanna talk back to your momma?"

"That's okay. I've got to go, but I'll talk to her later."

"Okay, then. Happy Thanksgiving."

"You too, Granny."

We thank you, dear Lord, for another day. We thank you for the food before us and pray for those less fortunate. I thank you for my family and ask that you continue to guide us in the direction of your Glory. We have been through some hard times but always knew you wouldn't give us more than we could bear. We also want to thank you for bringing Malik to our table, Lord. We know that in your eyes we are all family and to share our blessings is to share yours. In your name we pray."

"Amen," said those of us seated at the table in Malcolm's eat-in kitchen.

"That was lovely, Mrs. Williams," I said, emotions filling me like the aroma of the food before us. This was the first time I'd ever spent a Thanksgiving with a family other than my own and I almost felt as though I didn't deserve inclusion in her prayer of thanks.

"*Ms.* Williams," she corrected. "But just call me June."

Malcolm lived with his mother on 136th Street between Lenox and Seventh Avenues. Their apartment was a fourth-floor walk-up and each floor was divided into four apartments.

I'd felt uneasy approaching the building and a group of teenagers, ignoring the temperature, sat on the stoop, their boom box blaring Tupac. They sang along, practicing for their time in the spotlight, their claim to prosperity and fame. Though we were similarly dressed, they barely acknowledged me and provided my feet little space as I tried to make my way up the steps.

"This macaroni and cheese is slamming, Ms. June," I said after taking a bite of what was surely a heart attack in the making. She had filled my plate with food and I'd discreetly tried to keep the macaroni and cheese from touching the string beans from touching the stuffing and gravy from touching the yams from touching the rolls from touching the cranberry sauce from touching the turkey from touching the macaroni and cheese.

"Thank you, kindly," she said. "They don't let me cook it up like this on campus, not that they could appreciate it. Most of them kids just as spoiled as they wanna be and can't eat nothing. Either vegetarians or on a diet. Could pick 'em up with my pinkie but they on a diet."

"It's their loss. It's delicious."

"It's always good, Momma," said Malcolm, looking affectionately at his mother.

"Well, there's plenty," she said, refilling her glass with fruit punch. I had brought over a bottle of wine. Ms. June had taken it out of the bag and thanked me, but Malcolm later told me that alcohol wasn't allowed in their house. "You sure you don't want any of that wine you brought? I think we have a corkscrew in here somewhere."

"That's nice of you, Ms. June, but the punch is fine. I just didn't want to come empty-handed."

"You shouldn't have worried yourself with that. You're our guest. When we invite you, all you got to bring is yourself."

I felt something sliding along my shin, and thinking the worst, I quickly jerked it up, banging my knee on the table.

"Sorry," I said as Shantelle, Malcolm's younger sister, started giggling.

Malcolm and his mother both looked at Shantelle, who focused on her food as though she hadn't heard the commotion.

Shantelle was eighteen and had brought her two children, who were asleep in the bedroom, to see their grandmother.

Maurice, Malcolm's older brother, had also come over but didn't join us at the table. He had taken his plate into the living room to watch the football game and every now and again could be heard screaming like he was on the fifty-yard line at Giants Stadium.

"He's got money on the game," said Shantelle as she again ran her foot up my leg. I looked over at Malcolm. I picked up the paper napkin and wiped my mouth and as I put it back on my lap I lightly pushed her foot away.

"I still don't see why he can't eat in here with the rest of us," said Malcolm.

"Just let him be, Malcolm," said Ms. June, barely raising her voice. "Let's just have our meal in peace. I'm glad he came. He's been through a lot."

"Run it. *Run it. Yes!*"

"We're trying to eat," screamed Malcolm.

"Eat then," said Maurice.

The temperature in the kitchen was warm from all of the food that had been prepared and the window was open, offering a stingy draft. I focused on my plate, but constantly found myself looking up at the wine sitting on the olive-green magnet-covered refrigerator, certain if I stared at it hard enough I could unwrap the foil and uncork it with my eyes.

"You eat so slow," said Shantelle. I scanned the other plates and they were nearly empty and I had barely made a dent.

"I know," I said, trying to remain light. "My mother always said it was because I was an only child and I didn't have to fight for the last piece."

"I know that's right," said Malcolm. "You always had to eat fast around here."

"Yes, yes. Touchdown!" screamed Maurice. "That's what I'm talking about! That's what I'm talking about!"

Malcolm stood from the table and his mother grabbed his arm. She held on for a moment and he sat back down.

"You know you can't tell that fool nothing," said Shantelle as she put her foot on my seat. I looked over at her. "You know we can't all go to some fancy school acting all white."

"Yeah, but it's all right for you to get knocked up and act all black."

"Tsk. Whateva."

"Both of you need to stop it," said Ms. June. "This ain't the time. Is that any way to carry on in front of company? Malik, I apologize."

"No need, Ms. June. It's just like this at my house around the holidays."

I could envision the twenty or so family and friends gathered at our house, making light conversation. The drinks would be flowing and one of the kids would have graduated to the adults' table, but still in view of the kids' table, a step forward, a look back.

The meal would be served and the men would gather in one part of the house discussing their latest 3-wood or wedge discovery. Only the women would ask of my whereabouts. The men would just assume that a man has to do what a man has to do. But it would be my mother who would have to explain, just like Ms. June apologizing for her kids. No matter what my mother would say, the other women would draw their own conclusions, and their stories would only intensify until the next time I showed my face and they could examine me in full. I felt sorry for putting my mother through that.

Maurice came into the kitchen with his empty plate. It was so clean it looked like it had been washed. He was bone-thin, which made his big belly look awkward.

"I'm glad you could join us," said Ms. June.

"Commercial. Just came in for seconds."

"I guess you must be winning," said Shantelle.

"Bet. My niggas is playing that D."

"Don't use that word in my house. I told you about that," said Ms. June, getting up from her seat and taking his plate.

"Oh, don't be mad," he said, coming up behind his mother and wrapping his arms around her waist. She couldn't stay mad. She put more food on his plate. "But this nigga's about to get paid and I'm gonna hook you up."

"She don't need no hookup," said Malcolm. "What she needs is the money you owe her."

"Why don't you just tend to your business? You the one still living here having Momma carry you like some li'l ol' bitch."

"Maurice," said Ms. June, slamming down the top of a pot. "Malcolm is trying to better himself. He's getting an education and that's what counts."

"Yeah, it's always about him being in school. Always been about that. Many a men been paid and not ever set foot up in no *uni-ver-sity*. There are niggas in the joint that got more sense than this li'l nigga."

"You oughta know," said Malcolm.

"Excuse me," I said, putting the paper napkin over my half-eaten plate. All eyes seemed to look more at the plate than at me. "Where's the rest room?"

"The rest room?" said Maurice. I began to feel uncomfortable, even threatened, just as I had on that first day in Harlem when Malik, the real Malik, had mocked me. *Black boy blending.* "The rest room? Malcolm, you hanging out with punks now?"

"Maurice!" This was the second time that Ms. June had raised her voice but this came out with urgency. She then calmed herself before adding, "Take your plate and go on back in the living room."

He took the plate from her and smiled at us. "Awright," he said. "I see how it is. Gang up on ol' 'Rice. That's cool. The game's back on anyway."

Maurice walked out of the kitchen and I began to breathe again. "The bathroom?"

"I'll show you," said Shantelle, pushing her chair away from the table and getting up.

"He can find it on his own," said Malcolm, barely opening his mouth. "It's down at the end of the hall."

"Thanks." Shantelle refused to sit and made me rub my body against hers as I passed between her and her mother.

"Offsides. Offsides!"

I walked out of the kitchen and down the hall. The door to the bedroom was open and one of Shantelle's kids was sitting on the edge of the bed, while his little brother continued to sleep.

"Hi," I said. He didn't say anything. He just stared at me. I looked down the hall toward the kitchen, then went into the bedroom. I squatted so that our faces were parallel. He had an earring in each ear and a gold chain around his little neck. "What's your name?"

"Latrell," he said. I could see scuff marks on his skin from little-kid falls.

"Hi, Latrell," I said. "I'm M.R." I couldn't bring myself to say "Malik." I couldn't lie to a child. They always know. I stuck out my hand and he shook it. "Nice to meet you. I'm a friend of your uncle's. Malcolm." I wanted to clarify which uncle I meant. "Did you have a good nap?" He shrugged. "How old are you?" He held up his hand. "Five! Wow. You're getting on up there. Your momma's in the kitchen. Do you want to go out there with her?" He shook his head. "You gonna stay in here and watch your brother?" He nodded. "That's good. That's what big brothers do. What's his name?"

"Laron."

"Well, it was nice meeting you, Latrell," I said, standing. His eyes followed me. I walked to the bathroom and when I looked back he was standing at the bedroom door, eyes locked on me as I closed the door.

I turned on the cold water faucet as I looked at the mirror. I stared at my face; a face below the twists of hair and the earrings; a face minus any visible scars or hardness.

Feeling dehydrated, I cupped my hands to catch the water so I could drink and not wanting to mess up one of the towels hanging neatly on the bar near the basin, I dried my mouth on my shirtsleeve. I sat on the edge of the bathtub, the yellow plastic shower curtain brushing my back. The drip of the tub faucet amplified through my head and I felt as light as bamboo and just as hollow.

I slid down to the cool of the black and pink floor tiles. I couldn't stay in there too long without Malcolm's family thinking that I was avoiding them or, worse, rifling through their belongings. I took a deep breath, then stood up.

I flushed the toilet for effect, turned off the cold water and turned on the other faucet. It immediately spewed scorching water. When I turned off the water I looked in the mirror, took another breath, then opened the door. Latrell was still standing in the doorjamb of the bedroom.

"You my daddy?" he asked. Again, I longed for the cool of the bathroom floor, and though I couldn't lie to Latrell, I couldn't bring myself to say no. Instead, I said nothing; when, even for a five-year-old, nothing says it all.

He finally took his eyes away from mine and walked back into the bedroom. I stood stunned with my back against the wall. I counted to ten trying to prepare myself to return to whatever would await me in the kitchen. When I passed the bedroom door I looked in. Latrell had climbed back into bed and his arm was draped over his little brother.

H ad I known my sorry-ass brother was going to be there, I wouldn't have invited you," said Malcolm as we walked out of his building. A warm front had traveled up from the south and a fog hung over the night.

"It's cool, man," I said, holding the C-Town plastic bag that held a plate of food Ms. June had insisted I take. "Your momma can really throw down. I would have been eating Chinese food by myself if you didn't have me over."

"Where's your roommate?"

"Carmen?" I said, a smile quickly appearing on my face. "I don't know. Doing something great I'm sure."

"Yeah, I bet."

"Your mom seems really supportive."

"She's the love of my life. I don't know what I'd do without her. You close to your moms?"

"Not really. I've always been closer to my old man."

"Why's that?"

"I don't know. Nothing I ever do seems good enough for her. Everything has to be in order. My old man's a bit more laid-back."

"I don't even know who my old man is."

Latrell's eyes returned to mind.

"Didn't you ever ask your mother?"

"Nah. Some things you just don't talk about. Anyway, I never wanted to know. It was like I've never had a father." Malcolm said this as though it was common. No bitterness in his words. "Me and my moms weren't always close, but when I think about all she's gone through to raise us it made me take notice."

Malcolm stopped and sat on the steps of a building. It was quiet. The tryptophan-filled turkey dinners served through the neighborhood had evidently run their course, leaving the streets empty and sofas, beds and floors of apartments filled with languid bodies; stomachs as tight as snares.

"Every day I pass this building," he said, pointing to the Countee Cullen Branch of the New York Public Library.

"Are you a fan of his writing?"

"Not really. I mean, no disrespect, I've read his stuff, but before this library was here this used to be where Madame C. J. Walker had her house and beauty salon, and then home to the Dark Tower. I mean, right here where I'm sitting. That's Harlem, baby. Here was a woman who used to wash people's clothes, then she became the first self-made female millionaire."

"So it's just about the money?"

"No. It's about knowing things can get better. Living right down the street from this spot shows me that it can get better."

"You're on the right track, man. You're doing it."

"Trying to make it," he said, getting up from the step. "Trying to make it."

"You're doing more than that."

"What are you gonna do?"

"I'm trying to figure that out."

"Well, don't get too comfortable in that place you're staying. People like her, with money, only look out for their own. Just like those two dudes last night."

"Nah, man. I know how it looked, but Justin's good people. Yeah, Dale was bugging, but Justin is good people."

"If you say so," he said. "I gotta get back and help clean up, but just know I got your back. We don't have much, but we look out for our own too."

"Thanks, man," I mumbled. "I'll check you later."

"Bet. Later. Malik."

"Yeah. And thank your mother for the plate."

"Enjoy it."

I turned the corner onto Lenox Avenue for the walk home.

Ran into an interesting old man today on 133rd Street. "You got a smoke?" "No, sir. Sorry." "Don't be sorry. I don't need to be smoking nohow." "You're right." "White folk make me smoke." He stared across the street, a few men in suits looking at the boarded-up buildings. "You know they're gonna kill you." "Yeah, I know." I meant the cigs. I'm not sure that's what he meant. "I ain't seen you around here and I know everybody. Where you from?" "Just a few blocks down." "Uh-huh. But where your people from?"

"Louisiana." His face lit up, which was nice to see. "Lawdy, lawdy. I used to swing it with a yella gal from down that way. A Creole girl. Fine gal. Cost me a left nut to keep her happy." "That's a high price to pay." "I don't know. I'd probably give her the right one if she walked up right now. Yep. Met her right across the street there. Almost right where they standing. Uh-huh. Yeah. This was the block. The buildings all boarded up now, but this was the block. Dickie Wells' was right there and the Nest right there, and Pod and Jerry's right there. The peoples would step out looking good. It was the Beale Street of New York. You could find any woman you wanted and all of them could dance. No matter what you'd been through that day, when you hit this street, all that was behind you. Uh-huh. All behind you. You gotta smoke?" "No, sir."

·11·

The pleasurable sound of Carmen's moans aroused me as I firmly pressed my thumbs against the arch of her foot.

With a thud, she'd dropped her weekend bag at the door.

"You look tore up from the floor up."

"Why, thank you," she said wearily, walking into the parlor. "That's exactly the look I was aiming for. I saw it in *Vogue*." I grabbed her elbow and slowly eased her down onto the sofa. "I feel like I'm about to die. And to make matters worse, I know I'm not. God wouldn't be that good to me. Oh, no. He wants me to suffer. Trust."

"Too much holiday cheer?"

"Hardly. I was with Jean-Claude at his place out on the Island and, against my better judgment, I was persuaded to ride Chastity."

"Kinky."

"Don't be cute. I'm in too much pain for cute. Chastity is one of his horses," she said, slipping out of her shoes and putting her feet up on the coffee table. "I hadn't been on a horse in years and I just don't have the back for it anymore."

"I always thought that it wasn't how well you rode but how you looked on the horse."

Without asking, I'd taken Carmen's feet, put them on my lap and began to massage them. I rubbed her left foot, gradually at first, but when I saw that she wasn't resistant I'd gone up as far as her knee, my breath increasing as I did. She'd closed her eyes and let me caress her smooth calf. I could feel her relaxing; muscle pulling away from bone.

"That feels wonderful," said Carmen, audibly exhaling. "I can tell this isn't your first time."

"No. I've always been down with massaging. You can tell a lot by feeling a person's body."

"Oh, really," she said, slightly opening her eyes and looking at me. "And what is my body saying to you?"

Many scenarios flashed through my twenty-one-year-old mind, but I knew hesitating would prove too suggestive. "That next time, you might want to try sidesaddle."

Carmen tried to keep from laughing, but little painful sprouts of joy burst from her mouth. "Please don't make me laugh. It's just too painful."

She again closed her eyes and I found myself transfixed on her pedicured toes. I wanted to take each of them in my mouth, starting with the smallest, working my way up to the largest, licking them until they relaxed.

My pulse vibrated through my body like the tremble of a railroad track confirming the approach of a train not yet in view.

I looked at her face and saw it slowly release itself from the public to the private. It was a gradual transition: a ripple in a wading pool rather than a wave in a river. But when all the muscles acquiesced, a dawn of a smile sat on her lips and she looked as innocent as a baby with a fruit juice stain on its chin.

Hoping not to wake her, I gently lifted her feet, placing them on the sofa, and backed away like the loyal retinue refusing to turn their back on their master's supine body.

I had helped her release the tension, ease the pain, and when I reached the door, she rolled onto her side, opened her eyes for just a moment, like waking from a dream, said, "Thank you, dear."

Carmen napped for about an hour. I'd gotten so into the massage that I'd forgotten about the box from Tiffany's that had been delivered earlier that day. I placed it on the coffee table so when she woke up she'd immediately see it.

"For moi?" she said, stretching, suddenly revived.

"Yeah," I said. "A messenger dropped it off. You think it's from Tad?" I asked, trying to veil any hint of jealousy and get her to open the card—a card that I'd held up to the light to read, unsuccessfully. I had also tried to steam it open, but for my effort received nothing more than a burn.

"Who?" she asked, distracted by the box.

"Tad," I said, taking on his tone. "You know, the clothesless wonder who was here a couple of weeks ago."

"Oh, no," she said, ignoring the card, pulling at the pearl-colored ribbon. "He was just a familiar face sitting at my table at the Make-a-Wish benefit. Both of his parents are rather known painters and he's desperate to step out from behind their canvases, so he's been working on a novel. I suppose I was research. I give him E for effort, but I for incomplete," then focusing on the box and becoming frustrated, "Why must they put so much tissue in here?"

It was a rather large box, but once she pulled out the tissue all that was inside was a little pouch with a white drawstring. On the bag were the words "Tiffany Money."

Carmen pulled open the pouch, emptied it, revealing large coins, all of which were silver except for one, which was gold.

"Wow," I said, picking up one of the silver coins. It was heavy and as thick as three quarters. It appeared that Tiffany's provided coins rather than a gift certificate. One side of the coin read, "Redeemable in merchandise at Tiffany & Co.," and on the other side was a "C" and an "o" with a solid "T" stamped on top, and at the bottom the words "twenty-five dollars."

I put the coin back on the table and noticed that some of them were for fifty and the gold one was for one hundred dollars.

Carmen finally opened the card, discarding it just as quickly. "Jean-Claude," she said with a smile.

"I guess that helps ease the pain from Chastity."

"A wee bit," she said as she stood and stepped over the tissue paper carpeting the floor around her. "I think I'll have a bath."

Her steps were lighter and as she climbed the stairs I heard her warm laugh rise through the well. I assumed she was chuckling about the fashionable five hundred dollars' worth of Tiffany Money she'd leisurely left on the coffee table, but then I faintly heard her say, "Sidesaddle, huh?"

J ean-Claude treats me like a lady," said Carmen as we were huddled in a taxi. "I just feel good all over when I'm with him."

"Great," I said, but the words came out so false that even I didn't believe it. To me Jean-Claude was just another man in her life, someone to play with. It made me believe I was no different. "Great."

"I do hate feeling this way about him. I know he can hurt me and I hate that. I keep telling myself that he's the one, but I don't know."

"What about Christopher?" I said, a pinch of evilness behind the words.

The smile left Carmen's face as she looked over at me. "What about him?"

"I just thought . . . Nothing."

"No, Malik. What about him?"

"Nothing."

"Fine," she said, turning her head back to the window. "I can't think about that right now. Jean-Claude is a good man."

Then where is he? But I knew if he had been there, I wouldn't be, so all I could say was "I'm sure he is." We rode silently for a while. The cabdriver looked in the rearview trying to gauge our mood. What was once jovial became morose and it permeated the window guard that separated us from him.

"What do you write in that notebook of yours?" asked Carmen, still taking in the passing view.

"This and that," I said, but that didn't seem to be enough for her.

"This and that, huh?"

"Yeah. Thoughts, things I hear. It's like a journal."

"You probably write that I'm crazy."

"No. Nothing like that. It's all good."

"It's okay," she said. "I *am* crazy. Just promise me that you'll make me look good. If anyone ever reads what you're writing, make me look good."

"That won't be too hard," I said, trying to lighten the air in the back of the cab. I suddenly felt responsible for her change in disposition like I'd stolen her happy moment.

"I want to look good," she mumbled.

"Cream always rises," I said, sliding closer to her, still trying to win her over.

She turned from the window, looked at me and gave the best smile she was able to muster. She placed her hand on mine, then turned back to the window. "Yes, but it curdles too."

L et's just walk to the front," said Carmen as I paid for the cab. She'd decided that we should go to a club, and as I hoped that would make her feel better, I couldn't help but agree to go. The line spanned the length of the block of the Chelsea club and I could hear the pulse of deep bass refusing to be confined. House was in the house.

She took my hand and with determination in her stride and a presence that said, *I'm not going to wait,* we walked to the front of the line. The velvet rope was unlatched and without question we were ushered behind it. She was back to the Carmen that I knew, admired. I glanced toward the rest of the waiting crowd expecting some reaction, some mention of fairness, but they accepted the rules of the game, protocol.

Hey," said Carmen, returning from the ladies' room. I was standing near the wall swaying to the music, watching a beautiful Puerto Rican woman dancing on the speaker. She waved at me and I nodded with recognition.

"Oh, what's up?" I said, still looking up at the dancing woman, who appeared to be dancing just for me. She had on a halter top and tube skirt, clothes one would associate with a music video hoochie. As she squirmed around she reminded me of the woman on *Soul Train* who stood on the box jiggling and rubbing her body like battling poison ivy.

"I see something has caught your fancy."

"Nah, just window-shopping."

"That's probably wise."

"Jealous?" I said teasingly.

"I find it difficult to be jealous of a woman who used to be a man. But if that's what you're into, do your thing."

"What?" I said, looking at Carmen, then back to the woman. I zoomed in to search for the Adam's apple, which I had always heard was the telltale sign, but with the smoke, *why so much damn smoke,* the flashing lights and her gyrating motions, it was hard to get a clear look. "No way."

"Way," said Carmen with a laugh. "Yes, she's beautiful and is probably more woman than most, but the feet don't lie. Trust."

I looked down at the woman's feet and sure enough, they were protruding from her strapped heels. There was no doubt that these were the feet of a man, perhaps even one in the NBA, and even if Pearl Buck was doing the binding, it couldn't change their enormity.

While I stared in awe, a man walked up to Carmen. He was older than most of the other patrons, and perhaps that gave him confidence. One had to have confidence to pull off a leisure suit. He looked very much like L.A.'s finest, Lieutenant Columbo, mouth perched. *Just one more question, ma'am.*

"Hello, lovely lady," he said to Carmen, placing his arm on the wall behind her.

Carmen looked down at him. "Come on, now," she said, barely above a whisper, then going even lower, "Come on." The man immediately knew that these words were not meant for him to advance. He walked away and would certainly die from blood loss before he realized he'd been slashed.

"I can't believe you just did that. That was amazing."

"What?" she said with a coy grin, enjoying every minute of it.

"Said that to him. I mean, all you said was 'Come on, now,' and he walked away."

"No. I said, 'Come on, now,' a brief pause, then, 'Come on.' It's in the delivery and the eye contact."

"But you basically laughed in his face."

"No. No, I did not. He felt strong enough to make a move. I just assured him it was the wrong one. If I had laughed in his face, then it would have gotten ugly." She draped her arm over my shoulder. "Quickly and quietly, my dear. That's the key to avoiding catastrophe."

"I need a drink," I said.

"Make it a double and you might not care that that Chiquita over there is really José."

"Funny. You want something?"

"Yes, the usual," she said. "I think I'm going to check out the VIP room."

"Can we get in?"

Carmen looked at me with mock disappointment. "You're with me."
I watched as she sauntered toward the stairs that led to the VIP room,
which was a glass room overlooking the rest of the club. I stood there
for a moment, thinking about being out on the town with Carmen,
and even the deceiving woman added to the night. This was New York.

As the thought simmered in my head, a white guy came and stood
next to me. He moved in real close and whispered, "You holding?"

"What?" I said, but he mistook the inflection of my question.

"Coke?" he said, showing me a folded twenty, looking at me knowingly. I didn't even have on my bubble coat.

I felt as though I'd been stabbed in the stomach, but I refused to let
him ruin my night. *You buying, I'm selling.* "It's forty," I said, taking on
a tough posture. I could have just said no and he would have gone on
his white way, but I wanted to play along.

"Forty?" he said, shocked.

"Yeah, forty, motherfucker," I said. I didn't know what drugs went
for, but it seemed reasonable to me so I went with it. "This ain't no
used-car lot. You want the shit or not?"

He took out his wallet and turned his back to me while he pulled
out more money. With his wallet safely tucked back in his pocket he
turned back to me, looked around and handed me the money. "This
better be good."

"Nothing but the best for you," I said. "Wait right here."

"Where are you going?"

*Oh, I see. It's all right for you to roll up and ask me for drugs, because
I'm black in this club so I must be selling, insulting me, but you don't trust
me with your measly forty bucks.* "Man, I don't hold the stuff," I said,
fully feeling it now. "Five-O has been cracking down and shit and I ain't
about getting busted. I'm too pretty for jail." I paused and, for effect,
looked around as though scoping for undercover cops. He still looked
hesitant. "Psst. You know what? Fuck it," I said, passing his money back
to him and starting to walk away, happy to rid myself of the situation.

"No. It's cool," he said, grabbing my arm. I looked down at his hand like he had lost his mind and he quickly let go.

"Nah, man. Squash it. I don't need this shit."

"No. It's cool," he said, as though we were old friends and he was sorry he'd offended me. *Drugs truly do bring people together.*

"Say you're sorry," I said. He looked at me. "Psst," I said, walking away.

"Look, okay. I'm sorry."

I stopped, turned around and rolled back over to him.

"We cool?" he asked.

"Yeah, we cool," I said, palming his money. "Stay right here."

"I will. I'll be right here."

"Cuz I ain't gonna be looking for ya ass."

"Nah, I'll be right here."

I took the money from him and started walking away.

And the Academy Award for Best Black Performance of a Drug Dealer goes to . . .

"Well, if it isn't *Malik.*"

I turned around to find Jim, standing with his usual smirk. "You're enjoying that, aren't you?"

"Every minute of it. I like the sound of it. *MA-LIK.*"

"Yeah, well don't forget that I was in Barcelona and if I recall, you told that girl you picked up at the Picasso Museum you were single, which I'm sure would have been news to Lisa. You remember Lisa, don't you? Your girlfriend?"

"Oh, it's like that, is it?"

"Just like that," I said. "Come on, I've got to get drinks."

"Wait," he said, reaching into his back pocket and pulling out a wristband. "I'm about to head out, but here, why don't you go up to the VIP room? There's a private party tonight for an album launch. The party wasn't too good but the drinks are our favorite price."

"Free ninety-nine," we said together.

"Who are you here with?" he asked.

"Carmen. I'm supposed to meet her in the VIP room."

"And how is Ms. Thang?"

"She's cool," I said.

"I asked my mother about her. She didn't know her."

"If I took as many pills as Reeva I probably wouldn't remember either."

"Fuck you," he said with a laugh.

"Look, I better get up there. Thanks for the hookup."

"No prob."

I walked around the other side of the club so as not to run into the guy waiting on his delivery. I could see him still standing where I'd left him. He was joined by some friends. I could just hear him bragging about how he'd scored. How he was the man.

I started climbing the steps toward the VIP room, pride in my step as I snapped on my wristband, already tasting the free drinks, and as I was turning the landing I heard a confrontation.

"But I'm on the list," said Carmen.

"Yes, you keep saying this," said the doorman, trying to maintain his cool. "Hold on."

I stepped back behind the corner as other people climbed by me. Carmen stood there completely flabbergasted and couldn't believe this was happening. Heads would roll.

"What's the problem?" asked another bouncer.

"This *gentleman* won't let me in. I was told that my name would be on the list. Carmen England."

"Yes, ma'am, well there must be a mistake because there is no list tonight. This is a private party. Wristbands were sent out and if you don't have one, then I can't let you in."

"I see," said Carmen.

The bouncer seemed to get great pleasure in this. Other people were showing their wristbands and the bouncer let them through. They all looked at Carmen as they walked by. I could see her posture sink, then quickly return to upright as though she had more to say but chose not to. She slowly turned her chin up and started down the steps. I ripped off my wristband, put it in my pocket and just as she turned the corner on the landing I started back up.

"Oh, I was just coming to look for you," she said enthusiastically.

"Sorry it took so long," I said. "But the line at the bar was so long I thought it might be easier up here."

"You didn't miss anything," she said, still walking down the steps. "I did a quick walk-through and it hardly warrants my presence. I know you don't get to do things like this often, but would you be terribly upset if we left? I think the music and the smoke have given me a headache."

She was trying to keep a good face.

"Okay," I said. "It's not my sort of crowd anyway."

We started walking across the club toward the front door. Carmen was walking as though she couldn't get out quickly enough and unless she got some air on her face she would pass out. I was trying to keep up with her.

"Hey," shouted the guy I'd taken the coke money from. I'd forgotten about him. He grabbed my arm. "Where's the stuff?"

"Oh, I was looking for you," I said, yanking my arm away.

"Yeah? Did you think I was outside?" he said, moving in close, his friends in tow. "Just give me back my money and we'll call it even."

Even? "I suggest you roll up off me," I said, reaching into my jacket in a threatening fashion, beginning the sequel of my award-winning drug dealer performance.

"Malik, what's going on?" asked Carmen, coming back over to me.

"Nothing," I said. "I just ran into someone. I'll be right there."

"I really want to leave," she said, still reeling from her experience outside the VIP room, trying to escape before any witnesses could spot her.

"I'll be right there." I then turned back to the guy. I grabbed his arm and moved him farther away from Carmen. "Don't ever call me out like that in front of my lady, you hear? I don't know where you're from but uptown we don't play that shit. That's asking for a beat down." He didn't say anything, and I could see he was getting nervous. His friends sheepishly looked on. I couldn't believe he was buying it. "I couldn't find you so I had to get up out of here, but you see that lady over there dancing on the speaker?" He looked over at the speaker where the Puerto Rican *woman* was still dancing. She noticed me and could see that we were talking about her. I put my hand around the guy's shoulder and started to smile. She waved as she shook her booty a little harder. *Sell it for me, baby. Sell it.* I winked at her. "She's fine, huh?"

"Yeah."

"Unsuspecting, huh?"

"Yeah," he said, still looking at her.

"That's right. That's why she holds the stuff for me." I looked up at her and pointed toward the guy, then at her. She shook her head invitingly, encouraging him to join her. "Just go over there. The stuff she has will fuck you up. Okay?"

"Okay, dude. I'm sorry about that. I just thought you were trying to bail with my money."

"I wouldn't disrespect you like that." I walked off as he started toward the speaker.

"What was that about?" asked Carmen when I caught up to her standing at the exit.

"Just trying to bring the races together."

·12·

I knew I shouldn't have answered," said Carmen.

"Who was it?"

"Christopher," she said as though the weight of her head had tripled, and was more than her neck could hold.

"Everything cool?"

"Yeah," she said. "Yeah."

Though Carmen had proven she had no problem attracting the fancy of men, including her most recent beau, Jean-Claude, who she'd met through Judith "our apartment ain't that goddamn big" Steinman, I had patiently waited for her to tell me about Christopher. She had mentioned him, as had Rose, the cleaning lady, and the women at the party after the art opening. I'd also seen his name on various pieces of mail and even a photograph of him.

We'd been in Carmen's bedroom, catching up on the events since we'd last seen each other. I had to make most of it up: complain about the manager at the café, my coworkers, a nasty customer who didn't know the meaning of the word "tip." I'd spent many hours hanging out and writing in cafés, so it was fun to jump into that life, if only in my imagination.

"Could you look in the drawer and pass me that pill bottle?"

I opened the drawer of the night table. There was an eye mask, and various things that get stored away in a bedside drawer. I dug around until I found the pills, and under them I saw a small picture frame.

"Did you find them?"

"Yeah," I said, passing her the bottle, but still looking down at the frame. I pulled it out to see a photograph of Carmen and a man. He was snugly standing with his hands wrapped around her and his chin resting on her shoulder. Carmen looked puckish but comfortable in her pose as she rested her head against his chest. The photo was inscribed at the bottom, "To Carmen: For always making me look good. Love, Chris."

"Is this Christopher?" I said, somewhat surprised he was black. All of her other gentlemen callers had been rather white.

"Oh," she said, looking at the picture, then twisting the top off of the bottle. Her face tensed and her mouth hardly opened as she simply said, "Yes."

She walked out of the bedroom and went into the bathroom. I could hear the water running, hitting the porcelain with great force, as if to drown out my question. I got up from her bed and walked over to the His and Hers basins. She popped the pill into her mouth and swallowed without the use of water. I could feel it making its way, dry and bitter, down her throat, lodging in her chest.

"What?" she asked, looking at me by way of the mirror. "Can't a lady have a moment to herself?"

"Sure," I said, turning to leave.

"Wait," she said. "Shit happened. That's what happened."

She picked up a jar of cold cream and began covering her face, rubbing in small circular motions as though wanting to pierce the skin rather than rid it of debris.

"Rough breakup?"

"Technically," she said, raising her head to rub the cream on her neck, "we're still married."

"Oh." I wasn't certain how to digest that information. My face held a mixture of shock and disappointment.

Carmen stopped rubbing the cold cream and again looked at me from her mirrored view, then, turning to me, she said, "Don't look at me like that. It's not as it sounds." She again focused on her face and turned on the hot water. She dropped a facecloth into the basin, then picked it up without the slightest hesitation and placed it, steaming, on her face.

"It's none of my business," I said, still hoping to make it mine.

She took her time sliding the cloth over her face, relinquishing it of its mask, opening the pores.

"You're right," she said. I walked out of the bathroom back into the bedroom and started to head back downstairs. She immediately followed. "But if you must know," she said, sitting on the edge of her bed and opening the lid of the Vaseline. She two-fingered it before rubbing it in her palms. "Christopher and I met five years ago. We were sitting on a sofa at a party and he struck up a conversation. He told me he was a photographer, which he was. He did those pictures of me sitting in the corner there."

I'd thoroughly gone through those photographs since gaining entrance to Carmen's boudoir, and each time, the allure of her poses had piqued more than my interest.

"We fooled around," she said, rubbing the Vaseline over her face, then two-fingering it again and applying it to her elbows. "I didn't expect much from him. We were just having a good time, seeing how it would pan out. But he was wonderful."

She stopped moisturizing for a moment and her posture released as though the wonder of their relationship were passing in cinematic form before her. But when the credits appeared, the Vaseline again took focus and was rubbed between her palms before being applied to her knees and calves.

"I thought he was the one I'd been waiting for. We did everything together, practically inseparable. Socially we were unstoppable. We could go anywhere and work it. It was as though he could see through me and still not judge me. He was the only one who didn't take any shit from me and that's no easy job. Don't say it," she said, looking at me.

"I wasn't going to say anything."

"Good."

"If it was so great, what happened?" I asked, moving over to sit next to her on the bed.

"Life. Reality," she said, propping her left foot on the bed and rubbing it until it began to glisten. "He lost a job with one of the magazines and therefore his work permit. He had to move out of his tiny little flat. With no work permit he was going to have to go back to England.

"Then one night we went out to dinner to get his mind off of things. I'll never forget it. The Grange Hall, a lovely restaurant hidden away in the West Village." She put the top on the Vaseline and placed it on the night table. She fluffed her pillow and reclined on the bed. She patted the space next to her, so I happily stretched out too.

"At dessert he asked me to marry him. Of course, I said yes. It's what I wanted, what I'd waited for. I got home and immediately called my mother, but she wanted nothing to do with it, which, as you can imagine, crushed me. Sure, we had our differences but I thought she'd at least be happy for me."

"You don't seem like the type who needs approval."

Carmen rolled over on her side and looked at me. We were both on our sides looking at one another as though we'd known each other all of our lives and this was a night like any. I felt so comfortable next to her, but in truth, we both knew little about the other.

"We all want approval, Malik," she said, reaching over and starting to play with my twists. "It's what makes us see we aren't excluded." Carmen rolled onto her back, away from my eyes. "But my mother didn't approve, and everyone knows that a woman should be married out of her father's house, but there was to be no Sag Harbor wedding for me."

"Your folks live in Sag Harbor?"

"Yes. Harlem wasn't good enough for them anymore so they settled on rustic comfort. They haven't been bitten by any ticks yet, but one can still hope that Lyme disease will grace their lives soon."

"Did they move out there before or after they sold the Laundromat business?"

"What?" asked Carmen. She sat up.

"The Laundromats? I heard someone say that your folks were in the Laundromat business."

"Really," she said. "What exactly did you hear?" Her sudden change in tone made me nervous and I wished I hadn't said anything.

"It wasn't anything bad. These women were talking at the party after the art opening. They said you looked familiar and thought your family was in the Laundromat business, but the other one thought it was real estate. They weren't sure which, but they'd remembered meeting you with Christopher."

"Did they say anything about him?"

"No. They were just talking about money. That seems to be all that matters in New York."

"Yes. Cash does move everything around us," she said, easing back down and rolling her back to me. "How word does get around. Well, yes, they sold the business and their real estate holdings, too early if you ask me, and moved. They wanted a clean start and that didn't include my husband-to-be and me.

"But I was not to be denied. The wedding was lovely, albeit small. Just about thirty of our nearest and dearest. There's a lovely pond right at the entrance of Central Park West and 103rd Street and we had everyone meet us there. Christopher had hired some freaky priest from Woodstock.

"The water level was low and there was a boulder sticking up, about two feet from the shore, so Christopher convinced the good reverend to hop out on the rock. It was lovely seeing him standing there, surrounded by water, perched like a crane.

"Christopher and I stood at the water's edge, sans shoes, covered in linen, and we exchanged vows. As soon as we kissed, the clouds opened and the rain came down, but we didn't care."

Carmen chuckled at the memory and I could imagine a well-heeled, cosmopolitan group of people frolicking in the rain in Central Park.

"Christopher moved in here and I had the phone and utilities switched to his name so we could assure INS that we were sharing the responsibilities of the household. It's really a nightmare what they put you through, but I thought it worth it. We had nothing to hide."

She told the story evenly, almost as though trying to access it in a different light, looking for the clues that she'd missed. "At first, everything was wonderful," she said. "Then it started to deteriorate. He was finding it difficult to get work and his pride wouldn't let me support him through his dry patch, which I was more than willing to do. But men are proud.

"Then there were whispers in the wind. People who were supposed to be our friends, people I no longer speak to, started saying he was using me for the green card. That he had hustled me." Carmen rolled over to face me. She grabbed my hand and looked at me so I could reassure her, but when I said nothing, she continued, "Maybe he *was* using me. But even if that's true, I would have married him anyway. He made me feel like I mattered. He needed my help and I needed his.

"I tried to make him feel like he was a contributing, but artists are the best—and the worst—people to fall in love with.

"For his birthday, I had the two upstairs guest rooms turned into an office and studio, anything to give him a chance, to make him feel things were happening and he was being productive. He had all kinds of suspect people from all over Harlem traipsing in and out, at all hours, but I didn't say a word. All of his equipment is still up there. I locked those rooms when he left and I haven't been in them since. They'll be just as he left them when he comes back."

"Why didn't you just divorce him?"

She took my hand and pulled it over to her and held it just above her breast, tucking it there for safekeeping as though the story gave her a chill. My pulse didn't quicken. It remained steady. I propped up on my elbow, placing my free hand on the side of my face so I could look down at her, envisioning a wound whose scar was still visible. "I suppose if I wanted to be evil . . ."

"You? Evil?" I said jokingly.

"Yeah, imagine that," she said. The telephone rang and she jumped. "You get it."

"Hello," I said.

"Mason?" It was my mother.

"Uh, hello."

"Who is it?" mouthed Carmen, looking panicked.

"My friend Malcolm," I said, covering the mouthpiece. Carmen relaxed back into bed, but I remained tense.

"Mason, is everything all right? You sound different. You're not in trouble, are you?"

"No. Everything's cool."

"Well, your father and I were wondering if you—"

"Listen, now isn't a good time. Can I call you back?"

Though I had expected her to protest, she didn't. "Sure," she said. "Give us a ring when you can."

"I will." I hung up, somewhat dazed, and slowly climbed back in bed. Now Carmen's temperature wasn't the only one that had dropped. Carmen continued talking but my thoughts were still in Louisiana, then she started laughing, which startled me. I was certain she'd heard the change in tone when I was speaking to my mother; a leopard minus his spots. "What?"

"I just thought that might be him. He calls every now and then. Collect. Usually a drink short of a blackout, saying he misses me, and when I begin to believe him, he ultimately asks me to deposit money into our joint account. The only way I ever know where he is, is by looking at the phone bill. I keep telling myself that the next time he calls I won't accept the charges, but I always do. I always do.

"Maybe I should divorce him, but I still believe he loved me. Loves me. Soon he'll have his papers and we'll see what happens. But you can't force someone to stay if they don't want to."

Carmen yawned and finally began to relax. "But this house is too big for one."

I felt a pang run through me and I wondered if I was nothing more than a replacement, a need fulfilled.

"And there you were," she said, turning slightly and looking up at me. "A spot in the crowd with your pitiful little twists, but I saw something, a need stronger than the others. I recognized it because I knew it well. You and I aren't so different, you know."

"Yeah."

I laid my head back on the pillow and Carmen nudged her body next to mine. I held her, thinking that we were more similar than she knew and the longer I carried the guise, the harder it would be to ever let her know that.

"Carmen," I said, determined to tell her my story, not wanting her to feel used twice.

"Shh," she said. "I'm fine. I'm fine."

As we cuddled, silence shrouded us like the mosquito netting over her bed, the pills soon ran their course and sleep found her. Though I held her close, I was certain she would dream of him.

·13·

Christmas decorations were strewn across 125th Street like those seen on any Main Street in Smalltown, USA. Music poured from the storefronts and the voice of Donny Hathaway singing "This Christmas" made it difficult to refuse the season.

Niku Henu, the artist, had just moved into a new apartment in Harlem and was having a holiday party to christen the place, and Carmen had tapped me as her date.

"Didn't Jean-Claude want to go?" I'd asked.

"Look, do you want to come or not?" she snapped.

"Yeah. Sorry."

"Don't be. Just get dressed."

I called for a car to pick us up because the odds of finding a yellow cab in Harlem, at night, were like trying to find a diamond in shit.

Carmen had let me take some of Christopher's clothes down to my room, stating, "They're paid for and just hanging there. Someone may as well get some use out of them." For the evening I went with the basic

New York uniform: black turtleneck, black slacks, and a pair of black shoes that I'd charged on an impulse buy.

"Are you ready?" she asked, stepping into my bathroom.

"Almost."

"You spend more time fooling around with your hair than I do."

"What can I say?" I said, wiping my greasy hands on a bath towel. "Black hair is hard work."

"Well, I must say that you are looking good."

"Thanks. You too. As always."

Carmen had on a wool pantsuit, a maroon shirt, and draped over her arm was a full-length fur coat. She handed me the coat and turned so that I could help her into it. We walked out of the town house and made our way to the car, which I was certain she would turn away, particularly as one doesn't normally equate a fur coat with riding in a faux-wood-paneled station wagon. Nonetheless, she climbed in without complaint.

"Was that a present from Jean-Claude?" I asked, referring to the coat.

"No. I bought this myself, thank you."

"It looks great. But aren't you worried about people throwing paint on it?" I blew on the coat, watching the fur separate, then settle.

"Please. This is Harlem. Nobody up here is anti-fur. This very second there are women—and a few men—trying to figure out how to get their coat out of layaway before Christmas. And I'll tell you, if you throw paint on a black woman's fur, you've got an ass whipping coming."

After a short ride, the car pulled up in front of Graham Court. I paid the driver and we slid out. The building devoured the entire block between 116th and 117th Streets on Adam Clayton Powell Jr. Boulevard, and though it was in desperate need of sandblasting there was no doubt of its opulence.

"This building was commissioned by William Waldorf Astor and cornerstoned in 1901," said Carmen as we were let in the iron gates, which secured the building. We walked through the two-story arched passageway with marble columns leading to a courtyard.

The doorman pointed us to the appropriate elevator. "There are eight elevators in this building," said Carmen, continuing the oral history. "It's a bit beaten now, but like everything else up here, it's becoming hot again. I remember coming to parties here with my parents. Fabulous parties, but I suppose when you're a child all parties that have adults are mystical. It made me feel grown-up. Then you grow up and wonder what it's all about."

Carmen opened the door of Niku's apartment and we were beckoned inside by a haze of marijuana smoke. She turned her back to me and slipped out of her fur, certain I'd catch it, and I did. A guy manning the door immediately took our coats and we were handed a glass of champagne, bubbling around a strawberry.

We walked down the hall and came to the living room. I gathered that this was ghetto fabulous chic because there was only one piece of furniture in the room: a large lipstick-red leather sectional. People, most in all black, were standing, or sitting on pillows on the floor. Miles Davis poured from the speakers and I could imagine him turning his back on the entire crowd, who seemed to have just flown in from the Isle of Pretensia.

Pinkie ringing. Hair slinging. Stares stinging.

At least one hundred various skulls were placed throughout the room, making it look like a sixteenth-century crypt, and aside from the glow of several blunts, candles provided the only light, casting shadows over the walls and ceilings.

Carmen took no time to jump right in, but I kept taking in the room, smiling at my being at another New York soiree. I walked out of the living room and down the hall until I came to the dining room and kitchen. The catering staff had taken over these two areas and everyone looked up at me.

"You're late," said one of the women. "But we'll deal with that later. Grab that tray over there."

"What?"

"Didn't the agency send you?"

"No," I said. "I'm a guest."

"Oh, I'm sorry. I just thought."

"No problem." It seemed I finally had the right look to serve, but at the moment that didn't please me.

I walked down the hall and found a room with a big white tent in the middle of it. I thought perhaps it was an installation, but I didn't have the confidence to venture inside. Stretched canvases covered the walls and people walked from one to the next as if in a museum. Two people were standing in front of a particular painting and I walked over and stood behind them.

"I like the way it veers to the left," said the guy, his wineglass clutched to his chest as though protecting it and himself.

"Yes," said the woman. "It makes it look a bit angry, independent . . ."

". . . belligerent even. On the lookout."

"And this is the bedroom and therefore the showroom," announced Niku, walking in with Carmen on his arm. Everyone stopped what they were doing to look at the two. "As you can probably tell, I haven't had time to have a decorator come in, but the tent serves as my bed for the moment."

"It's a jungle out there," said Carmen, and they clinked their champagne glasses. Niku was in a bright red sarong, a long orange nightshirt, and though he wore no shoes he had on what appeared to be a great many colorful socks on each foot, giving his feet a clubbed appearance. Again, cake makeup matted his face, and his hair was a geometrical illusion. If black hair is hard work, then Niku's had to be slavery.

"Niku," said the man who had been commenting on the painting. "We know Tony's here, and not that we're poaching, but if you find yourself wanting a gallery change, do give us a call. The new work is just so . . ."

". . . expressive," continued the woman.

"Cheers," said Niku. "Food for thought."

The man and the woman both nodded and were hardly out of the room before Carmen started up. "It's so. So . . ." and, together, she and Niku said, "Expressive."

"What kind of shit was that?" asked Niku.

"I think they were interested in this painting over here," I said, pointing to the painting, which looked like a canvas painted black.

"That one?" he asked. "That's just the primer coat. I haven't even started on that yet."

"Then you're obviously working far too hard," said Carmen. "Niku, you remember Malik, don't you?"

"Of course. Your protégé," said Niku. "I hardly recognized you. Your hair is getting longer."

I immediately wished my hair had grown long enough to cover my nose. Niku's armpit was in whiffing distance and the vapors radiating from him revealed the culprit.

"How's it going?" asked Niku, draping his arm across my shoulders.

"I'm good," I said, breathing through my mouth, attempting not to be obvious that I feared fungus was growing across my back.

"Great. Enjoy yourself. *Mi casa, su casa.*" Niku walked away to talk to some of the other guests.

"I hate to be a bad guest," I whispered to Carmen, "but does Niku normally smell like that?"

Carmen laughed. Other guests looked over at us, concerned that our laughter may be directed at them.

"It's part of his shtick. It gives the collectors something to talk about," said Carmen, darting her eyes around the room, adding to the secrecy of the conversation. "Though it is decidedly unpleasant, we ignore it. Artistic freedom."

Uptown," said a guy talking to Carmen. He had a shaved head, a goatee, and was dressed in baggy jeans, a John Starks Knicks jersey over a T-shirt, and Air Jordans. He was introduced as Precious D, a downtown poet who had become so popular on the slam scene with his singsong verse that he ended up a V.J. on MTV, "getting paid." I was intrigued; one hardly uses "poet" and "getting paid" in the same sentence.

"Are you still living down in the East Village?" asked Carmen.

"Yeah." Carmen looked at him, waiting for him to elaborate. He didn't. Poets are economical with their words.

"Perhaps you can help Malik. He's always scribbling in a notebook." Precious D looked at me but didn't respond. "He works down in the East Village."

This seemed to interest him more. "Where?"

"Café Orlin," I said, almost mumbling the words.

"Speak up," said Carmen, like a proud mother.

"Café Orlin."

"Yeah?" said Precious D, his face lighting up. "I know the owner. James."

Everybody in this damn city knows the owner of something. Just so in the know. "Yeah," I said.

"Yeah," he said. "When I was starting out he used to hook me up with free meals and shit. Cool cat."

"Yeah," I said. "James is cool like that."

"So when do you work? I'll have to stop in."

Oh, so now you wanna get chatty. "You know, it changes from week to week."

"Hey, if you want, I'll talk to James, make sure he gives you the best shifts so you can make enough money to do your writing."

Carmen was hanging on to every word, happy that Precious D had engaged us. Her eyes darted around the room to see who was looking, and under different circumstances I probably would have been doing the same. I chugged the rest of my champagne. The strawberry rolled down the flute and popped me in the lip, almost as punishment.

"Nah, that's okay. I'm cool. I don't know how much longer I'm gonna be working there," I said. "Some other opportunities are shaping up."

Carmen looked over at me, surprised. "Oh, really?"

Again, I nervously put the empty flute up to my mouth. "Anybody need another drink?"

"Nah," said Precious D. Though I'd never seen her pass on a drink, Carmen also declined, but continued looking at me with curiosity. I walked away wondering if he was good with names. He must meet tons of people. He wouldn't mention me and even if he did, and James— *God bless him, whoever he is*—didn't have a clue of who I was, Precious D would just think he had made a mistake. Even poets, particularly those who appear on MTV, make mistakes.

S o how do you know Niku?" asked the woman, leaning against the wall, evidently trying to brace her back. Her hair was naturally blond but dyed black at the roots and her double D-imension breasts were hardly contained by a black T-shirt with white studded letters that read, Sex Worker.

"I met him at a party," I said, then motioned to Carmen, who was standing next to me. "He's a friend of Carmen's."

The woman gave Carmen a discerning look, which was returned in kind.

"And you?" asked Carmen, bored. She had given up her champagne and moved to her standby, Jack Daniel's.

After taking a sip of champagne, the woman said, "We met in rehab. Had it not been for him I would have been bored to death. Everyone was so uptight, you know what I mean? I mean, I remember when re-hab used to be a fun place to just unwind, make some contacts, but no one fun is ever there anymore, and sports stars are such a bore. Niku made it worthwhile."

"I'm glad to hear it wasn't a total waste," said Carmen, not even looking at the woman, yet waving at another guest down the hall.

"I mean, you're really not supposed to get involved with the other 'visitors' but Niku's so hot, and a woman has her needs. I mean, he's really good. I mean, you hear all these things about black men, which I can assure you aren't always true," she said. She took a suggestive bite of her strawberry as she briefly slid her view down to my basket as though wanting to see if a "Thank you, Easter Bunny" was in order.

The champagne and the marijuana smoke wafting through the air made me feel high, so I opened my stance as to not obstruct her perusal. "But Niku. I mean, it was just magical. You know what I mean. Really hot. The sweat between us made these amazing sounds and I know people were wondering what was going on. I mean, I'm not obsessed about size, but I do like a big—"

"Honey," said Carmen, quickly turning and placing two fingers an inch away from the woman's mouth. "It's okay to keep a secret."

The door to the bathroom opened and Carmen slipped in, leaving me with the woman who was proof that the tongue was the body's strongest muscle.

"You know, you look familiar," she said, inching closer to me. "What do you do?"

"Whatever it takes," I said.

"Oh really." She slowly started running her hand up my inseam.

"Careful. It bites."

"That's okay," she said. "I've got my shots."

I bet you do. "Maybe we can talk later," I said, sliding away.

"I hope so." I took a few steps away, then turned around, but she had already idled up to another guy. I walked into the living room. Niku had just sat down on one of the pillows. He looked up with a smile and motioned me over.

"Have a sit-down, shorty," he said. I sat on the pillow next to him. "I see Natasha was about to rape you."

"Can't rape the willing." Niku laughed. I don't know what had come over me. But I was feeling it. *Mackin' and attractin'.* "She said she was in rehab with you."

"Yeah," he said nonchalantly, as though I'd said they went to grade school together. "Too much heroin, man. Not too long ago I had so much horse around me you could have shot a western. But we all have our addictions. Natasha's is dick."

"I hear ya. But you must be glad you kicked it."

"No doubt. Smack'll kill ya. I prefer opium. It's just as addictive but more user-friendly." I almost laughed, thinking he was being ironic, but he wasn't. "So how's life with Ms. Carmen?" he asked, passing me the Sunday-*Times*-size joint which had made its way to our side of the room.

"It's all good," I said, taking a toke and passing it back to him.

"Hold on to it for a while," he said. "I'm sure you need it. Old Carmen is a character, but you've gotta love her. She pulls it off better than anyone I know. I wouldn't have a party without inviting her. Is she still rolling with Jean-Claude?"

"Yeah."

"That girl," he said. His tone let me know he didn't mean Marlo Thomas.

"She is something else," I said, trying to be discreet, loyal to her.

"Is she charging you to live down there?"

"Yeah." I still felt a bit uncomfortable by this line of questioning.

"How much?"

"Four fifty."

"Not bad. She must be getting soft in her old age."

"She's holding up."

"Listen," he said, leaning in close, the funk rising from his armpit. I envisioned ferns growing there. "You seem like a decent kid. But I wouldn't get too comfortable if I were you."

"You mean because of Christopher," I said. I could feel the pot creeping, taking over my brain. Like a saturated sponge still trying to retain.

Niku looked surprised. "So she told you about him?"

"Yeah."

"Then she must really like you."

I didn't want to give too much information—my loyalty was to

Carmen—but I was enjoying the idea that he could see how important I was to her.

"And you don't have a problem with that?" he said.

"Hey, man. That's on them. Carmen was good enough to help me out. It's all good."

"Live on, my brother," he said, taking the joint from me and taking a toke. "You'll learn that Carmen doesn't do anything unless it suits her needs. Just watch your back."

"I thought you two were close."

"We are. I've known her for a long time and that's why I can say what I'm saying. Look around. These people are here because I'm hot right now and doors and legs swing open when you're hot. This place wasn't just handed to me. I had to work my black ass off for it and I'm working harder every day to keep it. Nobody gives you shit. Carmen has a problem with that concept. She feels she's owed something. And it's a shame too. Her mind is years ahead of Wall Street or Madison Avenue, but she goes around thinking somebody's gonna save her life, make everything right. No one can save your life if you don't value it. It's not about the power of the master, but the strength of the slave."

I began to feel dizzy, like focusing on the passing horses of a carousel. I tugged at the collar of my turtleneck hoping to get the blood flowing back to my brain. The laughter and chatter of the other guests pinballed in my ears, irritating me; their faces distorting. I turned my gaze back to Niku.

"You seem like a nice enough young brother. There's something more to you than you're featuring, and that's cool. We all have our parts to play, but what I'm saying is sleep comes easiest for those who have their own, and Carmen . . ."

"Oh, there you are. I can't leave you alone for a second," said Carmen, looking down at me. I immediately started to get up, which took some effort, and she looked down at Niku. "What are you boys talking about?"

"You, my dear. What else?" said Niku, meeting her gaze, two animals ready for the next move.

"As it should be," she said, her tone verged on a warning. I feared my face had revealed that Niku was being less than complimentary toward her, but I forced a smile, still trying to absorb his words.

Niku stood up from his pillow and kissed Carmen. "I'd better check on my guests." Carmen watched him as he walked away, then she looked back at me.

"What was that about?" she asked.

"Nothing," I said. "Just shooting the shit."

"Are you stoned?"

"It's all good," I said, not at all sure that it was.

C armen's party mood dissolved and we abruptly left Niku's. She decided that "weather be damned," she wanted to walk home.

We strolled the streets of Harlem, which were gray from the salt, and cat-size rats scurried through trash cans looking for a meal. I watched with amazement as one ran down the sidewalk with a drumstick clamped in his jaws; not a drumstick bone, but a whole drumstick. But even the sight of that couldn't gnaw my mood.

A small group of men were huddled outside of a store, which had no other name than Liquor Wine Lotto. At one point I would have felt proud to be walking the streets with Carmen, but Niku's words kept filtering in.

Watch your back.

Carmen walked as though she owned the world, her hands slid deep into the pockets of her fur.

"Are you okay?" she asked.

"Yeah."

"One-word answer. That's never good."

"I'm cool. Just cold."

"It's only a few blocks. I need to clear my head and it looks like you do too."

I became aware of the tension padding my shoulders and I let them drop to comfort, which immediately seemed to warm me. Carmen kept walking but looked over at me. She then turned her eyes back to the horizon and said, "It looked like you and Niku were getting rather chummy."

"Not really."

"What did he have to say?"

"Nothing. He was just asking me about myself, what brought me to New York, shit like that."

"You wouldn't be keeping good party gossip from me, would you?"

"No." Though I looked ahead, I could sense her eyeing me.

"You should listen to Niku," she said. "He's done well for himself. Living the life, wouldn't you say?"

"I guess. It's a nice place."

"It'll do when he has someone come in and decorate."

"I think it's pretty cool the way it is."

"You would."

This hit me from marrow to flesh, but I tried to remain steady. "No, it's not as nice as the town house, but he sleeps in a tent. That's pretty cool. Who sleeps in a tent?"

"Niku does," she said. "He deserves his success. From the projects to Graham Court. You should let him be a lesson to you. If you work hard, one day you'll be able to change your situation."

"Yeah. Maybe."

"And what's this about leaving the café?"

"A few things are on the burner."

"Like?"

"Just things. Damn. Get off me."

"My. So secretive all of a sudden. Just know that staying with me is fine, but . . ." Carmen tilted her head sideways and raised her eyebrows, letting her expression finish her sentence. Our steps, which just seconds earlier had been walked with the precision of a drum corps, faltered.

"But what?" I said, stopping. Carmen stopped too, but only for a moment, and pleased that she had incited me, she started walking again, which made me trail after her.

"A slice of bread buttered on both sides increases the chance of heart attack."

"And what in the hell is that supposed to mean?"

"That mouth of yours really has gotten vulgar of late."

"I'll make a note," I said, my confidence returning. "What did you mean by bread buttered on both sides?"

"Let's face it, Malik. You can't live with me forever."

I'd gotten used to Carmen's Fahrenheit fluctuations, which came without telegraph, but this time I wasn't backing away.

"It's not my intent to live with you forever."

"Not your 'intent.' My, my, my. Nice word," she said, trying to put her arm through mine. I pulled away. "Don't get angry, Malik. Face it, you're letting your life pass in front of you. You're not in school. You're working in some café, for tips and a free meal. You *claim* to have something else in the works, but can't articulate what. Even the clothes you're wearing aren't yours."

"You said I could wear these. I can get my own clothes. And no, I'm not in school. Maybe I'll be an artist like Niku or a poet like Precious D."

" 'Maybe' is the hardest-working word in town," she said. "A poet? Hah. You and every nigger in town, scribbling in some notebook about your silly little life, like the world gives a damn about your black ass. People have to know you exist before they care about your pain."

My feet remained firmly planted on the sidewalk, but the top of my body swayed back as though a medicine ball had been thrown at my stomach. The DON'T WALK sign began to flash as we approached the corner. I thought of running ahead, making the light, leaving her, but I couldn't.

"Is this about Christopher?" I asked, trying to find some rationale to her sudden change in manner. "Are you asking me to move out?"

"No. I'm not saying that you should move, but this is my life, mine," she said, pulling at the collar of her coat. "If you want to make it here it can't be on my coattails."

"Fine. I'm sorry if—"

"You're always sorry and it borders on boring." The words came out so cold that ice wouldn't have melted in her mouth. "You think I've gotten where I am by being sorry? You'd be wise to learn that Sorry doesn't pay the bills."

"So everything is about money?" The shrillness in my voice surprised her, surprised me, and though the street sign said it was safe to walk, I couldn't stop myself. "You're always talking about who has this and who doesn't have that. You're a classist and it's tired."

"We're all classist, my dear. Nobody wakes up saying, Thank God I live in the projects and the elevator, when it does work, smells like piss and the alarm has been going off for three days. And certainly, no woman sits around dreaming about falling in love with a broke man."

"That's fucked-up. Why are you so cynical? So it didn't work out with Christopher, but that doesn't give you the right to go around judging people on what they have. So Jean-Claude can take you to his place 'on the Island' and buy you presents from Tiffany's. Big deal. You think—"

"Don't be so damn naive, Malik. You yourself said your parents didn't have insurance and couldn't afford your mother's medication."

For a moment, like a slap, this took away some of my steam, but I shook off the sting.

"This is a world of haves and have-nots, period," she said, grabbing my arm so tightly that it felt as though my coat wasn't even there. She looked into my eyes but seemingly through them as though trying to pierce my brain, make things clear. "Whether we like it or not, that's reality. The poor are trying to make it and the rich are trying to make more. The only people who can afford to give a damn about anyone else are those stuck in the middle and the only reason they do is because they feel guilty that they aren't poor, yet it provides them with a justification of why they don't have what it takes to be rich. Yes, sir, Mr. Malik. People love to walk around basking in their difference, then get upset when someone reminds them of that difference." She released my arm, but her grip remained.

"Malcolm was right about you."

Carmen left out a laugh. "You mean your little friend? He should talk."

"What does that mean?"

"He stopped by the house the other day."

"What? Why didn't you tell me?"

"Because he's a bad influence."

"I can't believe you," I said, disgusted, feeling this was something my mother would do.

"Be that as it may. Everyone in Harlem knows his brother served time for running a drug ring."

"What does that have to do with Malcolm?"

"How do you think he pays for school? Columbia isn't cheap."

"Have you heard of scholarships and financial aid?"

"Wake up, Malik! You can't afford to get self-righteous with me. I've been at this a bit longer than you have."

Her words were enough to make me cross the street. This time it was she who had to catch up with me.

"Since everything is about money to you," I said, pulling out change from my pocket and throwing a coin toward her, "here. Here's a penny. But feel free to keep your thoughts to yourself."

Carmen stopped midstride in the middle of the street and began to laugh.

"Well. I see being around me has finally paid off." She started walking again, continuing to laugh, which only made me more upset.

"This is all just a game to you," I shouted, missing the irony in my words. My voice had gotten louder with each step and I saw several noses pressed against Christmas-lit windows from apartments above, making me revert to a harsh stage whisper. "Am I just a little plaything for you, at your beck and call when Jean-Claude isn't available or until Christopher calls and needs money and you need an ear to moan in?"

"You're acting out of place." Her body was relaxed as ever but hate was settled in her eyes. I looked at her thinking that Niku's words had a ring of truth to them and anger took over like a whistling kettle.

I wasn't angry with her. The anger was toward myself, the worst anger of all. I walked several steps ahead, plowing through wind, her laughter piercing me.

People love to walk around basking in their difference, then get upset when someone reminds them of that difference.

I knew this pain, had felt it before, but had left it tucked away in Louisiana; never had I expected it to resurface on the streets of Harlem.

I couldn't help but think about Natalie Hill. We'd been best friends at Elixir Elementary and Junior High School. We'd been inseparable, spending hours on the phone or riding three-wheelers. Nothing could separate us; our own posse of two.

I'd been the only black student at Elixir, a school that was supposed to provide me with a superior education. Lisa Landau was having her twelfth-birthday party in the party room of Linden Recreation Center, and due to the selective guest list, it had been the talk in class, the lunch room and the canteen for weeks.

When my mother dropped me off, the Mercedes barely found its way into park before I jumped out.

I went in with gift in hand. Balloons were taped everywhere and a huge banner had been hung: Happy Birthday, Lisa.

The red, blue, green lights moved in time to the tunes being spun by the local, popular radio disc jockey. Chairs lined the walls but no one sat.

The dancing was done in groups, eight people in a circle, swaying, often offbeat. But the slow dances were when people coupled.

Several times I'd asked Natalie to dance. She kept shunning me but would then go off to dance with one of the other guys. I eventually took the hint and found myself sitting on the wall, hardly a flower, but a weed, pulled from the root. I watched Natalie as I tried to determine what I had done, what had changed.

I saw Lisa's mother notice me and shortly thereafter Lisa came over and asked me to dance. A slow dance; a song by Journey, I believe. I got up and we walked to the dance floor. All eyes went toward us as though we were walking on the moon as opposed to moonwalking. There were some giggles and looks of amusement; some people had even stopped in midbeat to watch us make our way to the center of the floor.

Lisa put her hands on my shoulders and I put mine around her waist as we turned, systematically, free of feeling, to the music; "Faithfully," I believe it was. Not once did we look at each other.

When the song ended, I thanked Lisa and went back to my seat. No one spoke to me for the rest of the evening. One slow dance had made the difference.

Natalie and a group of girls huddled around Lisa at the refreshments table, their laughter refusing to be contained. These were people I'd known for years, and suddenly, being twelve years old seemed much older.

I sat in my chair waiting for the clock to strike nine so I could be picked up. When the time came, I left without a good-bye, wanting to make certain I was gone before the lights were turned on.

I walked out and my mother was sitting in the car. She smiled at me as I walked toward her. I opened the door and got in. Her smile vanished. My tears fell fast and hard, large and salty. My mother didn't ask what had happened. She just slid her hand across the top of my head and down my neck where she caressed it and though I would have normally pulled away from her touch, I didn't. I didn't have the energy to deny her touch. My mother had been anticipating the day, dreading the day, when it would become clear to me that I was different, in a world claiming otherwise. I knew the next Monday I'd have to return to school, return to Elixir, a school that was to provide me with a superior education.

But as I walked across 120th Street that December night, Carmen's laughter and footsteps clickclickclicking behind me, all my tears of difference had already been tapped.

With my new name and twist-heavy head, I looked down as I walked, laden, feeling like a New York City squirrel; wishing for softer grounds, yet forced to find the crack in the sidewalk where a portion of harvest had been stored for cold moments like this one.

·14·

The knock at my bedroom door woke me from a fitful sleep. It was a soft yet diligent knock, suggesting it had followed several moments of contemplation, a hand waiting to react to the mind's resolve.

"Ma'am?" I said. I was groggy but I lifted myself onto my elbows, aware that I wasn't in my bedroom in Louisiana, but in the town house in Harlem. The door opened slightly, presenting a sliver of light across the floor and far wall of the bedroom.

Carmen peeked her head in and her shadow loomed while the words of Dinah singing "Mixed Emotions" floated in.

"What?" I asked, and because of the hour, thinking the worst. Had my mother called?

"Nothing," she said, still standing in the door. "Are you still upset with me?"

"Just forget it," I said, nestling back into bed. "It's late."

"Can I come in?"

"It's your place." I rolled over on my side, making certain my back was to her.

"Malik?"

I refused to look at her, but I could see her shadow shrinking on the wall.

"Malik?"

"Listen, Carmen, I'm trying to get to . . ." I rolled over to look at her and my words were swallowed whole. Carmen had on a sheer white robe, leaving nothing to the imagination. She untied the belt and the robe opened like a curtain in an old grand theater, revealing the stage. She eased out of the robe and it fell, gathering around her feet.

"One shouldn't go to bed angry."

Carmen walked over to the bed and slowly pulled the duvet and sheets away. I tried to speak but she put her finger over my lips. I was naked, but didn't try to conceal myself from her. I attempted to focus on Dinah's voice but the words, of a song I knew well, seemed like gibberish as Carmen climbed into the bed and straddled me. She placed her knees on each side of my waist. She looked into my eyes. I held her stare, but my eyes soon closed as her mouth replaced her fingers over my lips.

The kisses were mere pecks at first, seductive. I wanted to stop her, stop this from happening. *Don't stop her. Don't stop this from happening.* My mouth opened, my tongue lingered, longingly, a knotted stem on a cherry.

She placed her hand on my shoulders and pushed herself up to look at me. I met her eyes. *Cheers.* Her face was still close enough to feel the warmth of her breath. She smiled. She leaned back down and grazed the tip of my nose with her lips, then made her way down to the neck. I could feel her nipples dusting my chest, bringing to attention what few hairs slumbered there. I couldn't control the sounds coming from me. They weren't words. *Exclamation.* She ran the tip of her tongue over the ridge of my ear, then found herself navigating its interior regions, expertly, before sucking the lobe. I could feel her tongue flicking the earring stud and I rolled my lips inward to keep from screaming. From the lobe she worked her way down my jawline, to my neck, over my Adam's apple, sucking gently, before again finding my mouth. This time the invitation of my tongue was accepted. The salty taste of my skin and ear soon dissipated as she sucked on my tongue, aggressively, until the pain timidly hid behind pleasure. I knew it was too late to stop. I knew it was too late to be practical. *Don't stop. Don't be practical.* I wanted this. I wanted it just for myself. I reached up and placed my hands on her hips, firmly, sinking my fingers into her skin and pulling her tighter into me. She stopped kissing me for a second as though surprised by my aggression. *The quiet ones are the ones to watch.* The grin on her face was comparable to the arch of her back. Her skin was smooth as I ran my hands over the curve in her ass and up her back. I cupped the side of her face, embracing it and rubbing my thumbs over it like it was clay for my fingers to manipulate. She pulled herself up and looked at me. She arched her eyebrow at me as she pushed the duvet and sheet away from my lower legs, until nothing but our brown bodies were visible. The smile never left her face. She took my hands and placed them on her breasts. After leading the way, she found appreciation in my caress and she removed her hands from mine. She closed her eyes and threw her head back. "Nice," she mumbled. I closed my eyes and, without forethought, worked my hands down her waist. Her upper body and pelvis began to sway to the music and like a ritual leading to the end result, mine began to move in time. Her fingertips slid down my chest, down my abdomen. Slightly lifting from me, her hand continued its trail like my body was a map and her destination was in sight. I opened my eyes, only a moment, but not wanting to reveal astonishment, I closed them as she gently tugged and pulled and words were soon added to the sounds. I felt more of her weight lift off of me as her body slid down. Her fingers were replaced by her mouth and my mouth unhinged. I opened my eyes, but I didn't look down at her. Rather, I concentrated on the detailed molding on the ceiling as my neck and back rose as though being connected and pulled up by a web from above. *Yes. Even a spiderweb can appear beautiful with the right light reflecting upon it.* Aware of her power, Carmen slid back up my body, again positioning herself on my lap and with a seamless transition my dick slid inside her. The shock rushed past terror, before merging on ecstasy. For the first time we shared control. I placed my hands on her lower back and made an attempt to anchor myself as my abdomen flexed and released. Again, I looked up at the ceiling trying to take my mind away from the feeling, prolong the sensation. But my mind couldn't compete with matter and my eyes rolled back into my head and my body stiffened; legs and feet rigid, like a dancer on point. I could hear my granny, *Use a condom every time.* I thought of warning Carmen. I didn't want to warn her. My closed eyes took control and squinted until the black soon revealed streaks of color and opening them was impossible. Every muscle in my body simultaneously relaxedtensedrelaxedtensed, then relaxed, becoming one with the mattress and my eyes opened with the release. Exhalation. I looked up at her with a bewildered smile on my face and a single tear fell from her eye, hitting my chest.

I sprang up on my elbows, lost. My heart was racing and the sweat-soaked sheets caused a chill. My focus was a blur and it took me a moment to adjust to the surroundings. The sheets and duvet were still covering me and there was no sheer robe on the floor. No light streaming in from the closed door. No Dinah. No Carmen.

I ran my hand over my face and my heart tried to find a rate it could live with. It seemed to take all of my remaining energy to pull the duvet tighter, hoping to regain my loss in temperature. Mind over matter.

I took a deep breath, closed my eyes, but I knew sleep wouldn't be so easily found; a reclined body running.

·15·

I now have to lock my door when I'm not home. It's come to that. I'd left my journal in the kitchen while I went to the bathroom and when I returned Carmen was flipping through it like it was some mysterious find that would lead her to a lost treasure. She couldn't have had more than thirty seconds with it but it still pissed me off.

"What are you doing?" "Nothing. I was just curious as to what you've been writing. I thought if it was good I could help you . . ." "I don't need your help. It's private. I don't go through your things so I'd appreciate it if you wouldn't go through mine." She gave me a look that made me certain she'd seen something that had given me away. "What?" "I didn't see anything, really. The journal was lying here and I was just flipping through." "Whatever, Carmen." "Malik." "Don't you have a party to go to or something?"

This role I've cast for myself is beginning to overwhelm. I find it difficult to even look at Carmen. It's like I had been seeing her through rose-tinted glasses and the prescription's been adjusted. The town house *has become my own bell jar. If she comes in, I go out, still saying, "Not now, Carmen, I'm late for work." Yeah. Right . . .*

I took the train down to Café Orlin, a small café on St. Marks Place, where people passed time, hoping to bump into someone else doing the same. Whether poor or pockets of plenty, filling the day can be a chore.

Orlin was where I'd told Carmen I worked, but with the money that I'd spent there, I could have easily been one of the owners. I'd been sitting there for hours nursing the dregs of what was my fifth latte.

I was sitting near the window, scribbling words in my notebook—I no longer called it a journal because Carmen, in one of her bitchy moods, had politely brought to my attention that men don't keep journals—and reading E. B. White's *This Is New York*. Orlin was quickly filling around me and I could hear the waiters saying they were "slammed" or "in the weeds," terms I'd picked up and used on Carmen to describe my shift.

Someone knocked on the glass, startling me, and when I looked up it was Jim, shooting me the bird. I got up, left some money on the table and went outside.

"What up?" I said, outside.

"Nothing," he said. "Where were you last night? I tried to call you and Carmen said you weren't in."

"I was out with Malcolm. I've been trying to stay out of the house. Why? You keeping tabs on me? I'm your bitch now?"

"Fuck you. I called to see if you wanted to check out a band at S.O.B.s."

"What time did you call?"

"Around midnight. Carmen started asking me all these questions and shit. You would have thought she was Inspector Poirot."

"What did she want to know?"

"Don't worry. I didn't blow your cover, Malik."

"No, seriously, man," I said, grabbing his arm. "What did she say?"

"Just asking me what I'd been up to and how my mother was and how I knew you. Shit like that."

"Come on, Jim. This is important."

"Damn. That was it. I said we met down here. You were a cool dude and were happy to be living up there. That's it. Take a chill pill. You're bringing me down. If I needed this shit I'd call my mother."

· 16 ·

Broadway was teeming with people, and the smell of pine reminded me of the season. I bought a Christmas tree from the hippies who had made their way down from Canada in an old VW van to capitalize on city dwellers unable to chop down their own tree. I was hoping the tree would warm the frigid environment that had coated the town house like dripping icicles.

"Look at this tree," said Carmen, like an enthusiastic child. "This must have cost you a fortune."

"Yeah, they're more expensive up here, but it was worth it."

This was the most we'd said to one another in two weeks as our curt notes on Post-its had become our main source of communication. Carmen walked around the tree.

"I hope you don't mind that I moved the furniture around. I just thought the tree would look better near the window."

"No, it's fine. It's absolutely wonderful, and the smell. Um. That's

Christmas. I'm so glad you thought about it. When you're alone, decorations just don't mean as much."

"But you're not alone."

"No. No, I'm not."

This is fun," said Carmen as we sat on the floor in front of the fireplace, stringing popcorn and cranberries. "I haven't done anything like this since I was a little girl. I used to love Christmas. I never believed in Santa Claus, but Christmas was always a happy time. You kind of forget all the bad things. Decorating the tree was always great. I'd put on the ornaments that I'd made over the years. As you get older you realize they were rather ugly, but my mother always loved them. She's always let me put the star on top. Yes, it was always hard to be sad around Christmas."

Carmen hadn't spoken much about her family and I could see that the memory was fond.

"Feel free to put any ornaments that you want on it," I said.

"I don't have any here. My mother has them."

"That's too bad."

"Yes it is."

"Are you going to visit your parents? Maybe you can bring some back."

"No," she said, focusing on the needle and the cranberry she was stringing. "We don't get along. But I will call her from Deer Valley."

"You ski?"

"Don't be so surprised," she said.

"I'm not. Nothing you do surprises me."

"Then I must be slipping," she said. "You know Deer Valley?"

I had spent five days there with some friends during my junior year in college, where we debated East Coast versus West Coast slopes. "I think I heard you talking on the phone about it, or maybe I read it in a magazine. I don't know, but it sounds like a good time."

I was pleased that we were talking, though tentatively, trying to slowly work our way back into each other's good graces. I started eating the popcorn, bracing myself to come clean with Carmen.

"Don't eat the decorations," she said, tapping the back of my hand.

"Sorry."

"Don't be," she said with less conviction than the times she'd said it before. "Malik, I would love to invite you, but I'm going with Jean-Claude and—"

"No. I wasn't trying to milk an invitation. It just sounds like a good time."

There was an awkward silence that was filled by the crackling of the fireplace.

"Are you going home?" she asked.

"Nah, I'll probably just call."

"I can lend you the money if . . ."

"No. No. Thanks though," I said, a bit surprised by the sincerity in her voice, surprised by the gesture. "I appreciate it."

I'd spoken to my parents earlier in the week. Since they hadn't heard from me they were going to Barbados for Christmas. I was shocked they had made plans without me. "We can't wait around for you," my mother had said. "We've got our lives to lead too."

"Malik, I don't mean to pry," said Carmen, looking for the appropriate words, "but what do you want to do?"

"Do?"

"In the future. Your dreams. When you were a kid, what did you want to be when you grew up?"

"A fireman," I said, trying to bring levity to the conversation. But when I was a kid I did want to be a fireman. Carmen looked at me and shook her head as though there was no hope, just as my mother had done so many years earlier. "A lawyer," I admitted. It was the first time I'd thought of it in a while.

Carmen looked at me. Her head slightly tilted back and her eyebrows raised. It wasn't a mocking gaze, but one that made her look at me in a new light and I allowed it.

The tree was dressed and I thought Carmen would laugh as I started making a star out of tinfoil but she watched with amazement.

"You put it on," I said.

"I couldn't," she said. "You got the tree and everything else. You should do it."

"No. I want you to."

"No, really. I couldn't," she said, taking the star from me. I brought out a chair from the dining room. I helped her onto it and held her waist as she placed it at the tree's peak. She put her hand on my shoulder and stepped down.

"That does it." I walked over and turned off the light, and the glow of the fireplace danced on the walls. I plugged in the Christmas lights and they began to blink in counter time. Where generations of ornaments would have hung on my parents' tree, here there were strings of popcorn and cranberries. Where gold bows would have been, there were strips of ribbon. Where the handmade black angel with each family member's initials stitched into the wings would have been, there was a tinfoil star. And under the tree where gifts would be piled was an empty space. Yet, this tree had more of an impact on me than the ones I'd had growing up.

"It's the best tree I've ever had," said Carmen, traces of blinking lights crossing her face.

"Get out!"

"No. I mean it. This is real. It's often easy to forget what's real. But this is real. Excuse me," she said, getting up and leaving the room.

I didn't know what to make of her mood. When she was up, the world was hers, but the downs were as unsettling as stepping on the mines of dog shit dressing the city sidewalks, busy sidewalks. Both made you aware of your next step.

I quietly climbed the stairs, but the creaks of the wood seemed to explode underfoot. I knocked on her bedroom door. No answer. I knocked again.

"Yes."

"What's up?"

"Nothing."

"Can I come in? I've got something for you."

There was no answer and as I was about to walk back down she opened the door. She was in a terry robe and clothes were still all over her room.

"I just got out of the tub so by now my bathwater should be touching the world."

"And the better for it," I said.

"Yes, I suppose." Without looking at me she walked out of the bedroom and I followed her through the dressing room and on into the den where she sat in the window seat. She put her legs up on the cushion as she looked out, seemingly at nothing in particular, just out. I stood behind one of the leather chairs, holding her present.

"What am I doing?" she asked. "I sit here all high and mighty and have the nerve to ask you what you plan to do when I've always run away from that very question. Soon I'm going to be forty-three years old. Forty-three years old. And what have I done? Nothing."

"That's not true," I said, trying to conceal my disbelief at her age, but I couldn't truly say I knew what she'd done in her life.

"Yes it is. I know how to play the game. That's what this city is and you can't run from your history, because history is the present." Carmen kept looking out the window as if she were talking to it. "You remember that night, the night of the first snow?"

I did remember, and the mood that had filled the kitchen that night had climbed the stairs and sat with her now in the window seat.

"Yeah. But it didn't stick."

"No. It didn't. But the reason I was sitting there all dressed up was because I was supposed to go to a benefit with Jean-Claude. He called to say he couldn't make it. Of course, he made up for it later and he's taking me on this ski trip, but that night I was just a cliché. All dressed up." Carmen took a deep breath, clouding a spot on the window.

"Then when we were walking back from Niku's party, you said some things that really hit home," she said, almost as though she knew she had to admit this but it pained her to do so. "I walk around with my nose up in the air, and all that really does is make it easier for me to smell the shit."

Carmen finally turned her gaze away from the window and looked at me. "At least when you were a kid you knew that you wanted to be something. You wanted to be a lawyer and that's something real, achievable, with an office and a degree. I never wanted any of that. You know what I wanted to be?"

"No."

"Known," she said, a pathetic laugh leaving her mouth. "I wanted to be so known that when I died some Jewish intellectual would see fit to write a book about me. Isn't that sad?"

"No. I mean, people know you."

"They don't know," she said. "Words can become truth if enough people speak them."

"True that," I said, knowing exactly the truth behind that statement. "But maybe this will help. I know you're leaving tomorrow for your trip, but I wanted to give you your present before you took off."

"I didn't get you anything," she snapped. The funk of the holidays had nestled deep in her spine.

"That's okay. You've given me plenty."

She shook her head as if in sympathy and pulled her knees closer into herself. I walked over to her and set the Tiffany box on the cushion in front of her and began to walk out.

"Take this back," she said, looking down at it, then pushing it away. "I can't."

"No," she said, putting her feet down and holding the box. "You have to take this back. Where are you getting money like this? What's going on with you?"

"Wheeling and dealing," I said, trying to raise the spirits. "It's just money. It wasn't much. It's Christmas. I wanted to give you something special. Something no one else would give you. Just open it."

Carmen stood up and walked toward me. "Take it back," she said, handing me the box, but I refused to take it. Our eyes met but as she walked away she put the gift on the settee and left the room. I heard her bedroom door close behind her and the lock turn.

I walked out of the den onto the landing. I stood there for a moment before walking back downstairs. I went into the parlor and placed the box under the tree, where it sat, alone.

· 17 ·

Either no one told Mother Nature or she was drunk and just didn't care, but the mercury rose to the mid-sixties and everyone was taking advantage of her merciful thaw; stone faces became smiling ones.

The Hungarian Pastry Shop on Amsterdam Avenue had brought up their outdoor café tables from the basement to provide Parisian flair for the springlike overflow, and the seats were at capacity.

I walked over to upper Broadway and into the West Side Market. The vivid colors of the produce neatly stacked and partitioned looked as fresh as when on the tree; a vibrant painting in a season of gray.

I reached in the plastic bag for a Granny Smith as I made my way out of the store and onto the sidewalk. "Oh, sorry," I said, bumping into a woman, her book falling to the ground.

"This time you got it right," she said, looking at me. It was Kyra, the girl from the "You're Invited" art opening. "But it was partially my fault. I suppose I shouldn't walk and read."

I bent down to pick up the book, which was by Leonard St. James, a novelist popular with black women. "Yes, I can see how it would be stimulating."

"No, it's not Henry James," she said, taking the book from me. "But that doesn't make it less valuable."

We stood looking at each other for a moment.

"You look familiar," I said. "Have we met?"

"Don't try it," she said. "Why do men do that?"

"Do what?"

"Pretend they don't know you when they know they do. It's stupid."

"Okay. I guess I'm busted."

"Yeah, you are." She was flirting and the sun was boosting my confidence.

"Kyra, right?"

"See, your memory isn't so bad."

"I remember what I want to remember."

"We all do. And you are?"

"Oh," I said, still surprised by running into her. "Well, huh."

"Why the pause? Don't you know who you are? Or are you one of those boys who'll just give a girl any old name to get what you want?"

"No," I said, trying to regain my composure. But her words hit so hard that the truth flew out of my mouth. "Mason. Mason Randolph."

"So, Mason Randolph, are we just going to stand here blocking the sidewalk or are we going to walk?"

"Let's walk. I tried going over to the Hungarian Pastry Shop but they were slammed. It's so nice out I thought I'd go over to Grant's Tomb."

"That sounds great, but I don't know you well enough to go into the park with you."

"I assure you, I'm perfectly safe."

"You're probably right," she said, looking at me. "I could probably take you if I had to. But how about we get a coffee?"

"Sounds good."

"There's a great place on Eighty-third Street."

"Should we take a cab?"

"No. It's nice out, let's walk."

B   ut Yale's a great school," I said.
        "I know but when I went for the visit I kept expecting to see all
these black folk who were supposedly taking up all these spots so white
folk couldn't get in," she said, picking at the flakes of her chocolate
croissant. "I was walking around campus screaming, 'Black people.
Black people, come out. It's me. Kyra. Where ya'll at?' "

She started laughing and there was an ease in her that immediately
calmed me. I'd found someone who could relate to my experience, and
irony was irony, and not considered anger.

"This is a nice place," I said. "I've never been here before."

"Yeah, I'm a regular here." Café Lalo provided the perfect first-date
environment. The stained-glass hanging light fixtures; exposed brick
walls, the glass wall overlooking the street; the pastries and desserts on
display; even the rude French-speaking waiters only added to the ro-
mantic surroundings, the City of Light transplanted to Eighty-third
Street.

Kyra was doing her master's in anthropology at Columbia but as she
sat across from me I wanted nothing more than to study her.

"I thought about Princeton, they've got a good program, but I grew
up in the city, just around the corner, and I knew I'd miss it."

And it would miss you.

"So you live on campus?"

"No. I live at home."

"With your parents?"

"Yeah, everyone I know tries to get out of the house as fast as they
can, but it just didn't make sense to get another apartment when I
could stay in my own room. I've got plenty of time to move out."

And move in with me. "Aren't you just daughter of the year?"

"Now, but I had my time when I drove my parents crazy."

"I find that hard to believe."

"Believe it. I was getting arrested quite a bit."

I looked shocked, and all these thoughts ran through my head: shoplifting, drugs, robbing a bank.

"Don't worry, it wasn't anything bad. I don't even have a record."

"Friends in high places, huh?"

"Sort of. I was demonstrating, so we'd usually have it all arranged with the police beforehand."

"Who is we?"

"You name it. If there was a cause, I was there. Slavery reparations, police brutality, female circumcision. I was everywhere."

"And your parents were cool with it?"

"Not at first, particularly because all of their friends were sure I was a lesbian because I was wearing my hair short and walking around in big clunky combat boots. But they never tried to stop me. I think they thought it was cool I was standing up for something. They're pretty conservative now, but I remember seeing pictures of them when they were my age, marching in demonstrations. I guess that stayed with me.

"Then one day I was in this cell with all these people and it felt like a party and I realized everyone in that cell could afford to get arrested. We weren't going to get lost in the system. It was like Monopoly. But not everyone has a Get out of Jail Free card."

I said nothing. I started looking around the café, letting her words sink in. I knew exactly what she was talking about.

"Hello," she said. "Mason. Are you still with me?"

"Yeah," I said, and my name falling from her mouth sounded right. "Just thinking."

"That's always good," she said, reaching out and touching my forearm. "And don't worry. I'm not a lesbian."

"No. I didn't think you were."

"Why? I could be a lesbian. You don't think I'm good enough to be a lesbian," she said, pretending to be insulted. The couple at the table next to ours looked over, with a smile.

"No," I said. "I'm sure you could be anything you wanted to be."

"And don't forget it."

"I won't."

"See that you don't."

"I won't."

"Just see that you don't."

"I won't."

"Okay." She took a sip of her coffee and sat back in her seat. "You're cute. A little absentminded but cute."

"Cute? So now I'm a puppy."

"You're supposed to just say thank you."

"Then thank you."

"You're welcome."

"Do you always say what's on your mind?"

"No. It just depends on who I'm talking to."

M ason, what are you doing tomorrow at five-thirty?"

"I'm free," I said. I had made plans to hang with Malcolm but I wasn't going to miss out on this opportunity. How things start is often a reflection of how they'll end up. "Are you asking me out?"

"Slow down, tiger," she said, patting my arm. "I work with these kids up in Harlem and they're doing their end-of-the-term program. Of course, it probably won't be as interesting as traveling around the world, but . . ."

"No. No. I'm down with that. I'll be there. Where is it?"

She dug around in her denim shoulder bag and pulled out a pen but was having trouble finding something to write on so I stuck out my hand and she wrote the information on my palm.

"So I'll see you then," she said. She turned and walked toward Broadway. I stood watching, waiting for her to give me a look back, but she didn't. I could see she wasn't going to make it easy for me and I enjoyed it.

Couldn't sleep last night. Thinking about Kyra. She's the girl that Justin and Malcolm were talking about and I see what the fuss is all about. I have to try to take a nap before I see her tonight. I don't want to look haggard. It would kill me if I showed up and she looked at me only to realize that I wasn't as attractive as she thought I was. But then again, how could she? I'm the man. I AM THE MAN.

I walked into the community center on 149th Street, dressed in a new outfit. The salesgirl hadn't been able to say "Will that be cash or" before I had slapped my credit card on the counter. I wanted to look good for Kyra and didn't feel my urban wear was going to pull it off. Since Carmen wasn't home I'd thought of wearing some of Christopher's clothes, but I wanted my own.

G ood afternoon," said Kyra, standing center stage. She glanced at me. "I'd like to thank you for coming. These young people have worked very hard on the piece you're going to see this afternoon and I'm sure you will see that. So sit back, relax and enjoy *The Three Fairy Sisters.*

The audience applauded and the children started appearing onstage. The little girl who was supposed to start was overcome with stage fright. She placed her hand up to her mouth and refused to relinquish her lines.

"That's all right, baby. Take your time," said a woman in the audience, reassuring her.

The little girl, with cotton stuck on her clothing, providing a cloud effect, looked over at Kyra, who was mouthing the words.

Another little cloud saw the problem and took over and the show ran smoothly as the clouds and angels came to life.

In a not so far away place, from
This place you see,
Lived Mother Life and Father Time
With their family.

Mother Life and Father Time lived under
A huge umbrella.
They lived with their three fairy daughters,
Evilene, Karmajean and Rationella.

I watched as the little thespians continued to act out their morality play. As I listened I was certain they were talking directly to me. I started hearing things that they couldn't possibly be saying.

Poor little black boy
With two names
When will time run out
On his game?

Lied to Carmen to get a room,
A need for space.
Still not certain of
His place.

I looked around to see if anyone else was hearing this, but the mothers were just smiling, beaming as their little angels paraded around the stage. I began to squirm in my seat just like many of the other restless children in the audience.

Called his friend Malcolm,
Changed their plans.
Don't he know God don't like ugly?
"Nah, he don't, 'cause he the man."

The audience jumped to their feet and their applause snapped me back to reality, or at least my interpretation of it. The little actors came out to take their bows. They motioned for Kyra to join them, but she wouldn't. Several of them went offstage and pulled her out, but she never made it to center stage; she just came out a few feet, waved, then extended her hands out to the kids, indicating that it was they who deserved the applause and needed it.

The crowd soon disappeared and I waited in the back watching Kyra as she dealt with each and every person who came up to her. When the last one was gone, she released a long and warranted exhalation and walked over to me.

"That was great," I said, hugging her, hoping she wouldn't ask me any questions about it.

"Thanks," she said, sitting down in a chair. "Those kids are so great." She seemed suddenly sad.

"You must be exhausted," I said, rubbing her shoulders.

"No. Not really. I'm just going to miss these kids. They've made so much progress."

"I'm sure you had something to do with that."

"It's not about me," she said. "It's not about me. Did you really enjoy it?"

"Yes. It spoke to me. I'm glad I came."

She smiled, summoning energy. "Good. I'm glad you came too. I need someone to help me fold up these chairs."

"Oh, is that how it is?"

"Nothing is free, mister."

So how about I take you out tomorrow night for a celebration?" I said as we walked out of the community center. I wanted to take her out then, there and everywhere, but I didn't want to appear too eager.

"You mean on a date?"

"Okay, Ms. Clarity. A date."

"I can't."

Ouch. "You're already seeing someone?" I asked, quickly trying to recover and find a way out.

"Oh, no. I do want to go out, but we're leaving for my grand-mother's tomorrow night."

"Where does she live?" I wasn't really interested but I wanted to make sure she wasn't just blowing me off.

"Sag Harbor. We always spend Christmas and New Year's there. It's quiet out there this time of year."

"Sag Harbor, huh? Do you know any Englands out there?"

"No. But I can ask my grandmother. She knows everybody."

"That's okay. It's no big deal," I said, fearing her having contact with Carmen's family wouldn't be beneficial.

"So can I get a rain check on that date?" she asked.

"Whatever," I said.

"Don't be a baby." She took out a pen and I stuck out my hand. "Don't you bathe?" she asked, noticing the information for the com-munity center. She took the other hand. "Here's my number."

"Great."

She stood there looking at me for a moment.

"What?"

"Aren't you gonna give me your phone number or are you holding out on me?"

Poor little black boy
With two names.
When will time run out
On his game?

"Mason?" she asked, pulling a twist.

"Oh, right," I said, trying to figure out the mess I'd gotten myself in. "I was just thinking about the play." I took the pen from her and wrote the number on the program as the text from *The Three Fairy Sisters* stared up at me. "There. But don't worry. I'll give you a call. When are you getting back?"

"On the third."

"Great. Then I'll definitely call on the third."

"You'd better. I move on rather quickly."

"I bet you do," I said. "Are you going to take a cab?"

"No. I'll walk to the subway. I need some time to decompress."

"I'll walk you."

"No. You don't have to."

"No."

"No, really."

"Okay, then. I may have to turn in my southerners card, but if you want to go it on your own, so be it."

"Okay."

"Okay."

We stood looking at each other and I grabbed her hand, pleased to be touching her again but worried about her number smearing before I could write it down on something more suitable. I stepped in close to her and we hugged.

"Thanks for coming," she said, her face on my chest.

"My pleasure. It was great."

"You don't have to say that."

"Just say thank you."

"Thank you," she said. I could feel her laughing and I found myself holding her tighter.

"Ooh, Ms. Jamison is getting her hug on," said a little girl, passing across the street, as we stood hand in hand, all smiles.

Hello," I said, answering the phone.

"May I speak to Mason?"

"May I ask who's calling?" I said, somewhat concerned. I knew it wasn't my mother's voice.

"Kyra."

"Oh. Hello." My voice immediately softened. "It's me. How's it going?"

"Screening your calls?"

"Yeah. The telemarketers have been driving me crazy."

"I see," she said. "Well, I was thinking about you and I just wanted to call and say that it meant a lot to me that you came tonight."

"No problem." We both remained silent for a moment, but our smiles could be heard.

"Okay, then," she said. "I just wanted to call."

"I'm glad you did. I'll call you on the third."

"Promise?"

"You can bank on it."

"That's what I like to hear."

Again, smiling silence.

"Well, have a good trip."

"I will. And what's that family's name again?"

"Oh, you know, I checked into that. They live out on the Vineyard. I had the places confused," I said.

"Oh. Okay. So I'll see you when I get back."

"Bet. Have a good trip."

"You too. I mean, have a good holiday."

"Okay."

I hung up and started jumping up and down, doing a dance that would have gotten me many stares at any club in town, but I didn't care what it looked like because I was feeling it. "You the man, Mason. You are the man." The phone rang again and I picked it up on the first ring, hardly able to contain myself, knowing she had to hear my voice again.

"Yes," I said, feeling very Teddy Pendergrass.

"Malik." The mood quickly changed. "It's Malcolm."

"Oh, Malcolm. How you feel?"

"I'm good. Damn, you were sounding all Rico Suave and shit. Are we still on for tonight?"

"Damn. Yeah. I was just about to call you about that. I'm not going to be able to make it."

"Oh, that's cool."

Though he didn't seem to mind, I felt the need to justify canceling. The guilty always speak the most. "Yeah. See, Carmen told some friends of hers they could crash here while she was away and I have to wait around until they get here."

"I see she has you on a short leash. I told you about her. When I stopped by there she looked at me like I wasn't even good enough to take out her trash."

"Nah, man. I'm sure that's your imagination."

"Yeah, whatever."

"Hey, look. I think I hear someone at the door. I better go check."

"All right."

"I'm sorry about flaking, but—"

"It's cool, man. Just remember what I told you. People with money only look out for themselves. They'll have you sitting around waiting and not think nothing about it."

"I hear ya," I said. "But I gotta go. I think they're here."

"All right man. Stay black."

"Yeah."

I've made the best of the holiday. Kyra called to wish me Merry Christmas. Carmen didn't . . .

I went to see the Alvin Ailey American Dance Theater at City Center. I had a great seat. But I wished Kyra were in town to see it with me because all the beauty onstage reminded me of her. I watched the first half in the orchestra, then during intermission I climbed up to the top where the diversity was more than I'd seen at any performance. I stood watching the crowd and there was a certain energy that didn't exist in the "good seats." Do we lose that sense of involvement, that sense of expression and emotions, once ushered front and center? Too good to feel, too good to show that we do? Applauding in the appropriate place, hands held just so as we cry "Bravo." Blending. Business as usual. I don't know. The lights started to blink. People immediately found their seats without being prodded to do so. No C.P. time here. I knew I wasn't going to be able to make it all the way back downstairs. "Is anyone sitting here?" "No, sit down. Did you sneak in at intermission?" "Uh, yeah." "I did that once. I just had to see it. But I bought this ticket. Have you seen Ailey before?" "No." "Well, you missed Cry. *They turned it out tonight. But you're in for it." The lights went down and the people around me started to applaud and scream; some even stomped their feet. "What's going on?" "Revelations." She said it as though that should say it all. The curtain went up and it did say it all. The people around me sang along, "I Been 'Buked," even moving their bodies in their seats. "Wade in the Water." Even the kids, there were kids there, "I Wanna Be Ready," and their attention was spanned across that stage. They knew every aspect of it as though they'd seen it a thousand times. "The Day Is Past and Gone." I tried to fathom what it must have been like when it debuted in 1960. What did that mean? "You May Run On." We were sitting in the rafters. Closer to heaven. "Rocka My Soul in the Bosom of Abraham." Yes, revelations.*

·18·

A word, please?" said Carmen as I was about to leave. Nothing she could say could dampen my mood. Kyra had returned and we were going out. "Aren't you forgetting something?"

I looked down at my clothing, even checking my zipper, which in winter I always seemed to forget, but it was on track. "What?"

Carmen just looked at me.

"The rent," I said. "Damn. It slipped my mind. I meant to leave it in an envelope. My bad."

"That's fine," she said. "I even hate to have to ask you, but business is business."

"No. You shouldn't have to. I just forgot. I guess I've been preoccupied. You were away and . . . It doesn't matter. I've got it." I'd made a point of always paying Carmen on time and in cash. I'd been to the bank that day to get money for my long-overdue date with Kyra and was thrilled to see that my monthly allowance was smiling up at me from the screen.

I counted out the bills and handed them to Carmen, which she palmed and pocketed without counting. "That's quite a bit of money to be walking around with. I hope you don't get mugged again."

I looked up at her. She *had* read some of my journal, but I didn't have time to deal with it. If that's all she saw, fine. "I'm running late," I said. "I'll see you later."

"Malik. We should talk," she said. Fear consumed me. I'd always known that by the time those words are uttered it is already beyond time to talk. "It'll only take a moment."

"Okay," I said, looking at my watch. She sat on the third step of the stairs. I remained standing.

"You look nice."

"Thanks."

"Is that a new outfit?"

"Yeah. I've been doing some shopping. It was all on sale," I said, then, trying to charm her, "I didn't want to make you look bad."

"No. We wouldn't want that, would we?"

"Carmen, I really have to get going. The car should be here in a minute."

"So you're taking cars now?"

"I'm not going far. I was going to take the subway but I'm running late."

"Malik, I'm concerned about you."

"Why? Everything is cool. Couldn't be better. I'm sorry about the rent."

"It's not about the rent."

"Then what's the prob?"

"I don't know. You tell me."

"Things are good. I finally feel like things are going my way. I'm making things happen."

"So your job is going well?"

"Definitely. Now that I've been there a while it's not bad. I've got some good shifts and a few regular customers that tip pretty good."

"And what's the name of the place again?"

I started to get nervous. I didn't like the line of questioning. Couldn't we talk about this later? "Café Orlin."

"That's in the East Village, isn't it?"

"Yeah."

"Peculiar. I called there yesterday to see if you wanted to meet me downtown for dinner. Not only were you not there but they'd never heard of you."

"You must have called the wrong place."

"No. Café Orlin. I spoke with the owner, James."

I thought of trying to twist my way out of it but I didn't have the energy.

"Carmen, I can explain. But right now I have to go." I turned for the door.

"Are you dealing?"

"What?" I asked. Though my hand remained on the doorknob, my face looked back at her.

" 'What?' is a question, not an answer."

"What makes you think I've been selling drugs?"

"I'm not judging you," she said. Her tone was condescending and it irritated me.

"What are you talking about?"

"Well, let's see, you purport to be working at a place where they've no knowledge of you, yet you're able to afford gifts from Tiffany's and when I asked you about it you said, and I quote, you were 'wheeling and dealing.' And though you're evidently not working, you're never here and the son of one of the most prominent women in the city calls here at all hours looking for you. What could he possibly want with you?"

I looked at her with disbelief. "So those things mean . . . Forget it, Carmen. I don't have time for an intervention. If you must know, everything isn't about you. I have a date."

"Yes, I know. She called earlier. Sounded quite sweet. Kyra, I believe she said her name was. She knew my name, but, oddly enough, she was a bit confused when it came to yours. She seemed to think it was Mason."

"What did you say to her?"

"Nothing. But if you feel the need to take on a pseudonym, you must be hiding something."

Carmen seemed more intrigued than angry, pleased by this tasty morsel that had fallen into her fold.

"Pleading the Fifth, are we?" she asked. "How lawyerly of you."

"It's nothing. Really." A horn blew and I looked over my shoulder to see the car outside. "I've got to go. I'll explain everything when I get back."

"Yes you will."

I n the car I began to panic. I rolled down the window, hoping fresh air would make me feel better.

When the car pulled up at the corner of Eighty-fourth Street and West End Avenue, I slid the driver a fiver. I pulled on the door handle, but the door wouldn't open.

"Seven dollars," he said, looking back at me.

"Seven? No way. From 120th to here? A taxi wouldn't cost that much."

"Then you should have taken a taxi."

After giving Carmen the rent, I only had ten dollars in cash, but I'd seen Carmen bargain with other car service drivers in Harlem and she usually got her way. She'd told me that I shouldn't ask them how much, I should just give them what I thought was appropriate, then get out. But this driver played by his rules, not Carmen's. "Five dollars."

"Seven," he said, starting to drive away with me trapped in the backseat.

"Okay. Stop. Seven," I said, passing him the other five. "But I'm reporting you."

"Do that," he said, giving me back three singles. "Here's the number, motherfucker. Tell 'em I told you to call. Now get the fuck out of my car."

As I got out and the car sped away, the doorman, standing at the entrance, gave me a less-than-welcoming look. I stood in the crisp air for a minute trying to shake Carmen and the driver from my system, assuring myself that my date was going to be fine. I walked toward the entrance and the doorman opened the door.

"Good evening, sir."

"Hello. The Jamisons, 8E."

"And you are, sir?"

"Mason Randolph," I said, suddenly overcome with confidence. That's right. I was Mason Randolph.

"Yes, there is a Mr. Randolph here," said the doorman into the phone as he kept his eyes on me. "Yes, sir. Go right up."

"Thank you."

The doors of the elevator opened and I stepped in, pushing 8 three times before I was on my way up. I gave myself a final once-over in the blurred brass reflection of the door, then focused on the numbers announcing each floor. In the right corner of the ceiling a small camera peered down and I waved at it, hoping to amuse or infuriate the doorman.

The magic number finally lit up and the door opened like the portals of heaven. I walked down the hall trying to decipher which way the letters of the apartments ran, until I finally ended up in front of the door. I rubbed my sweaty palms on my pants, then pushed the doorbell, and as I heard steps approaching I took one last breath. I hated that I hadn't brought flowers. I'd meant to pick some up on the way, but after having to contend with Carmen's interrogation, time was lacking, leaving me to arrive empty-handed.

"Hello," I said, surprised not to see Kyra.

"Hello. I'm Bill Jamison, Kyra's father. Come in."

I stepped in and Mr. Jamison led me down the hallway into the living room. Three adults, two women and a man, all dressed in khakis, cardigans and loafers, were there but no sign of Kyra. The man stood upon our entering.

"This is Mason Randolph," said Mr. Jamison, announcing me. "Mason, this is Mrs. Jamison and our friends the Coopers."

How you feel? "Nice to meet you," I said, shaking Mr. Cooper's hand and nodding at the ladies.

"Have a seat," said Mrs. Jamison. "Kyra's not quite ready."

There was a moment of polite silence, which propelled me to speak. "Beautiful room." The room was yellow with matching floral furniture. A black baby grand piano was in the corner and I could envision Kyra as a child sitting there with sheet music before her and little white patent-leather shoes reaching for the pedals as she tapped out a minuet.

African art and art by African Americans filled the room and served as the topic of the properly placed coffee-table books. "Is that a Bearden collage?"

"Yes," said Mr. Jamison, seemingly pleased at my noticing. "Are you an art buff?"

"A neophyte, really," I said in my best impress-the-parents voice. "I know a bit about photography, Van Der Zee, Parks. But I've recently been interested in Niku Henu's work."

"The painter," said Mr. Cooper. "We bought one of his pieces last year. He has a promising career ahead of him. He could be the next Basquiat."

They all laughed knowingly. Kyra's parents could have easily been my own, and the Coopers, family friends.

"Would you like something to drink?" asked Mrs. Jamison.

"No, thank you."

"Caviar pie," she said, gesturing toward the coffee table where a dish held a pie; the bottom layer was chunks of potatoes mixed with sour cream or crème fraîche and the top was covered by a layer of caviar.

"No, thank you."

"You don't know what you're missing," said Mr. Cooper. He picked up a toast point and scraped it across the top of the pie.

"Larry, don't just scoop up the caviar," said Mrs. Cooper with mock reprimand.

"That's the best part," he said, offering a black sitcom father's Santa laugh.

When the last laugh was laughed the attention returned to me.

"Kyra tells us you're from Louisiana," said Mr. Jamison.

Speaking of Kyra, where in the hell is she? "Yes, sir."

"Laissez bon temps roulez," said Mrs. Cooper, holding her cocktail glass up in the air, and the others followed suit.

"We had the most wonderful time last year at Jazz Fest," said Mrs. Jamison. "We saw Ed Bradley."

"The guy from *60 Minutes*?" asked Mrs. Cooper. "I didn't know he was in a musical group too."

"No, Barbara," said Mrs. Jamison, trying to conceal her contempt. "He was *at* the fest, not in it."

"Oh, silly me."

"Yeah. He's down there a lot," I said. "Mr. Bradley and my parents are good friends. They go way back."

They tried to appear unimpressed, but I looked in Mr. Jamison's eyes, and I knew what he was thinking. *If that's the case then you absolutely must date my daughter.*

"Oh, the food down there is so wonderful," said Mrs. Jamison. "I must have gained a pound a day."

"But in all the right places," said Mr. Jamison.

"Well played, Bill," said Mr. Cooper.

I wanted to throw up all over the caviar pie.

"So what brought you North?" asked Mrs. Jamison.

"I was doing some traveling and you can't rightly do that without spending time in the Big Apple."

"You should travel when you're young. That's what I say," said Mrs.

Cooper. "It's just so hard to get away when you start a career. It's all about work in the States. Work. Work. Work. In Europe they get so much more vacation time."

"Did you get to Europe?" asked Mrs. Jamison.

"Yes, ma'am." *In fact, I wish I were there now.* "But I spent most of my time in Southeast Asia."

"Really?" said Mr. Jamison. They all looked impressed and I began to relax, but wished I'd taken them up on their offer of a drink. Familiarity breeds contempt. "I did a seminar in India a few years ago for a classmate of mine from Harvard. Did you spend any time there?"

"No, sir. I knew a lot of people who had been there but the consensus was you either love it or hate it, so I went to Sri Lanka instead."

"Wasn't that dangerous?" asked Mrs. Jamison with a tone that made me wonder if she thought I was the sort who would put her daughter in harm's way. "I read in the *Times* that they're in the midst of a civil war."

"Yes, ma'am, since 1983, but it's still beautiful and after you're there for a week or so it just becomes a part of your life. It's definitely a different way of life than we're used to in the States, but it's a beautiful place. I recommend it. It was just nice to be completely surrounded by brown people."

They all looked at me curiously as though I'd made a mistake by bringing up color or were making a mental note to look into it when next their calendar called for travel.

"And you're going to be starting at Stanford Law next year?" said Mrs. Jamison, directing her statement not at me, but toward Mrs. Cooper.

Blah, blah, blah, blah, blah, blah. "Yes, ma'am. That's the plan."

"Great school," said Mr. Cooper, again digging into the caviar pie. "That is, if you must go West. We're Harvard alums, but I suppose heading West is better than going to school in the South."

"My parents were educated in the South and I feel it safe to say they've done quite well," I said with a smile to take the bite out of my words.

Silence fell over the room and Mr. Cooper diverted his eyes from mine. I looked over at Mrs. Jamison, who seemed more than thrilled by my rebuttal.

"There's my baby," said Mr. Jamison, standing. I looked over and Kyra had entered and it was worth the wait. She had on black leather pants, an unbuttoned denim jacket over a tan suede shirt, black cowboy boots and a blue mohair scarf tied around her neck. Her overcoat was slung over her arm. "We were just grilling Mason."

"Yes, I have a few questions myself," she said earnestly. "Ready?"

"Sure," I said. "It was nice meeting ya'll."

I helped Kyra with her coat. Mr. Jamison walked us out of the living room and to the door.

"Take care of my baby."

"Dad," said Kyra.

"I plan to."

The doors of the elevator hadn't sealed before she wanted to know why Carmen was calling me Malik. I told her that she was just kidding around and wasn't used to my being interested in anyone aside from her and that ever since I'd gotten my twists she'd started calling me Malik. I was shocked how easily the words came out, and without a degree from Harvard. Though I had been honest with Kyra up to that point, I couldn't bring myself to explain how my relationship with Carmen had come to be, and felt a first date wasn't the best time to be honest.

We walked over to Eighty-sixth Street and Broadway to take the subway. I bought two tokens and hoping to impress her I dropped the remaining fifty cents into the cup of a panhandler. We took the 1 train to the West Village. She apologized about the third degree from her parents and informed me that the Coopers lived in the building and were the only other black tenants. Mrs. Cooper had always hoped that Kyra and their son, Jamie, would end up together.

"Please," said Kyra. "Jamie met Clay his freshman year and they've been together since. His mother blamed it on the school, like Bennington had something in their water system, and tried to get him to transfer to Sarah Lawrence, which shows just how clueless she is. She still thinks he's in love with me, like a girl doesn't have enough to contend with in this town."

"So she came up to check out the competition?"

"Probably," she said with a smirk.

"Do they do that with all of your dates?"

"No. I don't date often."

"Living at home and all?"

"No. I'm just particular. That's why when I do bring someone home they tend to trust my judgment."

"I think you know a friend of mine," I said, trying to bring in another association. "Justin Lee."

"Oh, right. I've met him at a few parties. He's a friend of my friend Dale. But I think Dale wants him to be more, so he's been doing the wear-down."

"The wear-down?"

"Yeah. It's when you position yourself to be the loyal friend and pretend that you're not at all hurt when the person you're in love with talks about their interest in other people, because you know that one day they will come to their senses and realize that you're the only one they could possibly be with." Kyra said this with such theatrical flair that I had to laugh. "Oh, don't pretend like you've never done it," she said, elbowing me in the side.

"Yeah. I have to admit that I have, but I didn't know there was a name for it."

"High school is the name for it. Any later than that is just too pathetic for words."

This made me think of Carmen.

"I don't think Justin is into Dale," I said. "As long as I've known him he's been too interested in changing the world to be involved with anyone. But he did say that he thought we'd be good together."

"You and he?"

"No. You and me."

"So I see you did some research on me."

"No. He mentioned that even before I officially met you."

"Then we'll have to see if we can prove him right."

Many lines raced through my head, hoping to find just the appropriate one, but I decided that silence was the best line of all. She leaned in closer to me and placed her hand on my leg as we rocked to the rhythm of the subway. Her touch was different than Carmen's. It was natural and without thought. It felt right and I was pleased I had opted for loose pants.

The older couple sitting across from us were holding hands. They looked like they'd been together forever and could read each other's every mood, could look into each other's eyes and still see the very face they had seen on the first day they met. What more could anyone ask for?

Grange Hall was a former socialist speakeasy tucked on the corner of Commerce and Barrow Streets, one of the most beautiful areas of the city. It was where Carmen had said Christopher proposed to her, so I knew it had to be impressive. When you walked in, it was like being transported into a place Frank Lloyd Wright would appreciate, simplicity prevailing.

The older bar, the telephone booth and even the menu, "food from the American farm," provided comfort.

"This is a great place," said Kyra as we were seated in a corner booth beneath the Diego Rivera-esque mural of a harvest setting.

"I thought you might like it," I said. I'd never been there but I added, "It's one of my favorite places."

I could see that she was impressed with my selection. We ordered drinks: pinot noir for her, gin and tonic for myself. "To a second date," I said, certain there would be one.

"Let's just stay in the present," she said, grabbing my hand. Even when the waiter came up to take our order, we continued holding hands, assuring everyone in the place that our relationship was at its onset.

"Your hands are so soft," I said, trying to add as many compliments as possible.

"I soaked them in Palmolive before I came out."

"Really?" She just looked at me. "Okay. Jokes. I see." I stretched my leg under the table.

"That's my foot, not the table."

"I know," I said. She started laughing.

"What's so funny?"

"You just seem different than when I saw you at the art opening. I saw you with Carmen and I thought it was really cute that you were hanging out with your mother."

"I'm sure she'd love to hear that. For all you knew she could have been my girlfriend."

"Well, don't we just think highly of ourself," she said, holding out her fork toward me with a piece of salmon on it.

"No. Don't try appeasing me with food."

"Oh, shut up and take a bite." *That's right. Talk mean to me, baby.* I leaned in and ate the fish. "You were whipped. I could tell. That's fine. I'm not the jealous type. She's an attractive woman. If you're into mother figures."

I tried to stay in the moment, but I kept thinking about Carmen. She was onto me and if I was going to continue seeing Kyra, which I planned to, then I'd have no choice but to tell Carmen everything. Kyra made me feel confident enough to take that risk. If it meant I'd have to find a new place, so be it.

As we continued our meal, the owner, a buxom redhead with soul, whose smile lit up the room, came over to our table.

"How is everything?" she asked.

"Great," I said.

"It's wonderful," said Kyra.

"Is he taking good care of you?" she asked, sliding into the booth next to Kyra and looking over at me.

"He's doing all right."

"Just all right, huh?" I said.

"Was anyone talking to you?" the owner asked, shooting a look at me like a mother. "No. So just eat your food. Grown folks are talking." She then turned back to Kyra. "You've got to train them early, but don't leave the paper down too long. I'm Jacqui."

"Kyra."

"I'm—"

"Ah," she said, raising her hand. "And who is this handsome young man you're with?"

"Depends on who you ask," said Kyra, adding to the teasing tone of the conversation. She reached for my hand and I playfully pulled it away. "In some quarters he's known as Mason."

"Well, Mason, you've done quite well for yourself. I hope you all have a wonderful evening."

"Is it okay to say thank you?" I asked.

"Certainly. And that's all you should ever be allowed to say." Jacqui slid out of the booth and sashayed back to the bar area of the restaurant.

Jacqui sent over a wild rice pudding for dessert and I moved over to Kyra's side of the booth, going for a more intimate approach. I'd wanted to avoid the subject, but the drinks and the atmosphere and her company were taking over. "Sorry about the name thing."

"That's okay." We leaned in to kiss, our first kiss. The moment made me forget I was against PDA, when in fact I wasn't against it if I was the one doing it.

Our eyes were closed or at least mine were when I heard, "Well, well,

well." I looked up and it was Jim, my dreaded friend, walking up to the table, drunk. "What do we have here? If it isn't my boy *Malik*."

Kyra slid over a bit and looked up at Jim, then at me.

"Jim Ross, Kyra Jamison."

"So you're Kyra," said Jim, sliding into the seat across from us. "I was beginning to think he was making you up, just like everything else. But here you are. In the flesh. I gotta give it to him, he wasn't exaggerating. And look at him. Now that he's uptown he's all gussied up. What's that, Armani?" Jim leaned across the table to rub the fabric of my shirt and I flicked his hand away. "Looking good, Malik. Looking good."

Kyra's body stiffened next to me and affection was no longer in her eyes. I could sense that I was in for one long, cold time-out. Jim took a sip of his drink. "These Cosmos can really sneak up on you," he said. "I think this one might just take me over the top. I don't know," he said, raising the glass and talking to it. "We'll just have to see who wins."

"Are you having dinner here?" I asked, attempting to get Jim to move along so I could begin damage control.

"Nah, we're up at the bar. One of Lisa's friends is the bartender."

"Excuse me," said Kyra. I slid out of the booth to let her out and lightly touched her arm, which she moved from my reach. I watched her as she made her way through the dining room and over to the ladies' room. She didn't look back. Jim put his feet up on the seat where she had begun to get cozy.

"You hit it yet?" he asked.

"What?"

"Hit it."

"No, Jim, I haven't *hit it,*" I said, wanting to hit him.

"Well, you'd better take your training wheels off if you plan on riding that."

"Fuck you, Jim," I said, trying to ignore him and plan my rook move. "Can't you just stumble back up to the bar?"

"Do you need a menu?" asked the waitress tersely, noticing that Jim had his feet on the seat.

"No," I said. "He's not staying. Can I get the bill, please?" I knew I had to get Kyra out of there as quickly as possible.

"Look, she's coming back," I said. "Can you just go?"

"All right. All right. Damn. I know when I'm not wanted." Kyra hesitantly walked back to the table. "Watch this one," said Jim to Kyra as she arrived. "He's sneaky. He would have been homeless, but I let him sleep on my floor and you see how he treats me. Just kicks me to the curb. No appreciation. None."

"On your floor?" said Kyra, refusing to sit.

"It was a futon, not the floor, and I'd just come from . . . Jim . . ."

"I'm going, I'm going. Oh, my bad," said Jim, bumping into the waitress and spilling some of his Cosmopolitan. The waitress rolled her eyes so hard that only the whites showed, but Jim was oblivious.

As Jim made his way through the dining room, the waitress put down the check. Kyra finally sat, arms crossed, but she didn't look at me. I pulled out my wallet and placed the credit card on the bill, which the waitress couldn't scoop up fast enough. I knew I'd have to leave a good tip.

I looked at Kyra but there was no mollifying the situation. She just stared at the robust women in the mural on the back wall as though they were alive and warning her of the hardships of dealing with men.

"Jim and I met in Barcelona."

"Um," she said without enthusiasm.

"I know this seems strange. It's a really long story. It's funny, really," I said, starting to laugh nervously. "It's hilarious, actually."

"Sir," said the waitress, returning. She appeared suddenly happy. I just assumed she was pleased we were finally giving up the table. I reached for the bill to sign. "This card has been declined."

"Declined?" I said, briefly looking over at Kyra. It was her turn to roll her eyes. The waitress looked down at her as if to say, *Girl, get out while you can.* "That's impossible. There's no way it was declined, it's a gold card."

"It was declined," the waitress said. One decibel louder and she would have definitely been loud-talking me. She wasn't at all interested in the color of the card because it wasn't providing green. "Would you like to try another card?"

Don't take that condescending tone with me. "I don't have another card. That's the only one my parents . . ." I stopped myself, realizing how infantile I sounded.

Kyra stood and reached for her purse, which was next to me. She pulled out her wallet and handed the waitress her credit card. "Why don't you try this one?" she said nicely, like someone apologizing for the actions of an unruly relative. "This should work."

"Sorry about that," I said. "I don't know what the problem is. That's never happened before. I saw an ATM on Christopher Street on the way over here. We can stop by there and I'll give you the money back."

"Fine." I could feel the hammer and nails being put into my coffin.

I leaned in the booth and Kyra looked everywhere but at me. I feared that the wait staff had informed their tables and all the patrons were looking over at me. *Mr. Cool with the funky twists and the earrings, whose "gold card" didn't carry its worth in weight.*

The waitress returned and with a flourish placed the receipt in front of Kyra. She signed it, thanked the waitress, reached next to me and grabbed her coat and headed toward the front of the restaurant. I tried to help her on with her coat but she didn't want to be helped.

"Check you later, Malik," said Jim as we passed the bar.

"Wait. Jim, tell her my real name," I said, but it was for naught as Kyra kept walking. I rushed up behind her and as we stepped out of the door, Niku Henu and posse were coming in. "Hey, Malik, right?" he said. "Is your ol' lady here?"

Kyra stopped, looked at Niku, then at me, then started walking away. Famous artist or not, I ignored Niku and started following Kyra up Barrow Street.

The walk to Christopher Street was filled by traffic sounds and conversations, none of which were ours. Whenever I tried to explain, she just looked at me in a way that let me know she didn't want to hear it.

When we reached the bank she didn't come in, her feeling toward me colder than the weather. She stood outside, arms crossed, closed off from anything I had to say.

I slipped the card in and punched in my security code. I was certain that once I had the cash I could sit her down and rectify the situation. As I stood at the machine my confidence began to return.

"Please pick up the courtesy phone," read the screen. I picked up the phone, putting the disgusting earwax-filled holes near my ear. The operator came on. I provided her with my security information.

"Sorry, sir. That account has been frozen."

"Frozen? How can it be frozen?"

"One of the names on the account has temporarily frozen it."

"How? When? I just withdrew money earlier today."

"Sir. There is no need to shout."

Don't try that "sir" and "no need to shout" passive-aggressive shit with me. I own the copyright to that. "I'm sorry," I said, trying to gain my composure. Sugar not vinegar. "But you can understand my frustration. Can you just tell me—"

"Sir, I have no further information. You should call your local branch."

"But my local branch is in Louisiana and they're closed."

"Then perhaps call the other person on the account. Other than that, sir, there is nothing I can do from here."

I slammed the phone down, beginning to panic. I knew this had my mother's hands all over it. "Okay. Okay. Think. Calm down. This isn't as bad as it seems." I'd unknowingly started pacing and talking aloud in the ATM center. People waiting in line looked over trying to decide if they should call 911.

"What the fuck are you looking at?" I asked one of the people waiting. I walked out before any answer could be given, and started trying to come up with some explanation for Kyra. But that would have to wait. She was gone.

·19·

After Kyra bailed on me I went back to Grange Hall. I was relieved to find Jim and Lisa, his girlfriend, still at the bar.

As I walked up to the bar I saw Jacqui look at me and shake her head. The wine was corked.

"Strapped for cash, huh?" said Jim. "What, they don't take food stamps here?" Lisa just sat there grinding her teeth as if sharpening them to bite into me. I wanted to go off on Jim, but I couldn't. I needed him.

"I need to borrow some cash to get back uptown."

"I don't have any. I'm broke."

"That's bullshit," I said, trying to conceal the urgency in my voice.

"I'm serious. I don't have any cash on me. Lisa, do you have any cash on you?"

Lisa looked over at me, took a sip of her Cosmopolitan and began to cackle.

"Why don't you just sit down, have a drink?" said Jim. "You can crash at my place tonight."

It only served me right. I parked myself on a barstool, sitting in my own shame. I kept looking back at the booth where things had been going so well before turning into a catastrophe. I hoped that the couple now seated there would fare better, but I grew bitter watching their affectionate display. I couldn't stand being in the restaurant any longer. I still had a set of Jim's keys so I schlepped across town to the East Village. Outside of their building a group of pierced and tattooed teens sat soliciting change to get food for the dog that cost more than some people earned in a pay period.

"Come on, man," said one of the teenagers. "Look at you, dressed all smooth. You know you could hook us up with some change."

"Looks are deceiving," I said, turning the key, then heading into the building.

Hello, Mr. Jamison," I said, trying to reach Kyra. "I'm sorry about the lateness of the hour, but may I please speak with Kyra?"

"Kyra is in bed. And frankly, I don't think she wants to speak with you." I could envision Kyra in Paddington cotton pajamas, leaning on a wall next to her father, arms crossed and wanting to call me an asshole, if not rip me another one.

"Please, Mr. Jamison," I said, clenching my hand to hold back my frustration. "It's important. We had a misunderstanding."

"She doesn't want to speak with you and I trust you will honor that request. If not, I'll have no choice but to inform the authorities. I'm certain they can find out who you really are."

But I'm Mason. I'm going to Stanford. I know Ed Bradley. "The authorities?"

"Good night."

Noon the next day, Jim still hadn't made it home. I scoured the apartment, lifting sofa cushions and looking everywhere possible to find change. I found it difficult to believe I couldn't even scrape up enough for subway fare, which seemed like nothing. It *was* nothing, yet it was more than I had.

I called home trying to get in touch with my father to find out what was going on with the bank account and credit card. The answering machine came on. My mother's voice sounded annoyingly chipper but I didn't leave a message. I didn't want to let them know I was in trouble before I had to.

At two o'clock I was no longer able to confine my neurosis to the apartment and waiting for Jim to return seemed as futile as screaming at the wind.

I walked toward the Astor Place subway station looking at the ground hoping I'd be like Charlie from *Charlie and the Chocolate Factory* and money would appear, allowing me to buy a token. As I went down the steps of the subway, I looked at the straphangers, hoping to find sympathetic eyes in the crowd, but because of my lack of sleep and disheveled appearance I didn't get any help. I thought of trying to call Carmen, collect, but I already had more than my share of explaining to do with her and I couldn't bear hearing her laugh at my dilemma. I even considered calling Malcolm, but guilt squashed that thought. Not because I would have to call him collect, but I'd have to explain to him that I was out with Kyra. I was stuck. No one to call. I had wanted to start anew, be on my own. Now I was.

The words I'd often heard on the subway, *Good afternoon, ladies and gentlemens. Spare any change, ladies and gentlemens,* came back into my head. But I couldn't bring myself to say them.

I stood on the platform for twenty minutes trying to build up the courage to jump the turnstile. I looked back at the stocky woman in the booth, certain she was eyeing me, ready to scream through the microphone, "Boy, pay your fare," alerting an undercover cop waiting to bust someone just like me. No. I wasn't about to be a black man getting arrested for jumping the turnstile. I refused to be that. Refused to have to explain to my parents why I was in jail for the cost of a token.

· · · · ·

The first twenty blocks I tried to convince myself that this was good, that walking was the perfect way to see the city as well as provide me ample time to figure out how I was going to convince Kyra that this was all a big misunderstanding. My concern was no longer with how Carmen took the news of my deception. Either she'd deal with it or I'd move. And then it dawned on me that I had no money. No allowance. No credit card.

By the fortieth block, I'd been bumped, pushed and prodded more than the people at the running of the bulls in Pamplona. The tourists aggravated me as they walked in packs, spread across the width of the sidewalk, stopping to take in the smallest sight which most New Yorkers would now be blinded to, blocking those who just wanted to be on their way. I cursed them. I fantasized grabbing one of their purses from their tight clutch, initiated by my approach. *Give me that damn purse. Let go, bitch. Let go.* I could see myself pulling it off her shoulders and dragging her, pounding and kicking her until the value of life outweighed that of the contents of her designer bag, bought during this very trip. Even the cop on the street corner couldn't deter the fantasy, only adding to it. I looked at him with contempt, fully aware that no matter my background, I was born to fit the description. How many times had I seen a sketch on the news, a sketch that could have been anybody, could have been me or at least made others think so? Yes, I looked at that cop. I knew I could outrun his fat ass, but he wouldn't run, would he? But would he risk shooting into a busy midtown crowd? Probably so. I fantasized as I walked the avenue, cold wind tunneling through the canyon of buildings.

I was past the point of delirium and it started to suit me. It made me smile, even laugh, which immediately made people more aware of my presence and less apt to bump into me. I'd finally made my mark: the best-dressed bum in New York City. I stopped midstride and threw my arms up in the air, embracing my self-proclaimed title, not at all caring what another living soul thought. Freedom.

I continued on in my new shoes, and the soles, hardly soiled, couldn't compete with the soot that made the ice black, like me, deceiving. My futile grab at the air couldn't stop my fall. I hit the ground so hard the wind was knocked from me. My first instinct was to quickly get up, shield myself from embarrassment. But a voice in my head said, *Stay down. Stay down.* The crowd continued around me as though I were a flyer on the ground. *Back pain? We can help.* I knew in the South someone would have stopped, made certain I wasn't hurt. But this was New York City. It was cold and people had to be on their way. *Better you than me, this time.*

A man stepped on my hand. He briefly looked back, then kept going. *Stay down. Stay down.* I knew I had to get up.

I passed the New York Public Library and as my safari through the concrete jungle continued, Patience and Fortitude roared at me through stone mouths, assuring me I was not the king of my domain.

My hands stuffed in my without-a-prayer pockets, I climbed the steps and walked into St. Patrick's Cathedral. I habitually dipped my hand in the Holy Water, half expecting the water to begin sizzling as it touched my skin, and made the sign of the cross. I sat in the last pew, unable to go much farther. I looked at the beautiful marble work, the stained glass and the artwork portraying the life of Christ. That cross looked heavier than ever. I tried to pray but couldn't settle my mind enough to find any words other than *Oh, Mary, don't you weep. Tell Martha not to moan.*

I thought of asking one of the many people fingering rosaries to provide me with the change it would take to get home, but my laughter at the thought soon echoed through the beautiful, hollow structure, and the disapproving looks shot my way affirmed that I'd blown my chance for a collection on my behalf.

"Spare a dollar," said the man on the corner of Fifty-seventh and Fifth Avenue, definitely no place to ask for anything less.

"Nah, man. Sorry," I said. *Sorry. What am I saying "Sorry" for? Hell,*

I might be out here with you tomorrow. As a matter of fact, I'm coming back here and taking this spot, so you might wanna be gone when I get here.

I walked off, amusing myself with the thought of showing up on that corner the next day, staking claim to the midtown change. My head filled with Otis Redding singing "Mr. Pitiful" and I happily tried to walk to the beat, adding a slight spring to my weary steps.

I walked up Fifth Avenue along Central Park, looking at the museums and the mansions of long ago. Every time I saw a limousine heading toward me I walked to the edge of the sidewalk and stuck out my thumb. A few back windows were cracked and I got some quizzical looks, but no one stopped. Hitchhiking went out with the seventies.

I took a needed break at the Conservatory Garden at 105th Street. The sculpture of the three women dancing hand in hand in the fountain seemed to come to life and their flesh shook freely from their drenched clothes. Their carefree laughter seemed directed at me.

I was beyond exhaustion and I didn't care about Kyra. I didn't care about money. I didn't care what anyone called me. I just wanted to take my shoes off. I could feel my damp socks and imagined the bottom of my feet, wrinkled and white from moisture.

An involuntary smile came to my face, and my steps, by this point on automatic pilot, began to quicken as I turned the corner onto 120th Street. I don't know how Moses did it, but I'm almost certain that when he got to the Promised Land his first thought was comparable to mine. *What in the fuck was I thinking?*

As I climbed the stoop I pulled out my keys. When I reached the top step I turned around and looked at Marcus Garvey Park, assuring myself that I'd made it, if not back to Africa, then at least back to Harlem. Home. The sun was retiring and I was thrilled by the prospect of doing the same.

I opened the door and walked a few steps, my undivided attention directed toward the end of the hall and my bedroom. Never had a closed door looked so inviting. I thought of the cool sheets and the warm duvet embracing my aching body. A shower would have to wait. I heard Carmen's voice. I thought perhaps Judith Steinman was there, but even one of her stories about parties and hustlers and bisexual husbands couldn't stop me from going to bed.

"Mason," said Carmen from the parlor. I stopped, which took more energy than walking.

"Not now, Carmen. Please. Not now. I'll explain everything later."

I mentally summoned the energy to tell my throbbing feet to begin moving again, but then my heart was no longer in my chest. It had fallen, separated and placed in equal halves in my feet, becoming bass drums.

Mason.

So she'd found out. Fair enough. Good. I couldn't help but smile, which led me back to the door of the parlor. I was too tired to care. I leaned on the wall just outside of the doorjamb and looked in. Carmen was sitting on the sofa, refined and refreshed, dressed exactly as she had been that very first day I'd seen her. She said nothing, but motioned across from her where my mother was sitting.

My walk from downtown, 112 blocks, flashed before me and I savored every step with laughter. I didn't say a word. I just moved away from the door and started for my room.

·20·

Sleep was long and hard and I woke late the next afternoon rested but dreading the inevitable cross-examination. I took a shower, eyeing the dirt of the city tornado its way down the drain, wishing that I could disappear as easily. Every time I thought of Kyra I wanted to bang my head against the tile. Karmajean had caught up with me.

Carmen had called my parents by getting the number from the phone bill, a practice she had initiated when dealing with Christopher.

"Good morning," said Carmen. "Or should I say, 'Good after-noon'?"

"Yeah," I said, looking around for my mother.

"There's coffee. I made it myself, so I don't know how good it is. I've never really learned how to use that contraption."

Carmen was doing her best to act like nothing had happened and I appreciated her effort. I poured a cup of coffee and began drinking the cup's content as if it were a panacea.

"This is horrible."

"The coffee or your situation?"

"Both. Is my mother still here?"

"No. She's at the Four Seasons," said Carmen, raising her eyebrow. I looked away from her. "She wanted me to have you call her when you woke up."

So it wasn't a dream. "Yeah. Thanks."

Carmen took my cup and refilled it. Her back was to me when she said, "You've come to mean a great deal to me and I didn't know what else to do. I didn't want you to ruin—"

"It's all right, Carmen. This is on me, not you."

I walked back across the hall to my bedroom and began picking up my clothes. I pulled out the duffel bag which had been my faithful companion on my travels.

"What are you doing?" asked Carmen, standing in the doorjamb.

"Packing."

"You're going back with your mother?"

"No," I said. "I'll just find another place until I figure out what I'm doing. I'm sure Jim'll let me stay with him until I do."

Carmen walked over to the bed. She moved some of the clothing and sat down. I couldn't look at her so I went into the bathroom and started packing my toiletries.

"Can I ask you something?" said Carmen.

"No. I'm not doing drugs. I'm not selling drugs. I don't even know why you'd think that. Just because you thought I didn't fit into your world doesn't mean I'm dealing."

"Mason." Hearing her use that name sent a chill over me, like the sound of wind chimes before a storm. I let my toiletries fall into the basin, unresolved blemishes waiting. "Come in here."

I went back into the bedroom but refused to sit next to her. I stood with my back to the wall—Sheetrock to studs.

"I'm trying to comprehend why you felt the need—"

"To lie?"

"I wasn't going to use that word, but—"

"That's what I did. I lied and it got me in here, didn't it? You could have picked one of the other guys but you didn't."

"I picked you because I thought you needed it the most, and evidently you did."

"Yeah, I guess I did, but you were more than willing to play along. I'm sure it made for good party conversation, the *poor little boy* you've taken in. We both got something out of it."

"It should have been *spoiled* little boy," she said, still sitting, her tone steady.

"So now all of this is my fault?" I looked away from her.

"No. You look at me, Malik, or Mason, or whoever it behooves you to be today. Look at me."

"What?"

"So many people would trade places with you in a heartbeat."

"You're one to talk."

"Maybe. But look at you. You think your hair and the way you dress or any of this charade is going to change who you are? There are kids right outside walking around that never got to be kids because their reality demanded that they be hard, look hard, in order to survive in a world where people pounce on those considered soft.

"I've lived in Harlem a long time. People are moving up here, snapping up homes because they can afford to, and then there are people who live here because they can't afford to live anywhere else. Your friend Jim can dress any way he likes and people will give him the benefit of the doubt. But why in the world would you try being something that most of society already thinks you are?"

"Why not? Maybe it's easier."

"That's bullshit," she snapped. "Easier? For whom?"

"Everybody."

"Yes, I can see how easy it's been for you," she said a bit sarcastically. "Think about what you're saying. It makes no sense. You've had every opportunity in the world to show them different and you're fucking it up."

This shocked me. Not the use of the word but the urgency with which she said it, and it raised my energy level like a mongoose attacking a snake. "Why should I have to show people anything? It's not my job to teach them about themselves or me. I played by the rules, rules I never had anything to do with planning. So I think I'm paid up. I don't owe them anything."

"This isn't about them. What about what you owe yourself? Your family. Mason, I'm sure your life hasn't been all great. Whose has? But I still find it difficult to feel sorry for you."

"That's odd because we wouldn't even be having this conversation if you hadn't felt sorry for me."

Carmen looked wounded and I could see the tears begin to well, deep from a place that existed long before I'd moved into the town house. As I stood there it was as if our roles had reversed.

"Wants and needs are different things, Mason," said Carmen, standing and walking toward the door. "Very different. Stay here if you like, but if you feel the need to go, I understand. Your mother left you some money. It's on the kitchen counter."

M om, it's me," I said from the house phone in the lobby of the Four Seasons.

"I'll be right down."

I hadn't been looking forward to dealing with what had ultimately come about from my own doing. My mother had me right where she wanted me, a bug forever trapped in amber.

I stood from the chair in the lobby lounge as my mother walked off the elevator. I felt like an anxious child taking his first step because no one has told him he can't, awaiting that moment when the thrill is trapped in time. Yet, a step is not walking.

I was wearing baggy jeans, a hooded sweatshirt, construction boots and a silver bubble coat. I'd expect some comment from her about my appearance, perhaps even wore it for that purpose. But she came over to me, relief in her stride, and without a word hugged me. I don't remember the last time I'd been hugged by my mother. She wasn't patting me on the back; it was an embrace. My arms remained at my sides.

"Where's Dad?" I asked, stepping away from her.

"He wanted to come," she said. She tried to conceal her disappointment at my question. "But I wanted to come on my own. I thought it would be good for me to handle this alone."

The thought of being handled made me more withdrawn.

My clothes made me stand out as we walked toward the restaurant, and people looked at me with my mother, probably certain I was a rap star. Why else would I be in the Four Seasons dressed like that? Or perhaps they knew our situation very well and felt sorry for my mother and admired her restraint.

As we approached the door of the restaurant Judith Steinman walked out with another woman. I thought of trying to distract my mother and wait for them to leave, but Judith Steinman saw me.

"Well, look who it is!" she said. The slur in her voice let me know that she had halved her way through one or two bottles of white wine.

"How you feel?" I said, hoping that would be enough and she would go on her way.

"Gloria, this is Malik." I held my head down and could feel my mother looking at me. I expected her to correct Judith Steinman, but she didn't.

"Hello," said Gloria.

"Malik's a *friend* of Carmen's," said Judith Steinman. "You know, *Carmen England*," she said with a joking tone.

"That makes sense," said Gloria, and they both gave knowing smirks.

"I wouldn't expect to see you here," said Judith Steinman, taking a quick glance at my mother. "But I suppose I shouldn't be surprised. After spending time with Carmen it's only right that you'd learn how to get around."

"I'm here with my mother," I said, but I said it so weakly, I'm sure she didn't believe me.

"Oh, okay," said Judith Steinman, patting my arm as though letting me know my secret was safe with her. "Well, have a nice lunch." She and Gloria started to walk away but I could hear her mumble, "With your *mother*."

"I met her through Carmen," I said, trying to explain as we walked into the restaurant.

"Yes, I gathered," said my mother.

"Carmen knows all kinds of people. It's been interesting."

The maître d' walked us to our table. He made no small talk. I could only imagine the amount of frigid parent/child meals and deals made he'd seen, realizing it was best to remain cordial yet unfamiliar. I was nervous and immediately picked up my water glass after it was filled. I braced myself.

"I like your hair," she said.

"Yeah, right."

"No. I mean it. It reminds me of your father. He had this huge Afro when he was in college and he'd often get cornrows. He felt empowered, like he was going against the establishment. That's what attracted me to him."

"I never knew that."

"Believe it or not, you're not the first one to go out into the world and try to demand a place. We understand more than you give us credit for."

"I know, you were young once."

"Well, I'm not ancient," she said, attempting levity. "I think I'm holding up rather well, thank you."

"That's not what I meant," I said, looking at the attractive woman who was my mother, yet for the first time seeing that she was getting older, no longer timelessly trapped in my child's mind. It was also the first time that I realized that she looked much like an older Kyra. Maybe I'd seen it before but refused to acknowledge it.

"Carmen seems like a lovely woman." Though it was a statement, it also had hints of a question.

"We have our moments."

"Regardless, she seemed concerned about you, and from what I understand, rightly so."

"The word seems to be that she's only concerned with herself."

"Then why are you living there?"

"I needed a place."

"Um," said my mother. She always said that when she wanted me to think about what I'd said, and the sense of it therein. I'd always rather she say more than that, but the utterance of "Um" more than said it all.

"Things are fine with us," I said, trying to reclaim my thoughts. "She just jumped to conclusions."

"Conclusions you've evidently helped in leading her toward."

"What do you want me to say? Okay. I lied about my name. I lied about having a job. There, I said it."

"You also told her I was mentally unstable," she said with a devilish smile.

"My bad. I shouldn't have involved you."

"Your *bad*?" she said, raising a brow.

"Yeah, my bad."

"Yes," she said, reaching for a sourdough roll. "Evidently mine too." She picked up the knife, slicing the bread, then began to spread butter on it. She looked back up at me. "Are both of your ears pierced?"

"Yeah," I said. *Here we go.*

"I'd noticed one," she said, buttering another piece of the roll. "Um. It looks nice." I just shook my head, hardly believing the words coming from her mouth.

"Can I get you all something to drink?" asked the waiter.

"A glass of red wine for me. Mason?"

"Ice cubes, floating in Jack Daniel's."

I had expected this to shock my mother, yet she looked up at the waiter, who had looked down awaiting her permission.

"What are you looking at her for?" I snapped. "I'm the one ordering it."

He looked at me for a moment, then rolled his eyes back to my
mother, still waiting for her to respond.

"And a Jack Daniel's on the rocks," my mother said. "Thank you."

There was something different about my mother; an ease that I'd
never seen or, perhaps, never looked for. It had been almost eight
months since I'd last seen her. But I wasn't going to play into it. I knew
she was just waiting for an opening so she could attack.

"That's a strong drink for this time of day," she said, brushing the
bread crumbs into her hand and putting them into her napkin.

"Well, somewhere in the world it's later and maybe after a drink I
can pretend I'm there," I said, smiling, adding injury to insult. Still my
mother remained restrained. Usually by this point we would have been
swapping words, but she refused, which made me nervous.

"Um," she said.

"Are you ready to order?" asked the waiter, returning with our
drinks.

"Not just yet," said my mother. "A few more minutes, please."

"Then I'll let you enjoy your drinks," said the waiter, looking down
at me, hardly concealing his disdain.

"Thank you," said my mother. The waiter walked away and on his
heels my mother turned back to me. "Mason," she said, then, pausing to
reassess her approach, she continued, "I'm not here to fight with you."

"Then why are you here?"

She looked at me as though I'd taken the knife away from her and
stabbed her. "If you have to ask, then there's nothing I can say." She put
the rest of the roll on the bread plate and took a drink of her wine.
"You're twenty-one years old . . ."

"Yes, I know. *I'm an adult.*"

"Yes, but adulthood doesn't come with the blowing out of candles.
It's not as easy as that." She moved her silverware around straightening
it, then placed it back in the very spot it had been. "I just don't under-

stand this need you have to be . . . this," she said, viewing me as if I were a dish she'd ordered but was disappointed by when it arrived.

"What is *this*?" I asked. "You mean black?"

She started to laugh. It was surprising. I'd never heard my mother laugh so loud. Sure, she would smile or even laugh, but it was hardly audible. But this time she laughed without trying to hold it in. "It must be horrible to be so all-knowing."

"You should be happy," I said. "At least your money wasn't wasted on my education. It's just too bad you never really realized that the lesson plan wasn't all I was learning in those classes."

"Believe me, I do have some idea," she said. "But is it so bad that we wanted . . ."

". . . the best for me. Yeah. Yeah. Detergents always say 'the best, nothing better' until 'new and improved' comes along. The best is always changing. The only thing staying the same is the separation. I'm the one dark shirt that got mixed in. Lucky me."

My mother seemed taken aback, then, again, suddenly burst into laughter, which irritated me.

"I wasn't trying to be funny," I said.

"Yes, I know," she said. "That's the humor of it." She continued laughing. She looked at her wineglass and started circling the rim with her finger. She took a deep breath and looked around the dining room at the other patrons. She wiped the cloth napkin at the corners of her mouth, then turned her attention back to me. "Did you know that your grandmother used to be a maid?"

"What?" I said. I hadn't really thought about what Granny did. She was Granny and as far as I was concerned her job was to do whatever she pleased. She'd raised her children and now she was reaping the benefits of their success, her success.

"Yes. She worked for the Clark family, cleaning their home and caring for their children."

"No one's ever mentioned that before," I said, picking up the glass of Jack Daniel's. But even that couldn't distill the words.

"No. Just because we don't talk about the past doesn't keep it from existing. We as a people were shackled for so long, we feel not talking is a way of protecting ourselves from it happening again. You see—"

"Excuse me," said the waiter. "Are you ready to order?"

"Sure," said my mother, looking up at him, seemingly thankful for the interruption. "I'll have the mixed greens."

"I'm not hungry," I said, though starving.

"Mason, you should eat something," she said, concern feeding her voice. I looked up at the waiter, who seemed hesitant. I thought about how it must have felt for my mother to be sitting across the table from a son she didn't recognize, a son that had done everything to distance himself from the world he knew, all while sitting in the Four Seasons.

"Steak frit. Medium rare," I said, handing the menu to the waiter.

"Very good," he said.

"Thank you," said my mother to the waiter, who backed away. Then she looked across the table at me. "The funny thing is you don't really know you're poor until you see what else is out there and if you don't know it exists, life doesn't seem so bad.

"Each day after school I'd meet your grandmother at the Clarks' and play with Danny, their youngest son, until it was time for us to take the bus across town, or maybe even one of their older children would drive us across town. I did that for years and it was wonderful. I thought my mother had the best job in the world, working in a beautiful house, and Danny had these great toys and we'd run around like children do.

"One day Mrs. Clark pulled into the driveway and Danny and I were wrestling, rolling around in the front yard. It was all very innocent, but she made us stop and come inside. That look on her face confused me but we went inside. As we walked in she called your grandmother into the kitchen. Being kids, Danny and I eavesdropped and we heard his mother tell your grandmother she no longer thought it was a good idea for me to come over, that it would ultimately cause trouble in the house.

"Danny and I both looked at each other, wondering what we'd done. I had my ear pressed to the door, waiting for your grandmother to tell her how ridiculous that was and that there wouldn't be any conflict, but she didn't. She just said, 'Yes'm.' I'll never forget that day.

"So rather than go over there after school I'd walk home and wait until she'd go off to work. I felt she'd chosen the Clark kids over me, and it made me angry and I closed myself off from her. All I could see was the attention that the other kids were getting.

"I thought of running away," she said with a chuckle. "You'd always see the little white kids on television running away and it seemed so exciting, but black children didn't run away, because you knew you didn't have any money and would have to come back and didn't want to have to deal with the ass whipping that would ensue. But I guess times have changed."

My mother using the term "ass whipping" surprised me but she laughed after saying it.

The waiter returned and placed our plates in front of us but my throat had constricted, making it hard for me to swallow.

"Fresh pepper?"

"No, thank you," said my mother.

I think I shook my head and the waiter walked away, wearing the mood that surrounded our table.

"When I went to college, your grandmother used to get bomb threats at her house."

"Bomb threats?" I knew my mother had a tendency for the dramatic, but I couldn't imagine her making up something like this.

"Yes. Some people felt I shouldn't go to college or at least not to that particular college. I didn't know about the bomb threats until much later. She'd kept that from me, but she'd worked hard to send me and even though it was a hellish experience, I went. I had to take different tests than other students, and papers I'd turned in would mysteriously disappear. But I never told your grandmother any of this. We were both trying to protect the other. I wasn't going to let her down. I wasn't going to be the example for a world that seemed set on my failing, on our failing."

Again, my mother looked around the opulent dining room, a place she fit in with ease. She turned back to her plate and closed her eyes. I didn't know if she was praying, or trying to find the words that would let her continue. The steak frit was of no interest to me because what my mother was serving went beyond mere meat and potatoes.

"Danny and I were in the same graduating class," said my mother, her fork in hand, never making its way to her salad. "I hadn't seen Mrs. Clark since that day she'd called your grandmother into the kitchen, but I knew her the moment I saw her. I'd seen Danny on campus over the years, both of us aware of the connection we would always have but ran from nonetheless. My mother had practically raised us both. We'd see each other and give a knowing nod, but we never spoke. That just wasn't done. We were on the same campus but in different worlds.

"Mrs. Clark walked over and hugged my mother, then looked at me and said, 'Well, you've turned into a fine girl.' I was seething. But my mother just smiled at Mrs. Clark and said, 'Yes'm,' just as she had done years ago. But that time it had meant something completely different. Mason, you're not the only one in the world to be the only one."

I wanted to resist her story, resist her. I looked around, trying to find a waiter so I could order another drink. Not seeing a waiter, I stood up. I wanted to leave.

"Sit down," she snapped. This caught me off guard. I looked at her and she held my gaze. "Sit. Down."

I couldn't believe she had raised her voice in public, but she no longer seemed to care about her surroundings. There was determination in her eyes. People around the dining room began to stare and I slowly eased back into my chair.

"Is there something I can do for you?" my mother asked a couple at a nearby table. The couple, surprised, as was I, by her confrontation, didn't answer, but she remained focused on them until they looked away. "Good," she mumbled.

"Everyone used to always say to me, 'You're so lucky you have a son. Sons love their mothers more than life itself.' I believed that. But every time I've tried to talk to you, you seemed to think that I wanted to run your life, like the experience I had to offer meant nothing. The harder I tried, the more you resented me. And I hated you for it. That's a horrible thing for a mother to say to her child, but that's how I felt."

"Well, I . . ."

"Just wait," she said, cutting me off, which I was more than pleased by as I tried to keep the tears from leaving my throat. "Since you've been on your sojourn I've had a great deal of time to think, and when Carmen said she thought you were in trouble all I could think of was not being able to do anything, fearing you'd shut me out again. But I was willing to accept that."

"You didn't need to come," I said, feeling wounded and wanting to take a jab at her.

"I don't need you to tell me what I need to do, Mason." She didn't say this with any hint of venom. She had a peaceful smile on her face as if this realization had been long in coming. My mother was still smiling but her voice started to tremble and I again leveed the flood running through me. I picked up my glass and sipped the melted ice with its hint of liquor and again began to look around for the waiter.

"Look at me." I couldn't. "Look at me," she said, taking the glass from my hand.

I looked at her, stared at her, hoping to keep my eyes dry. "Yesterday I sat on that plane, and the woman next to me asked why I was coming to New York," she said. "I told her I was visiting my son. She asked if you were doing well in the big city and I was about to say yes and talk about all the things you've done, but I couldn't. I looked at the woman and I told her I didn't know. That was the truth. I didn't know.

"For the rest of the flight she didn't say a word to me. I sat there wondering what I'd done wrong and I realized that just being there doesn't mean providing. If I could protect you from the wrongs of the world I would, but I can't be everywhere at every minute. I used to think I could. The world is just too large. I know that, but I'm here. Now. But I can't make you appreciate that."

I thought about the many teachers' conferences and her being the only black parent at PTA or picking me up at day camp. I thought of the tennis matches where the umpires saw everything I hit as long, and when I'd complain she'd simply say, "Mistakes are made. That's part of the game." I thought of the times that I'd not been able to spend the night at the homes of others, and even though I could have kids over, I never wanted to. It didn't seem like it would be as much fun. Yes, the world is large, I'd traveled much of it, but it seemed much smaller as I sat across from my mother. I thought of the driver I had hired in Sri Lanka who had looked at me and asked if I was Sri Lankan. I'd told him no, that I was from the States. I thought of how he looked at me certain I was one of the privileged Sri Lankan kids who are sent to the States or Europe for their education, no longer wanting to associate themselves with their homeland; too good to do so. As I sat quietly in the backseat of the car, there was no convincing him but he drove on.

My mother finally looked away from me. She reached down for her purse, opened it and pulled out an envelope, which I recognized as a bank envelope revealing the face of a president. My mother slid the envelope across the table toward me.

"Your grandmother sends her love."

·21·

How'd it go?" asked Carmen as I walked into the parlor. She threw aside the copy of *Vanity Fair* she was reading and got up from the sofa, then sat back down, just as I had done right after she had chosen me as her housemate, not certain what I should do or what was to come.

"It went well," I said. "Surprisingly. But Judith Steinman was there, which didn't help."

"Judith Steinman?" asked Carmen, again standing from the sofa. "Did you talk to her?"

"Briefly. I think she thinks I'm a hustler and my mom was a sugar momma." I laughed at the thought, but Carmen didn't.

"Did she say anything about me?"

"My mother. Yeah, she thought you were—"

"No. Judith. Did Judith say anything about me?"

"Not really. She just told her friend that I was a friend of yours. Don't worry, I didn't embarrass you."

"Oh, no. I'm not concerned about that," she said, looking at me to see if I'd told her the whole story. "Well, I'm glad things went well with your mother. I suppose you've convinced her that you're okay?"

"Yeah. Now I have to convince myself. She's been in therapy and thinks I should go."

"Therapy? Please. If you think you need therapy, do what I do."

I expected her to say yoga or massage or some Eastern philosophy emptying pockets all over the city.

"Watch reruns of *Little House on the Prairie*," she said. "No one's life is as miserable as the Ingalls'. If the house isn't on fire, then the church bell is broken. If the church bell isn't broken, then someone's gone blind. Hell, after three episodes you see your life isn't so bad. Trust."

"I guess you're right," I said. I was grateful to Carmen for making light of the situation. "As always."

"Not always," she said, putting another log on the fire. "Speaking of, are they letting you stay? I mean, here in New York?"

"Yeah. My mother's heading back tomorrow, but she wrote up this contract on hotel stationery and made me sign it. It basically said I could stay but I'd have to go back at the beginning of summer to work for my father to pay off the money I've spent on the credit card because they've decided not to foot the bill anymore."

"Oh, poor baby," said Carmen, as if that wasn't a satisfactory punishment. But then she caught herself and her tone changed. She turned toward me, but her hands were behind her back, welcoming the heat of the flames. "I've been thinking about the conversation we had earlier."

"Me too. I'm sorry about all this."

"Don't be."

"No. I mean it. You let me live in your home and I misled you."

"You misled yourself," she said, then she said, "We misled each other." She walked over to the liquor cabinet, took the top off a decanter which normally held the Jack Daniel's. It was empty, but she picked up a glass and held it. "You *were* what I wanted you to be."

"Maybe we were meant to meet each other."

"Maybe," she said, walking back to the fireplace. "I'm pleased things went well with your mother." She put the glass on the mantel and looked up at the mirror. "I waited too long for that to happen with mine and I've nothing to show for it."

"There's still time."

"My dear boy," she said. "Yes. Maybe we were meant to meet."

I got up and walked over to her. I hugged her and she returned the embrace. We held each other for a few seconds and then I let go and started to leave the parlor.

"You'll explain to Judith, won't you?" I said, turning back to her.

"Sure," said Carmen. "I'm sure she'll get a good laugh out of it," and then as though stating it for her own benefit, "Judith loves a good laugh."

Carmen has taken everything in stride, which I guess I shouldn't find surprising. But there's something different about her now. She may be playing around with this Jean-Claude, but I know she still thinks about Christopher. Every time the phone rings I can see it. She's convinced Christopher used her and now I've done the same. In a way we were both after a green card, a passport to freedom. I'm going to have to make it up to her. Mind you, she still hasn't thanked me for my Christmas present, and after all that's happened, I can't rightly bring it up.

Tried to call Malcolm but he hasn't been around. Kyra keeps hanging up on me. I thought of asking Carmen to give her a call, try to explain everything, but she's done enough for me already. Everyone has . . .

"Carmen, it was a pleasure meeting you," said my mother, shaking Carmen's hand, then deciding to hug her. I couldn't believe this was my mother. She handed Carmen a bag from Bergdorf's, which was conveniently down the street from her hotel. "Just a little something."

"No, I can't," said Carmen.

"Please. I appreciate your concern for Mason. I can see you've been a good influence on him."

"And he on me, Joyce," said Carmen, accepting the bag. I was surprised to hear her say it and even though I didn't see how that could be true, I was pleased she'd said it.

It was peculiar standing in the hotel lobby watching these two women speaking of me as if I were someone other than who I was; someone other than they had known. I thought of how easy it is to determine the impact another has had on you, but gauging your impact on others can be daunting. I carried my mother's suitcase outside, which the bellhop frowned about, a tip missed.

"If you're ever in our neck of the woods, do look us up," said my mother.

"I may just hold you to that," said Carmen. "I already know the number."

"Yeah, we know that," I said, putting my arm around Carmen's waist.

"Mason," said my mother, again becoming formal, ridding herself of emotion, "it was good to see you."

"You too. I appreciate that you came."

"That's all I've ever wanted," she said, my words a rush of relief.

"And don't worry, I'm not going to ruin my life. If I don't go to law school, I'd figure out some way to survive."

"I'm sure you will, but that doesn't keep me from worrying. But just know that I plan to spend every cent before I die, so you'll either get it together or starve."

"Ah, Mom's got jokes," I said as my mother started walking toward the waiting Lincoln Town Car.

"Try me," she said, standing at the car door. "Earrings in both ears. What is the world coming to?"

"Hey, some African kings wore earrings in both ears and their noses too."

"Oh, so now you want to use your knowledge. Lovely." She took off her gloves and put her hand up to her ears and pulled out her diamond studs. She placed them in her palm and held it out to me. "If you must wear earrings, wear the best."

My hand started itching, thinking about the diamond studs rather than the little silver hoops I'd graduated to. I reached for her hand, which she quickly shut and pulled away like in a child's game.

"But you've got a lot of work to do before you have your own tribe, so get busy," she said, sliding into the backseat of the car, leaving Carmen laughing and my jaw dropped. The driver closed the door and as the car pulled away in the morning midtown traffic the window slid down. "And I lied too," she said, putting on the earrings. "That hair. It's a mess."

·22·

The late January day was gray and the pregnant cloud-coated sky had yet to decide upon its offspring. The snow, once pristine, was now nothing more than banks of smut making my journey, if not longer, less pleasant.

My numerous calls to Kyra went unanswered. I felt like the Christmas trees, their sentences served, that had been piled on the street curbs, tinsel blowing in the wind. The merriment that was recently a part of the holidays had vanished with the new year.

I'd been hanging out at Café Lalo hoping to run into Kyra. To no avail. So I bundled up and went up to Columbia's main campus. I walked around the quad sitting on the steps of Low Library, which made me think of Malcolm and his thoughts of the tours of Harlem. I gathered I was out of favor with him as well because every time I called he was either on his way out or not home.

I began to feel my turn at stalking was pointless so I walked to the 1/9 train at 116th and Broadway and as I started down the steps there was Kyra, coming up with some friends, an angel coming from the depths of the underground. They were chatting jovially, and laughter fell freely until she looked up and saw me. She and her friends walked by without a word.

"Kyra," I said, following her on the street. The other girls stopped and looked back when they heard her name, and though she stopped she refused to turn around. "Kyra," I said, grabbing her arm.

"What?" she said, pulling her arm away. She stepped back, standing regally, and gave me a less-than-inviting look but I refused to budge. I'd never seen the other girls but they all struck a defensive pose as if they were a gang ready to protect one of their own.

"Hello, ladies," I said. Eyes arched and mouths were turned up but no salutations presented themselves. "Do you mind if I speak to Kyra for a minute?"

"Why are you asking us?" said one of the girls in a tone that mixed Valley Girl with ghetto superstar. I looked at Kyra, hoping she would help, but she remained firm in her silence, comforted by the support of her friends. Her eyes more than let them know that I was the one they'd heard about.

"May I have a word with you?" I asked.

"As long as it's 'bye,' " she said, turning to leave. The group of girls started walking with her, laughing more than they needed to.

"Kyra," I said as I followed them to the gate of the campus. I ran in front of them and blocked her way. "Kyra, come on. I can understand your not wanting to talk to me, but at least let me explain."

"Your wanting to explain has nothing to do with me. It's about making yourself feel better, and I don't owe you that."

"O-kay," said her friends as if they were in a choir and they had rehearsed for just this moment.

"You're right." I moved out of her way, making it easy for her to go on if she so chose. A few coeds timidly passed like children hoping to go unnoticed during a fight between parents. "I'll leave you alone, but I thought you might like this." I reached for my backpack.

"If it ain't her money, then you need to keep stepping," said one of the girls.

Though I had wanted it to remain in my head, the words "Would you shut up?" shot out of my mouth.

"Oh no he didn't," she said. "Oh. No. He. Didn't."

"Oh. Yes. I. Did," I said, shaking my head and waving my finger just as she had.

This made Kyra smile a bit. "Okay. Let me just get this over with. I'll catch ya'll later," Kyra said to the girls.

"Girl, are you sure?"

"Yeah."

The girls all looked at me like they wanted to ingrain my face into their memory for a future beat-down. They slowly backed away, kung fu masters keeping their eye on the opponent.

"Look, I thought you might like this." I pulled out the gift. She walked over to a bench and sat down. She unwrapped the package and looked back at me. The mercury slowly began to rise.

I had remembered that one of her guilty pleasures was the novels of Leonard St. James. She had already read *Don't Mess with Mama's Malt Liquor* and *Aw, You Done Made Mama Mad Now* and had been anticipating the publication of the final installment of the Mama Trilogy, *Get Mama Her 'Stention Cord.*

"It's an advanced copy," I said, still not wanting to look too pleased with myself. "I practically had to beg, borrow and steal to get it."

"That doesn't surprise me," she said, standing from the bench and looking at her watch. "You're so resourceful."

"Come on, Kyra. You can't avoid me forever."

"Why not? You seem set on avoiding yourself," she said, starting to walk away, enjoying every moment of it. "Anyway, I have to meet someone."

"How about a cup of coffee?" I said. "Just a cup of coffee and I'll leave you alone." She stopped and looked at me. "I even have the cash to pay for it."

She looked at the book then back as she started walking past me and toward the gate. "What are you waiting for?" she said. I started walking to catch up with her and as she led the way I placed my hands in the prayer position at my chest and threw my head back toward the heavens, and Kyra, without turning around, said, "Don't get too happy."

S o your name *is* Mason," she said as we sat at a back booth at the West End Gate, a publike restaurant near campus.

"Yes, everything I told you was true. All of it. You can even ask Justin. We were suitemates in college."

"Let me get this straight," said Kyra. "You went around pretending to be someone else."

"Yes, but when I met you, I wanted to get to know you better. I'd already heard about you. You just seemed like the sort of person I would want to get to know, someone I wouldn't have to pretend with."

"And I'm supposed to find that flattering?"

"I was hoping so."

"So you're saying that it was okay for you to lie to everyone else but not to me?"

" 'Lie' is such a strong word," I said. She stood from the booth. "No, wait. Sit back down. Yes. Yes, I lied and it was pathetic. Okay. Is that what you want to hear?"

"It's not about what I want to hear, it's about what happened."

"Okay, you're right," I said, almost in a whisper, noticing that people were watching. "Just sit down. Let me try to explain."

She sat, as though it was a chore.

"I have issues, okay."

"No, you have items, and they need to be marked off, but I can't help you with that."

"I know. But for some reason I thought you would understand. Maybe I just wanted someone to understand, you know? Maybe it's just different up here. Everyone is just so enlightened. The great black North." A certain sense of bitterness tinged my words. I sipped my coffee, thinking of what to say next. I couldn't even look at her, but I kept going. "The first day I looked at Carmen's place this guy started coming at me. He said I was a black boy blending. No one had ever said anything like that to me so I never had to deal with it, you know? Yeah, I've seen the looks I get from some black people and I feel it, which is fucked-up, you know, but when you're walking through Harlem and you hear that, it fucks with you." I found myself chuckling.

"What's so funny?" she asked.

"I'm trying to explain this and I can't put the words together; that's the only time I really ever use profanity. It's just not me. But it's frustrating not to be able to find the words, to not be heard. And I'm supposed to be a smart guy. Mr. I'm-Going-to-Stanford. I used to think maybe if I went to an all-black college things would have been different. Maybe an all-black experience would have been better. But it would have probably been the same shit—I mean stuff—no, I mean shit. Shit. It would have been the same shit, just different-color noses pointed in the air, and there's something more painful about being rejected from what you believe to be your own. So the familiar seemed less painful and for me familiar was white. I knew how to deal with that.

"I guess what I'm saying, or trying to say, is I thought you were one of my own. Someone who would give me a chance." I looked at her and I knew I had her attention, finally. "All my life I've been 'the black guy.' If someone didn't know me, that's how I was referred to. 'You know, the black guy.' Sure, everyone has ways to describe people, we all do. He lives here, or she drives this, or his parents own that. But many people can live in a neighborhood, drive a car, own something, but when they said, 'the black guy,' that meant me.

"This isn't something you can explain to your white friends because every time you mention anything that has to do with race, they just clam up. My presence is a reminder, so why bring it up? If they say something biting or witty, it's irony. If I do, it's anger."

"Do you all want to order food?" asked the waiter coming up to the table. I looked over at Kyra. She didn't speak or look up, she just shook her head.

"No, the coffee is fine," I said. The waiter walked away in a huff and I didn't care, but his presence had provided me with the example I was looking for. "Before I left Louisiana a friend of mine got married. It was a formal wedding at a beautiful plantation and me and the ties were the only black things there." Kyra grinned, unwillingly, and the tension eased. "The slave quarters were still there, shacks away from the main house, and as I walked around I got really emotional. I dreamed of one day buying one of these plantations and whenever I had white friends come over I'd make them stay out in the slave shacks. Of course, I'd fix them up, but I'd put them out there. Make the reminders work for me, for once.

"But I was still glad to be at the wedding because I'd known this guy for years and it wasn't about color with us. I knew he was good people. He'd proven that. I wasn't just something exotic to add to the mix.

"After the ceremony, cocktails and hors d'oeuvres were served on the grounds. I'm walking around decked out in my tux, looking and feeling pretty good, and a woman, I believe his great-aunt, made a beeline for me and asked where I was hiding all the Cajun shrimp and could I make sure that when I brought out the next tray I come find her. I could have gotten all belligerent and caused a scene that my friend would still be talking about on his first anniversary, but she was an older woman, from a different time, different landscape, so I told her I'd check. Of course, I didn't."

"Did you mention it to your friend?"

"No. What would have been the point? It wasn't about me. It was about her perception of me, of black people and their place. Serving with eyes down. But on that day, my place just happened to be sitting next to her at the reception dinner, where I knew I impressed my charms upon those at the table enough for them to later chat about how 'articulate' I was. It's funny how both white and some black people seem shocked if you're black and articulate."

"You mean, when you don't use 'shit' and 'fuck' and 'you know' in a sentence to explain yourself," said Kyra with a sly grin.

"Touché," I said. "I guess I'm just trying to get to a point where I don't care so much. You seem to have it down, or maybe I've been presumptuous in thinking your experience was like mine. Like I said, it's different in the North."

"Not really," she said, holding her coffee and warming her hands, her silver thumb ring clinking against the mug. "We're just better at pretending that we're above it. From the sky you can't see the lines on the map."

I waited for a moment, hoping she would have something more to say, hoping she was scanning her memory of a time when being in a cocoon seemed preferable to being a butterfly. She kept looking at her cup, as though the coffee had been replaced with tea and she was looking for guidance in the leaves.

"I just wanted to explain," I said. "I hope I made sense, though I can hardly make sense of it myself. But I'm working on it."

I reached into my back pocket to pull out my wallet. "Here is the money for dinner at the Grange Hall," I said, reaching my hand toward her. "I understand if you don't want to see me, but I just wanted to clean up the mess. I just hope I'm not—"

"What up, Malik?" said Malcolm, coming up to our table. He put his hand on Kyra's shoulder and she looked right at me. The rest of my sentence rested in her eyes like someone taking coins from a well; wishes stolen.

Too late.

Malcolm slid in the booth next to Kyra and put his hand over hers until their fingers joined.

"Trying to make it," I said.

"You two know each other?" asked Kyra and Malcolm simultaneously.

"Yeah," I said. Malcolm looked puzzled but I kept going. "Long time no see. I guess I see why you've been busy." He looked at Kyra and smiled. I tried to hide the hole in my chest, stifle the cough huddled there. "So you two are going out?"

"Yeah. For a couple of weeks now," said Kyra.

"That's great. Good. Good," I said, sliding out of the booth. I left the money on the table. "I'd better go."

"Mason," she said.

"Mason?" said Malcolm.

"You didn't tell him?" I said, looking at her. Malcolm's face slowly drifted away and in its subtle transition I could actually see that it did take more muscles to frown.

"Tell me what?"

"Nothing," I said. "Nothing. I'll see ya'll around."

·23·

I walked back into the town house and headed for my room. I looked into the kitchen and Carmen was sitting at the kitchen island. She was unkempt, and looked as if she'd just gotten up. A bottle of one of my Forties of Ballantine ale was sitting next to her.

"What? Out of Jack Daniel's?"

"Yeah. I've been meaning to pick up another bottle but I haven't gotten to it. I suppose I had a taste for something different. I'm sure you can understand that." She didn't have a glass, she just picked up the bottle and took it "to the head" as I'd heard it referred to in the hood. I was impressed with the ease with which she handled it.

"What are you doing here?" I asked.

"I live here, remember?"

"Sometimes I wonder," I said, walking across the hall toward my bedroom.

"What do you mean by that?" asked Carmen, coming up behind

me. I fell back on my bed, throwing my arms above my head in search of my breath. "Malik?"

"Don't call me that."

"What did you mean by sometimes you wonder?"

"Carmen, I've had a bad day and I thought I'd come back and be able to moan in private."

"What happened?"

"Kyra."

"You're still after her?"

"I *was* still after her, but she's moved on."

"So you spoke to her."

"You're really quick today, can't pull anything over on you."

"My, my," said Carmen. "I take it it didn't go well."

"No. No, it's safe to say it didn't go well," I said, finally sitting up. "At least not for me. But Malcolm is doing more than 'trying to make it.' They've been going out."

Carmen walked over and sat on the bed next to me, which made me get up. I didn't want to be near anyone. I didn't want to be touched or reassured.

"If it makes you feel any better, my day wasn't ideal either. I was supposed to be going to St. Lucia this afternoon with Jean-Claude. The car never came. I called him, and his assistant said he'd already left."

"You don't need him. Why don't you just do it on your own?"

"Do it on my own? You mean like you've been doing?" she said. I let it go. I deserved it. "Christopher called," she said abruptly.

"Did you accept the call?"

"He didn't call collect this time. He just wanted to let me know he's coming back in three weeks. February fifteenth. Isn't that a laugh? Not the fourteenth. The fifteenth, which is fine because I hate Valentine's Day anyway." The doorbell rang. "Jean-Claude."

Carmen sprang from the bed and went into my bathroom. I watched her look at her face and put her hair in place. She came out of the bathroom and rushed past me. I recognized the look of desperation as she quickly moved down the hall. I knew that look well. It was her sense of power that had drawn me to her and now she was hoping that a man was ready to sweep her away to sandier shores. When she reached the door, she took a moment to reposition her clothes, then opened it.

"Oh," she said, her posture slightly sinking. Malcolm looked past her and our eyes met. "I think it's for you."

"I need to talk to you," he said, refusing to enter the house.

"Yeah. Come on in."

"Nah. We'd better talk out here."

"Right." I walked down the hall, picked up my coat off the rack and stepped outside. Carmen remained standing at the open door like a mediator.

"Oh," she said. "I gather you two want to speak in private."

"Yeah," I said. I was ready to handle whatever he had to bring.

"Remember. Black-on-black crime has to stop." She slowly closed the door, but I could see her standing behind the frosted glass looking at us.

I welcomed her tension breaker and tried to shrug off a laugh. Malcolm leaned on one side of the stoop's railing, I on the other.

"Did Kyra send you?" I asked.

"No. She didn't want me to come but I wanted to set some things straight."

"You don't have to apologize. It's cool. You deserve her. I had my chance."

"Apologize?" he said. "You arrogant mother— Look, I don't need you to tell me I deserve her."

"That's not what I meant, but you were the one who said you didn't think she'd be interested in you. You've got her, you win."

"You amaze me. Here you are in this big house, with your cleaning lady and Ms. My-Shit-Don't-Stink, and you think I came to apologize to you?"

"What does where I'm living have to do with it? This isn't my house. I told you that. I rent a room—"

"Squash it. I know her type and yours too. This has just been play-time for you, but this isn't a game to me. It's life," said Malcolm, motioning to the neighborhood before turning his focus back to me. "On Thanksgiving, I brought you into my house with my family and filled your stomach with food . . ."

"I know and I—"

"You don't know," he said, his voice rising. "You brought your act over, sat at our table, and you ate our food. What, you thought you'd come and see how the other side lives?"

"No. It wasn't like that."

Malcolm stood from the stoop's railing like he was dizzy and my words were akin to food poisoning. For me, Thanksgiving was long gone. But it still stuck with him.

"I have to walk on that campus every day while other people wonder if I really belong and I bust my ass to prove that I do. I suck it all up to make sure I get mine. But when Kyra told me your weak story all I could think about was that you came to my house and ate our food. So don't tell me you know. Because that's bullshit.

"You don't know what it's like for you and your brother and sister to get dressed up to take the subway out to the Bronx to visit your aunt and your mother telling you beforehand not to take any food from them because she didn't want them to think you were hungry, even if she knew you were. No. You don't understand."

"So this is, your blues ain't like mine?"

"Nah. Your blues are definitely worse, 'cause you're the one with the access and the tools and you still can't manage to do the work, so why not just steal it from the people with ability but no access."

He looked at me, then started down the steps.

"Malcolm. I didn't mean . . ." He put his hand up in the air and shook his head. "I'm sorry."

"Yeah. You sure are," he said. I watched him walk down 120th Street. I wanted to go after him, say something, but my feet were leaden and words escaped me.

Carmen opened the door and peeked out.

"Is everything all right?"

"Yeah," I said. The habitual answer is always easier than the truth, jumping out like a child at play. But I'd grown weary, and pretending no longer served its purpose. "No, Carmen. It's not."

"Why don't you come in out of the cold? We'll talk about it."

Come out of the cold?

"I think I'm going to sit out here for a bit." When she saw that I wasn't going to change my mind she closed the door.

The streets were empty, providing me the only peace I'd had that day. I sat on the stoop, biting the skin on my chapped lips, looking across the street at what was once Mount Morris Park but was now Marcus Garvey Park and irony was more than just a Shirley Jackson short story, and my number was up.

The trees were bare, their limbs ashen from the unyielding elements. A black plastic bag, sailing on gossamer wings, got hooked on one of the branches and wallowed and popped, hoping to continue its undetermined journey.

For ten minutes I sat on the stoop, numb to the cold, beyond it even, hoping with the help of the wind the bag would break free. But it didn't. It remained in the branch's grasp; merely lifeless litter.

·24·

I'd heard it said that February is the cruelest month and I believe it to be true. The calendar had changed and warmth was hard to find.

Carmen's mood fluctuated and even though I'd bought a bottle of Jack Daniel's for the house, she seemed to take a liking to having a Forty with me. She didn't mention Christopher but I could tell that his impending return weighed heavily on her.

To try taking her mind off of the negative, I had invited her out to dinner and was to meet her at M&G, a no-frills soul food joint on 125th Street.

I sat at the counter for twenty minutes, not ordering, awaiting her arrival.

"You keeping that seat warm?" the waitress asked, pointing to the empty stool next to me where I'd placed my coat to assure Carmen would have a seat.

"Yes, ma'am."

"Good, I'm glad to hear it, but unless you wanna pay rent on it, I recommend you hang up that coat and order something for that seat you sitting in." The two women who worked there were always curt, but in a loving way. They didn't let you get away with anything and perhaps that was why I'd grown fond of the place.

"I was supposed to be meeting someone here."

"Well, honey, you've been stood up, so why don't you stand up so somebody else can have those seats?"

"But there's no one waiting," I said jokingly.

"That's because they look in and see that there ain't no stools, so they think to themselves, 'Well, ain't no stools, I'll just go on down to Popeye's.' See, everybody wants a counter seat so they can get close to me."

"Can't say I blame them for that," said a man sitting two stools from me. I looked down at him and he was eating scrambled eggs with what at first glance I took to be grits, but on closer inspection was rice. He'd mixed the two together and was plowing the combination into his mouth.

"Was anybody talking to you, Henry?"

"Like that ever stopped me," said Henry, then, looking at me, "Don't pay her no mind, young buck. She all talk. I told her whenever she ready she can take off that apron and I'll take care of her. Good care. But she's always trying to act like she not into it."

"You can just get that out of your head. I'm into insurance and insurance ain't no man."

The few women in M&G seconded her emotion and the men groaned, hiding behind six o'clock shadows. I kept looking at the door, hoping Carmen would walk in, feeling she could benefit from the conversation.

"I tell you what," I said, thinking it best for me to leave, but still wanting to get something for the time I'd occupied the stool. "Why don't you give me a piece of that chocolate cake? To go."

"That cake there?" the waitress asked, pointing to an unsliced cake, sitting temptingly on the cake stand.

"Yes, ma'am. That cake."

"Can't cut that cake. It's cooling."

I shrugged my shoulders and started to stand from my prized counter stool.

"Hold your horses, now," she said. She reached over the counter and sat me back down, then walked over to the cake. She picked up a knife from a plastic bucket filled with water. She wiped it with a paper towel as though this was her favorite part of the job.

I'd seen her have this type of banter with other customers and had always enjoyed it. I'd also seen her kick customers out if they got too loud or used profanity and it was a certainty that no matter how fly you thought you were, if you wore your hat inside, you'd only do so once.

She wrapped the generous portion of cake in aluminum foil and placed it in a brown paper bag. She jotted down the price and tore the bill out of her receipt book and placed it in front of me. Three dollars and fifty cents.

"See some places, they'll ask you if you need change," she said, picking up the five I'd put down. "But we don't do that here. The way I see it you shouldn't have to force somebody to tip." She turned to the cash register but her voice was at a level that all the customers could hear. "But here, we don't do that. Downtown, they might do that, but not here. That'd be rude. You shouldn't have to beg nobody for nothing. That's what I say." She closed the cash register and making certain Henry and anyone else who cared to look could get a nice view of her behind, she slowly made the four steps back over to me and placed my change on the counter.

"That's for you," I said.

"Thank you, honey." She immediately slid the money into her apron before the words were even out of her mouth. She then leaned on the counter, her ample breasts resting on her forearms. "Now, listen, 'cause this is for free. I don't mean to get all up in your tea, but was it a woman you waiting on?"

"Yes, ma'am."

"See, then that's your problem. You don't tell no woman to meet you nowhere. You supposed to be a gentleman and go and pick her up. We like that, you see. But young men these days, when you don't get your way ya'll walk around all hurt and angry, full of bitter butter in your batter, then you sit around wondering why Betty done gone out and found some better butter."

"I guess we have to learn that one the hard way," I said, getting up from the stool.

"That's the only way to learn," she said, raising from her elbows. She started to wipe down the space I had just occupied; stools are valuable at M&G.

I t's good to see someone is making use of this dining room," said Carmen, walking in and pulling out one of the chairs.

"Yeah, I thought I'd live a little," I said, looking down at the chicken, fries and rice and beans. "Since you didn't show up at M&G I brought back some Popeye's."

Carmen didn't say anything and I wondered if my chewing sounded as loud as the silence. She placed her hands on the table and her fingernails weren't freshly painted as they usually were, which made me look at her, really look at her. She looked tired. Her eyes looked heavy and her skin lacked its usual effervescence.

I pushed my plate away. I could see that there was no use in her painting her nails; she was biting them, scraping against her teeth what little color remained. "Now I've got to go back to a life of uncertainty. That's never fun. Trust."

"Have you talked to Jean-Claude?"

"Yes. We called it off."

"Really. Good for you."

"I hope so."

"Why were you attracted to him?"

"He said hello and I believed he meant it."

"Is that all it takes?"

"Sometimes. But whenever the phone rings I still hope it's him say-ing that he's made a mistake."

"And you'd take him back?"

"I'm not as strong as you think I am, Malik."

This wasn't her taking a jab at me. I was certain of that. It was the name she was familiar with and she, too, needed something familiar. I didn't correct her. She'd always said she'd chosen me because she thought I needed it most, but sitting across from her, I knew it was more than that.

I had some idea of what she was going through. My feelings for Kyra had gone below the surface and in my mind I had played the *what if* record so many times that it scratched, then skipped to the next cut.

Move on.

Easily said.

"I called my mother today. Asked her if I could come for a visit," she said, pressing her thumb on the crumbs on my plate like hoping to collect them all before placing them in her mouth. "Big fight. Noth-ing new."

"It'll pass."

"Sure it will. Hopefully sooner than later."

·25·

The air in the house was like a sickness hovering and Carmen was quarantined. There was no lift in her step and our verbal exchanges were brief at best. She wore the same clothing every day, a baggy, old warm-up suit, and the slightest sound made her jump.

I was worried about Carmen but I was no longer able to be at home as much. With all my secrets exposed I became freer, not at all concerned about what would be waiting for me around the next corner. My time in New York had evidently seasoned me, providing a certain scent, and with the appropriate name-dropping I had been able to get the highly fought-over job of checking coats at one of the new places-to-be restaurants, which filled my life with cashmere, fur and the occasional poly blend to keep me grounded. Still, at a dollar tip, at least, per coat, I was just making, as Carmen would say, "cute money" for a few hours' work.

I'd asked Carmen what her plans were for Valentine's Day and she'd said that she was doing her best to block it out. I knew it would be a lucrative coat check night—men always tipped well on special occasions—but I took the night off. To take Carmen's mind off of Christopher's return the next day, I wanted to show her a good time, particularly as I knew once he arrived I had no idea where I would fit in. I didn't think she would ask me to leave—she'd probably need me more than ever—but I wasn't quite sure.

"What are you going to do?" I'd asked one night after coming in from work. She was sitting in front of the fireplace like it was all the warmth she needed.

"Do?" she said.

"About Christopher?"

"What I always seem to do. Move on."

"Good for you," I said. But from the way she looked at me, the light from the fire cascading across her face, I knew it wasn't going to be as easy as that, as easy as putting another log on the fire. "You can do it."

"Knowing you will and wanting to are altogether different."

"Maybe you and Judith Steinman can go away, have a girls' outing."

"No," she said. "Whether I like it or not, I'm going to have to deal with this on my own."

Yes, Carmen definitely needed a night out, a chance to forget, a chance to remember. I walked up the stairs. As usual, her door was closed but the sign deterring Rose from entering was no longer there.

"Enter," she said upon hearing my knock.

I opened the door and, to my surprise, the room was tidy. There were no clothes, shoes or magazines on the floor. The bed was made, the pillows aptly positioned, and the suitcases were closed and placed neatly in the corner. The photograph of her and Christopher that I'd seen in the drawer of the night table was now in view. It immediately caught my eye but I chose not to comment on it.

"I see you've taken your ban off of Rose."

"No," she said from the dressing room. "I cleaned it myself. I thought it was time I put everything back in its place."

"Well, you don't have to let him come up to your bedroom," I said, trying to support her, plant the seeds of strength that she no longer seemed to have.

"I did it for myself. Not for him," she said, walking out of the dressing room in a long red sequin dress. Her hair was pulled up and my look of approval seemed to better her mood. "It being a mess wouldn't at all surprise him. He'd expect it, and I couldn't have that." She did a quick spin-around for my pleasure, and hers.

"You look great."

"Yeah, I love dressing up. I'd almost forgotten what a drug it can be."

"For you or for those looking at you?"

"Both," she said with a laugh, quickly turning back into the Carmen I knew. "So you're still not going to tell me what we're doing?"

"No. It's a surprise."

"What are you up to, Mason Randolph?"

"Nothing. Can't I take you for an evening out without there being some hidden agenda?"

"You're still a man, aren't you?"

"I'm trying," I said. "Cut the lip service and get your coat. The limo's waiting."

"A limo?"

"Only the best for you, my lady," I said, bowing. I didn't mention that the limousine driver was a guy I'd met at my coat check job. He was an artist but made his money by driving a doctor from his apartment to the hospital in the morning and picking him up in the evening. He'd also been known to use the limo to drive his artist friends around to run errands. "You'd be surprised by the service a starving artist can get when stepping out of a limo," he'd said one night while dropping me off at home.

The champagne had been chilling in the limousine and I popped the cork as Carmen and I settled into the backseat.

"Kyra doesn't know what she's missing," said Carmen.

"That's nice of you to say," I said, but I knew I was the one missing out. "But this is your night. Christopher doesn't know what *he's* missing."

At the mention of his name her body sank into the leather seat as though it were the end of the night rather than the beginning. Her head rested back and she looked out the window at the buildings of Harlem. She started to bite her nails and I took her hand and pulled it away from her mouth. I held her hand in mine and she looked over and smiled. It was a weak smile, like it had to be summoned from a place outside of her. It was clear to me that it was going to take more than a *Little House on the Prairie* marathon to pull her out of her funk.

"Mason," she said, "I want to talk to you about Christopher. As you know he's due back and—"

"Don't," I said.

"No, I need—"

"No. Not tonight. I shouldn't have brought him up. I know he's coming back, but if you could just enjoy tonight. With me. We'll worry about him tomorrow. Let's just take it one day at a time."

"Yes. One day at a time," she said, again turning her gaze to the window.

L adies and gentlemen. We at Birdland are thrilled to present the legendary styling of Little Jimmy Scott!"

Carmen perked up and looked over her shoulder waiting for him to appear, and then she looked back at me.

"Happy Valentine's Day," I said.

Jimmy sang in a way that I'd never heard; a small man with a smoky voice, second to no one. Carmen sat there like a child, free of all bad thought, swept up in the moment.

The champagne flowed and the evening was as light as the bubbles. Jimmy began singing "For All We Know" and Carmen put her hand over mine. She seemed entranced listening to him and as he reached the end of the song a tear trickled from her eye as she sang the last line with him: *Tomorrow may never come, for all we know.*

Thank you so much," said Carmen as we walked back into the town house. "How in the world did you pull that off?"

"I saw an ad and was lucky enough to hook up a table. I was afraid you'd have other plans, but it worked out. I'll probably be a little late with next month's rent, but I thought you'd understand."

"Let's not worry about that," she said as she threw her fur coat over the back of the chair and the broken arm fell off. I rushed over to pick it up. "Leave it there. Let's not worry about anything." She walked over to the turntable. "This was the sort of night I've dreamed about. It was even better than when I went with . . ." Her voice trailed off but where hers stopped, Jimmy's took over. His voice seeped through the speakers and it was easy to imagine ourselves back at Birdland.

I used to visit all the very gay places,
Those come what may places.

"May I have this dance?" she asked.

"Certainly," I said in my most gentlemanly manner. "I like a woman who's not afraid to go after what she wants. I knew you wanted me."

"Lush Life" was one of the songs that Jimmy had sung that night but it was more potent with Carmen's arms draped over my shoulders and her body pressed close to mine.

"I've never thanked you for your Christmas present."

"No you didn't," I said, my eyes closed as we swayed back and forth.

"I didn't really know how to thank you. I felt bad that I hadn't gotten you anything. Then more time passed and it just seemed too late to say anything."

"If anyone knows that feeling, it's me."

"Yes, I suppose you do," she said. "But I loved it. It was the best gift anyone has ever given me. I'll always remember that."

"I thought you thought it was hokey."

"Oh, no. Saying hokey is hokey. Malik never would have used the word 'hokey.' "

"No, you're right about that. But I'm not Malik."

"No. You're not. But I loved it. It was perfect."

"It was from Tiffany's."

"It was from you," she said, stopping the flow. "That's enough."

"I've got to get to bed," I said. "I think I've had too much to drink."

"Yes, one should really only drink champagne during the day. Trust," said Carmen, suddenly a diva again. She shook her head. But not at me. "There I go again. One would think after all of this I'd give it a rest."

"We can't change who we are."

"Sure we can," she said. She held out her arms for a hug and I walked over to her. "Thank you so much. For everything. I'll always remember this night."

There was a distance in her voice. A chill. It raised concern. "You're welcome," I said, holding her until she stepped away. "To many more."

"Yes," she said. "Good night."

"You too. See you in the morning."

"For all we know."

She left the parlor, her come-fuck-me pumps swinging in her hands. I listened as she climbed the stairs. Valentine's Day was over.

Tonight was great. I could tell Carmen was moved, which is no easy task, particularly of late. We were finally able to let down our guards a little and everything was out on the table. I've been living here but it wasn't until tonight that I felt I actually belonged here; felt welcome, just for being me. I know if I was at M&G and the waitress asked, "How you feel?" the answer would be "I feel good." Damn, we should have gone to M&G. That would have been perfect. I could just see us walking in there all dressed up. It would have been perfect. Some other time.

Tomorrow, I've got to pick up a new notebook, fuck it, journal, why can't a man keep a journal? I've reached the last page. I always get a strange feeling when I've filled another journal. I feel somewhat disjointed, like a baby whose blanket has been taken away only to find something else to attach himself to. Some things you remember, some you forget. It's all for the viewing. The story continues. We keep going. "How you feel?" I feel good. Good night.

I woke up late the next day. Fresh snow covered the garden, concealing the signs of life waiting for spring to shine upon it.

The steam from the shower filled my small bathroom and I ran my hand over the mirror and liked what I saw. The evening before played in my mind and I was certain Carmen, too, had a smile on her face.

I stepped into the shower and as I lathered my body I started singing, "You're the best thing that's ever happened to me."

Those were the only words of the song I could remember but each time I sang them, I got louder, almost screaming them out, wanting the world to know and not at all embarrassed about it. I was certain Gladys Knight could hear me all the way down in Georgia where she rubbed the back of the man that couldn't handle L.A. She'd hear me and tell me to forget law school and become a Pip.

A knock at the bathroom door caught me off guard and I stopped singing. "Come in," I said, sticking my head out of the shower curtain. "Sorry. I guess I got carried . . ." But when the door opened it wasn't Carmen. A man stood there looking at me. He was about my height and had shoulder-length dreads. He startled me and I pulled my head back into the shower as if that would protect me from this stranger. I then felt the urge to face whatever was coming.

"Are you a friend of Carmen's?" I asked. *Had she gone back out last night?*

"Something like that," he said. "But the better question is, who are you?"

"Mason."

He passed me a towel. "Mason, huh? I'm Chris. Would you mind telling me what the hell you're doing in my house?"

I couldn't believe what he was saying to me but certain lines kept echoing.

"Green card?" He laughed. "I was born in this house. It was my grand-parents'. Damn," he said, looking at the broken arm of the chair on the floor. "That girl. I told her to be careful with this chair. I'd better get this fixed before my mother visits or she'll shit a brick and I don't need that."

I could hear Carmen's words of that first day: "When fine things be-gin to fall apart, only then do they reveal their true essence. Trust."

I kept watching his mouth, kept trying to wake from a champagne-induced dream. But there's no waking from what's real.

"She was evicted from her apartment so I told her she could house-sit for me while I was on assignment. I wanted to help her out. You know, she can be a bit much but she's harmless."

"But couldn't she go out to her folks' place in Sag Harbor?" I asked, still trying to grasp his words, find some semblance of sense through my denial.

"Sag Harbor? Carmen's mother lives somewhere in the South. Mississippi, I think. She was always vague about it. She wanted to leave that behind, start anew. She took a bus up here and hasn't looked back. I met her here in Harlem when I was shooting different people from the neighborhood and I took a liking to her. What can I say? She's an enigma."

No real estate.

No Laundromats.

No marriage.

Even the people she knew, she'd met through him. My mother had always told me the importance of a proper introduction.

I listened to it all but I still didn't know what to believe; who to believe. Maybe this was just Christopher's way of getting rid of me. But where was Carmen?

I went upstairs to her bedroom. The room was sterile, like a hotel room. It was completely free of her except for the photographs stacked in the corner and the one of her and Christopher on the night table. Next to it was a robin's-egg-blue box and an envelope.

"I think those are for you," he said, standing behind me.

I recognized the envelope. It took me right back to the day when I'd walked into Tiffany's in search of a Christmas gift for Carmen. The store had been crowded and I couldn't decide what to get her.

"What about stationery?" suggested the saleswoman. At the time it seemed like the perfect recommendation; there is permanence in stationery. She had a look of concern when I told her what I wanted on the letterhead, but that hadn't stopped me.

I walked over to the night table, my name on the envelope pulling me. I opened the box and there was the stationery. I picked up the envelope. *This was all a joke. I was sure of it. She was going to come out at any moment, saying, "That'll teach you to lie to me."* I turned back around and focused on the envelope. I lifted the flap, which she'd left unsealed for easy access. I know she didn't want this to be difficult for me. I pulled out the piece of paper and ran my fingers across the Solid Antique Roman engraved words; words I'd chosen: The Queen of Harlem.

I didn't want to look at the words she'd written below. I turned back to Christopher. I even smiled at him, hoping to assure him that all was well and this was just a misunderstanding. He returned my smile, but there was no hiding something from someone who knew the truth.

My dearest Mason:

Sometimes freedom is slavery in disguise, and even after change we are more or less the same.

I've never regretted anything, but I regret not being able to be me, at least with you. I trust you can understand that. Just remember, if or when you should think of me, playing poor isn't a privilege afforded to all.

Trust.

The Queen of Harlem
Reading Group Companion

For anyone who has ever felt caught between two worlds, or anyone who simply enjoys a fresh and satisfying storyline, *The Queen of Harlem* is fertile ground for conversation. The questions that follow are designed to enhance your discussion and personal reading of *The Queen of Harlem*. We hope they will also lead you to further topics of inquiry about this rich tale and its vibrant locale.

1. Jackson prefaces his novel with a quote from Marianne Williamson: "We ask ourselves, 'Who am I to be brilliant, gorgeous, talented, and fabulous?' Actually, who are you not to be?" In what ways does Mason fear his talent and economic power? What does the final chapter tell us about Carmen's true fears?

2. How does the evolution of Harlem reflect the lives of its residents? What does the opening scene convey about Harlem's Second Renaissance, especially compared to its first one in the early twentieth century?

3. What is the symbolic role of Jim, Mason's dread-headed white buddy from college? Besides being the character who knows the truth about Mason, what does Jim's presence say about authenticity in general, particularly among whites who appropriate aspects of black culture? How does Malcolm's role compare with Jim's?

4. When Mason steps off the number 6 train and receives his stinging introduction to Harlem from the real Malik, what keeps Mason from heading back downtown? What drives him to stay and invent a "ghettonian" version of himself?

5. How is Mason transformed by his mugging? What kind of turning point occurs during that scene, particularly when he orders his mugger to listen to the stolen CD?

6. Mason receives a lot of mothering. Compare the mothering styles of Joyce and Carmen. How do those two differ from Granny and her generation?

7. How is Mason's attraction to Carmen different from his attraction to Kyra? What do both women teach Mason about "keeping it real"? Why is Kyra able to navigate the fine line between privilege and greed so successfully?

8. Though the chasm between rich and poor is a universal source of friction, why is this friction sometimes particularly intense in black America? Why is the real Malik so personally offended by Mason's clean-cut appearance? What does Jackson tell us about the way wealth and destitution coexist in Harlem today?

9. As part of his disguise, Mason has to learn a new dialect. What does his new speech style suggest about the urge to shun the language of your oppressors? What are some of the empowering characteristics of

Mason's new way of communicating? How does he feel about his old mannerisms when he has to make small talk with Kyra's parents?

10. New York is often thought of as a city where it's possible to reinvent yourself an unlimited number of times. As Mason travels among several neighborhoods, and particularly when he is forced to walk a hundred blocks to get home, what does he observe about the many identities of New York itself?

11. What does Mason's mother reveal to him at The Four Seasons? Does her arrival provide him with an even bigger dose of reality than Harlem?

12. As much as Carmen wanted to be the Queen of Harlem, didn't Mason equally enjoy playing the part of her courtesan? What does the final chapter say about the imaginary quality of all self-perception?

13. In her farewell note to Mason, Carmen says, "Sometimes freedom is slavery in disguise." When has that phrase proven true in your life? What has enslaved Mason and Carmen throughout the novel?

14. Discuss some of the ways in which Mason's Harlem experience plays out in your town or neighborhood. When have you felt compelled to hide behind a false self? What are some of the daydreams that keep you going?

For other suggestions for books for your reading group, and more Reading Group Companions, visit www.harlemmoon.com.

© CHRISTOPHER BEANE

About the Author

BRIAN KEITH JACKSON has received fellowships from Art Matters, the Jerome Foundation, and the Millay Colony for the Arts. *The Queen of Harlem* was named one of the Best Books of 2002 by Black Issues Book Review, and won Mr. Jackson a Distinguished Writer Award from the Mid-Atlantic Writer's Association. *The View from Here* won the American Library Association Literary Award for First Fiction from the Black Caucus of America. Jackson lives in Harlem.

6100
1-800-242-0100

9 T-PAIN : "BARTENDER"

8 Kanye West : "Stronger"

7 Audio Club : "Hot Brown Supersea ver?"

6 Rihanna & Neo : "Hate That I Love you"

5 Good Charlotte : "I Don't Want to
                    Be Alone"

4) Sean Kingston : "Me Love"

3) The Fray "The Great Escape"

2) Backstreet Boys :
             Inconsolable

1)
   Hurricane Chris:
             Ay Bay Bay